Prais

"When I pick up a Manda Collins book, I know I'm in for a treat."   —Tessa Dare, *New York Times* bestselling author

"[Manda] Collins is a delight!"
                    —Elizabeth Hoyt, *New York Times*
                                    bestselling author

"Manda Collins reminds me why I love historical romance so much."   —Rachel Van Dyken, #1 *New York Times*
                                    bestselling author

"Manda Collins writes sexy and smart historical romance, with a big dash of fun."
                    —Vanessa Kelly, *USA Today* bestselling author

"A go-to for historical romance."
                    —*Heroes and Heartbreakers*

A Governess's Guide to Passion and Peril

"A fast-paced, fun romp."   —*Library Journal*

"Collins creatively fashions another beguiling historical romance."   —*Booklist*

"Collins' crime/romance combination continues to be a fun and successful formula."   —*Kirkus*

A Spinster's Guide to Dukes and Danger

"The mystery unfolds effortlessly, delivering a slew of suspects, tantalizing clues, and danger around every corner without ever overshadowing the love story. This sensual romance will have pages flying." —*Publishers Weekly*

"Compelling, evenly paced, and delightfully fun."
—*Kirkus*

"Collins keeps the heat smoldering between the well-drawn main characters in this installment, and the mystery keeps the pace moving nicely... [for] fans of Julia Quinn and Evie Dunmore." —*Library Journal*

An Heiress's Guide to Deception and Desire

"After delighting readers with *A Lady's Guide to Mischief and Mayhem*, Collins is back in fine fettle with another fetching mix of sprightly wit, nimble plotting, and engaging characters that is certain to endear her to fans of historical romances and cozier historical mysteries." —*Booklist*

"The mystery drives the action while the romance provides the heartbeat of the story, and the two weave together to create a well-plotted, entertaining tale for fans of both genres. Expectations and prejudice based on class and gender are scrutinized throughout, while the leads are witty, fierce, bighearted, and easy to love... A successful and thoroughly enjoyable mix of mystery and romance." —*Kirkus*

A Lady's Guide to Mischief and Mayhem

"A delectable mystery that reads like Victorian *Moonlighting* (with a good heaping of Nancy Drew's gumption)...*A Lady's Guide to Mischief and Mayhem* is wickedly smart, so engrossing it'd be a crime not to read it immediately."

—*Entertainment Weekly*

"This book is proof that a romance novel can only be made better by a murder mystery story."

—*Good Housekeeping*

"Smartly plotted, superbly executed, and splendidly witty."

—*Booklist*, Starred Review

"Both romance and mystery fans will find this a treat."

—*Publishers Weekly*

"Collins blends historical romance and mystery with characters who embody a modern sensibility...The protagonists and setting of this first in a promising new series are thoroughly enjoyable."

—*Library Journal*

"Utterly charming."

—PopSugar

"A fun and flirty historical rom-com with a mystery afoot!"

—SYFY WIRE

"Manda Collins smoothly blends romance and an English country-house whodunit...The twists and turns of the plot will keep readers guessing, but Kate's independent attitude and the interesting friends she gathers around her bring the story to vivid life." —*BookPage*

"With wicked smart dialogue and incredibly strong characters, Manda Collins reminds me why I love historical romance so much. Witty, intelligent, and hard to put down, you'll love *A Lady's Guide to Mischief and Mayhem*."

—Rachel Van Dyken, #1 *New York Times* bestselling author

"When I pick up a Manda Collins book, I know I'm in for a treat. With compelling characters and a rich Victorian setting, *A Lady's Guide to Mischief and Mayhem* weaves mystery and romance into one enthralling tale."

—Tessa Dare, *New York Times* bestselling author

"[Manda] Collins is a delight! I read *A Lady's Guide to Mischief and Mayhem* waaay past my bedtime, absorbed by its spot-on period detail, the well-crafted characters, and of course the intriguing mystery. Brava!"

—Elizabeth Hoyt, *New York Times* bestselling author

"Mystery, romance, and an indomitable heroine make for a brisk, compelling read."

—Madeline Hunter, *New York Times* bestselling author

A Wallflower's Guide to Viscounts and Vice

Also by Manda Collins

A Lady's Guide to Mischief and Mayhem
An Heiress's Guide to Deception and Desire
A Spinster's Guide to Danger and Dukes
A Governess's Guide to Passion and Peril

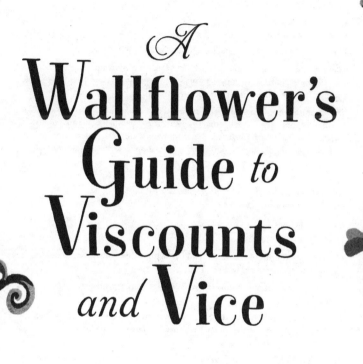

A Wallflower's Guide *to* Viscounts *and* Vice

MANDA COLLINS

FOREVER

New York   Boston

Copyright © 2025 by Manda Collins

Reading group guide copyright © 2025 by Manda Collins and Hachette Book Group, Inc.

Cover design by Daniela Medina
Cover illustration by Karen Gonzalez

Cover copyright © 2025 by Hachette Book Group, Inc.

Forever
Hachette Book Group
1290 Avenue of the Americas, New York, NY 10104
read-forever.com

@readforeverpub

First Edition: April 2025

Forever is an imprint of Grand Central Publishing. The Forever name and logo are registered trademarks of Hachette Book Group, Inc.

The publisher is not responsible for websites (or their content) that are not owned by the publisher.

The Hachette Speakers Bureau provides a wide range of authors for speaking events. To find out more, go to hachettespeakersbureau.com or email HachetteSpeakers@hbgusa.com.

Forever books may be purchased in bulk for business, educational, or promotional use. For information, please contact your local bookseller or the Hachette Book Group Special Markets Department at special.markets@hbgusa.com.

Print book interior design by Taylor Navis

Library of Congress Cataloging-in-Publication Data
Names: Collins, Manda, author.
Title: A wallflower's guide to viscounts and vice / Manda Collins.
Description: First edition. | New York : Forever, 2025. |
Identifiers: LCCN 2024047457 | ISBN 9781538769188 (trade paperback) |
    ISBN 9781538769201 (ebook)
Subjects: LCGFT: Romance fiction. | Detective and mystery fiction. |
    Historical fiction. | Novels.
Classification: LCC PS3603.O45445 W35 2025 |
    DDC 813/.6—dc23/eng/20241007
LC record available at https://lccn.loc.gov/2024047457

ISBNs: 9781538769188 (Trade paperback); 9781538769201 (ebook)

Printed in the United States of America

LSC-C

Printing 1, 2025

Author's Note

Dear Reader,

Have you ever wondered what it would be like to suddenly find yourself investigating a crime just like the ones that occur in your favorite mystery series? This is just what happens to Miss Lucy Penhallow when she and her friend Meg's gorgeous but cranky elder brother, Will, aka Viscount Gilford, witness a kidnapping during the most exciting ball of the London season. Not only that, but the kidnapping victim, Miss Vera Blackwood, just happens to be Lucy's American friend from the Mischief and Mayhem book club, which reads only mystery and detective novels. Of course, Lucy isn't content to sit by and wait for the police to investigate—in part because though she trusts her beloved cousin Superintendent Eversham she has less faith in his colleagues, who seem not to care very much about looking into crimes against women, especially women who aren't well connected to the English aristocracy. So, with

Will by her side, she'll look into Vera's abduction and will leave no stone unturned until she unravels the mystery behind it. And along the way, we'll watch the heiress Lucy and the newly penniless Will come to realize that they're perfect for each other for reasons that go beyond their respective fortunes.

Content Warnings: This book contains kidnapping, violence against women, more than one murder, attempted murder, and probably some other stuff I'm forgetting right now. But I promise that there are a corresponding number of cozy tropes like found family, bromance, female friendship, and most important of all: justice.

As always, thank you so much for reading.

All my very best,
Manda

For all the myriad healthcare professionals who have come to my rescue over the years. Most especially the nurses and doctors who quite literally shocked me back to life this past year. So grateful to still be here and able to write my historical mystery romance books.

A Wallflower's Guide *to* Viscounts *and* Vice

Chapter 1

May 1874, Paris

He was too pretty to die.

Not technically true, but who gave a tinker's damn about truth when one's brain matter was jostling about like a poorly sprung carriage?

"I'm too pretty to die, Temple." William, Viscount Gilford, clutched at his pounding head and fervently wished he'd not drunk that last glass of absinthe the night before. "You'd better mix up one of your foul concoctions."

"Already done, milord." The valet pressed a tumbler of his famous overindulgence remedy into Will's hand. "And ye'd better get it down right quick, begging yer pardon, because there's a Yankee gent in the salon waiting for yer."

Pausing the cup halfway to his mouth, Will blinked. "What?"

"Better to get it all down your gullet, Gilford. You're going to need it."

Will scowled at the American who appeared in the doorway. "What the hell are you doing here, Woodward? Shouldn't you be negotiating a treaty or something?"

A former diplomat for the United States, Mr. Benjamin Woodward, while not the last person Will had expected to darken his door this morning, was definitely in the running.

"Go ahead and drink your medicine," Woodward said with a gravity that was uncharacteristic of their previous interactions, and Will felt a surge of alarm course through him.

Shoving the glass into Temple's hand, he ignored his headache and stood. "Something's happened," he said, taking the trousers the valet had somehow conjured and pulling them on. "Is it Meg? Mother? Grandmama?"

He was the worst sort of scoundrel, Will thought, glancing around the bedroom of the pied-à-terre he'd called home during his sojourn on the Continent. Oh, he'd done his best to ensure that his mother and sister and whatever other relations with a claim on the Gilford estate would be taken care of in his absence. But he'd shirked the main of his responsibilities as Viscount Gilford, and they all knew it.

But his father's death at the hands of a man the whole family had considered a friend had sent Will into a spiral of grief, and, faced with living in the house he associated with his beloved parent, he'd fled.

Now, with the thought of the loss of his remaining close family, a rush of self-recriminations ran through him as he searched Woodward's expression for some clue.

The American raised his hands, palms out. "Nothing like that," Woodward assured him. "Finish dressing, and we'll talk about it in the breakfast room."

Before Will could press him for more, Woodward strode from the room.

"Better drink it like 'e said, milord," urged the valet, giving Will the malodorous drink again. "It sounds as if you'll need it."

Not even stopping to taste it, he downed the entire contents of the glass and handed it back to the valet. He was too preoccupied with whatever it was Ben had to tell him to care about such a trivial matter.

A quarter of an hour later, he strode into the little room he used for dining, and saw that Madame Lyon, the woman who did the cooking and cleaning for him, had made Woodward at home. A cup of coffee in his hand, the flaky remains of a pastry on the plate before him, the former diplomat looked up with a grin. "If I had any questions about why you had remained here so long, the coffee and baked goods alone would have put them to rest."

"I don't care about baked goods, dammit. Tell me why you're here."

Seeming to take pity on Will, Woodward put down his cup and reached into his coat to retrieve a large envelope.

"I don't actually know what it's about," the American said, handing the parcel of papers to him. "We share a man of business, and when I overheard him discussing sending a courier to you, I offered to bring the documents myself. He didn't seem happy about whatever it was, and I thought you might wish to receive the news from a friend."

Woodward had been nearby when Will had been given the news of his father's murder, so he was doubtlessly remembering that occasion.

"But I do know," Woodward said, interrupting Will's thoughts, "that it has nothing to do with anything dire happening to your mother or sister. I saw them both in the park yesterday, and they were well."

That was something, at least, Will thought as he broke the seal on the packet and saw that the top page was indeed a letter from his man of business. A quick scan of the pages below revealed what looked to be account sheets.

Dropping into the nearest chair, he set the financial documents on the table and began reading the letter.

As he took in the words, certain phrases leapt out at him: "profligate," "crop yields," "overextended," "dire need," "she must be told," "cannot continue on this path," "an infusion of funds," "must marry well."

When he set the letter atop the other documents—which he now understood to be proof of what the accountant had told him—Will pressed his thumb and forefinger onto either side of his nose and squeezed.

"Bad news, I take it." Woodward's tone was sympathetic.

"You could say that." Placed alongside the news of other calamities—a dead parent, a train derailment, an ill child— the news that he, like so many other peers these days, was in danger of losing his expensive estates was trivial. Will now recognized that no amount of concentration or studied ignorance would save him from the reality that had come to his doorstep in the figure of an old friend.

His Continental fever dream was now at an inglorious end. However much he might have wished to elude responsibility, to pretend that his father was still alive and running the Gilford estates with the same efficiency as always, he must wake up now.

"It seems I am needed at home, Woodward." Feeling as if he'd aged twenty years in a quarter of an hour, Will leaned back in his chair and ran a hand over his eyes.

When he opened them, the expectant expression on the other man's face almost made him laugh. But only almost.

"It would seem that my estates are in need of a swift infusion of funds or the house of Gilford will collapse in on itself."

Woodward's eyes widened at the words. "I don't know what I was expecting, but it wasn't that."

Will sighed. "I assumed my father was just as adept at managing the estates as he was at handling the minutiae of foreign policy, but I suppose even he made mistakes. He left everything in the hands of a trusted steward. And foolishly, I kept the man on when I left England to cavort about Europe."

"He's mismanaged things, I take it?"

"Oh, he's done more than mismanage things," Will said with a growing sense of unreality. "He's been fleecing the estate for decades and now he's absconded with his spoils to the devil knows where."

Woodward bit back a curse. "Surely they have some idea of where he's gone. A man cannot simply disappear into the aether."

Will stood abruptly and shouted for Temple. To his friend he said, "The authorities are looking into it, but it seems unlikely they will find him in time to repair matters."

When the valet entered the room, Will instructed the man to book passage for them on the next packet bound for Dover.

"I am sorry, old fellow," Woodward said, pushing back his own chair. "Name whatever it is you need from me and it's yours."

Will sighed and crossed to the door leading into his bed-chamber. Before he went in, he said over his shoulder, "I require only your congratulations."

"For what?" Woodward called after him.

"My marriage, it would seem." Will was grateful the American couldn't see his face because he knew it betrayed just how morose he was at the prospect. "I don't know who she'll be. But she'll be a bloody heiress."

* * *

"Tell me what progress you've made on the murder of Mary Crosby."

As she flipped through a drawer in the massive file cabinets housed outside the office of her cousin, Detective Superintendent Andrew Eversham, Miss Lucy Penhallow listened shamelessly to his conversations.

She'd only recently become acquainted with Cousin Andrew, who had defied familial objections by joining the Metropolitan Police a few years ago. But she had grown quite close to him and his wife, newspaper publisher Lady Katherine, in that time. And it was to Kate that Lucy was certain she owed her minor position as a filing clerk in the offices of the police. Despite his relatively liberal views on the role of women in English society, Eversham was as protective as any man over his family.

"Mary Crosby?" Constable John Boddie asked, not quite keeping the note of contempt out of his voice. "I thought we'd decided to let that one go."

"Boddie."

There was a long silence, then Boddie gulped.

If one could hear a man's life essence depart his body, Lucy had. She wished she could turn and see what expression her cousin had leveled at the man to make him quake so.

"D-detective Super, sir?"

Lucy had come to know most of the men under Eversham's authority in the murder division, and she knew Boddie to be a conscientious but rather foolish young man. Certainly, he wasn't clever enough to hide his casual contempt for the people he was meant to serve. But then Lucy often found that those who hailed from the middle classes—Boddie's father was a well-known barrister—tended to be even more contemptuous of the lower classes than the aristocracy. It had something to do with pulling the ladder leading out of the slums up behind them, she suspected.

"Have we not discussed your attitude toward, er, those women who ply their trade on the streets?"

Lucy bit back a smile at Eversham's attempt to protect her tender ears from the words that would more properly name the profession of poor murdered Mary Crosby. Then, she mentally chastised herself. A woman was dead.

There was nothing in that to smile about.

"Yes, Detective Super."

"Then you'd best make a better effort at curbing your tongue," Eversham snapped. "Every case that is presented to us deserves our best work. And the victims deserve our respect."

Once Boddie had been dismissed, Eversham called out to Lucy in the filing room. "I suppose you heard that."

Slotting the last information card into place, Lucy shut the large drawer and turned to enter her cousin's well-appointed office. Taking in the dark paneling and brass fixtures, Lucy noted not for the first time how much the room looked like her late father's library in the Mayfair house where she lived with her mother.

Perching on the edge of the chair facing Eversham's desk, she smiled at him, startled as always to see her own eyes in his masculine face. "Of course I heard it. I must say that I am relieved that you are the man who gives the orders here. If it were up to Boddie and the like, only the murders of those with unblemished reputations would be investigated."

It was not a new conversation between them, and Lucy thought she saw a hint of weariness in the set of her cousin's shoulders. It couldn't be easy holding dozens of men to account—especially not in a world where the majority of them reckoned a woman's mental acumen somewhere just below that of a hunting dog.

"It is troubling to hear such cynicism in one so young, Lucy," he said with a shake of his head. "I hope your mother won't be proven right about her opinion of your working here."

Mrs. Frances Penhallow, the daughter of a viscount's younger son, and Eversham's paternal cousin, had argued vociferously against Lucy's going anywhere near Scotland Yard to assist Eversham. But since she was now above the age of majority and in possession of her sizable inheritance, Lucy was not bound by parental strictures.

"Mark my words, Lucy," Mrs. Penhallow had wailed, clutching a handkerchief to her bosom like Mrs. Bennet from Miss Austen's *Pride and Prejudice*. "Your reputation will suffer. As will your sensibilities."

"Since my reputation has, alas, not suffered a whit," Lucy

said with a half smile, "then I think you must be referring to my sensibilities. And I can assure you that on that front, I am as unfazed by male conversation as I ever was."

"And from what Kate tells me of the book club, you are imbibing nothing but lurid details of murder there as well," Eversham said. Though his words could be construed as chiding, his tone was one of amusement. "I wonder if an interest in solving crime can be passed through bloodlines in the same manner as eye color."

"It must have passed Mama by entirely," Lucy said with a rueful smile. Her mother had been appalled when her only daughter, and indeed only child, had come home from finishing school with an appetite for sensationalist newspaper stories about the grisliest of crimes. Lucy had tried to tell her that it wasn't the details of the crimes themselves but the apprehension of the perpetrator that truly caught her interest.

"I fear that if we didn't favor one another so much she would wonder if I was a changeling."

A great beauty in her day, Mrs. Penhallow had hoped to see her daughter repeat her own success in the ballrooms of the *ton*. But despite enduring multiple seasons, Lucy had not quite *taken*. This might be the result of her inability to stop herself from speaking her mind. It didn't matter the topic—Lucy had opinions and seemed unable to keep her thoughts to herself. And if her mouth didn't betray her, her countenance did.

She regretted that her unruly tongue had caused her mama disappointment in her only child's marriage prospects, but Lucy couldn't bring herself to be sorry on her own behalf. As much as she might one day wish to marry and have children, for now, she was pleased to have control of both her person and her fortune.

Since she'd come into her majority at one and twenty, she'd found a great deal of satisfaction in donating some of those funds to certain causes—such as the establishment of Newnham College for women at Cambridge a few years earlier and the continuing fight for women's suffrage—and she was not ready to cede that control to a husband. Though marriage settlements might be used to protect a lady from an unscrupulous husband's misuse of her fortune, to a degree, there was little a lady could do to keep out of her husband's control whatever funds she brought to the marriage. And since the majority of men who'd approached her since her inheritance had become public knowledge had been fortune hunters and grifters, she'd chosen to consign herself to the side of the ballroom at *ton* entertainments by refusing to dance, and sitting with the wallflowers and chaperones.

The clock on the shelf behind Eversham's desk tolled and Lucy sprang up from her chair. "I have to go. I'll be late for book club."

She retrieved her hat and umbrella from where she stored them and waited for Eversham to escort her to the rear door, where her maid waited for her.

"Please convey my best wishes to your mother," Eversham said, accepting a quick hug from Lucy before he disappeared back into the building.

"Did you have a pleasant time at the tea shop, Dora?" Lucy asked as she and her maid rounded the corner to search for the Penhallow carriage in the street beyond.

"I did, miss," Dora said with a sweet smile. Lucy knew that

the girl, who was close to her family, met with her mother and sister each week while Lucy was filing. "And I seen—that is, I saw your friends Miss Gilford and Miss Blackwood."

Lucy turned to judge whether Dora was serious. "At the tea shop?"

"Yes, miss. They said they were waiting for you."

Lucy hurried in the direction of Applegate's tea shop. If Meg and Vera were waiting for her, then they would all risk arriving late to the book club meeting.

She and Dora had just turned the corner when Lucy saw her friends, a single maid hovering right behind them. When they caught sight of Lucy they began walking toward her.

"I thought you'd never come," Meg said with an overdramatic shake of her head. "We'll be late for the meeting if we don't hurry."

"No one pressed you into waiting for me," Lucy said, embracing first Meg and then Vera. "You might already be settled into Mrs. Clevedon's drawing room enjoying the warmth of the fire."

The Ems, as the ladies called the Mischief and Mayhem Book Club, after the letters in the name, met at the home of one of the members once a month. And since the original founders, Lucy's cousin-in-law Lady Katherine and Lady Wrackham, had been forced to step away because of their increased familial and business responsibilities, Lucy and her friend Meg had offered to take up the mantle.

They'd met Vera Blackwood, whose family had traveled to London from their home in Boston earlier in the year, at a rout party given before the season officially began, and had become fast friends. Vera's forthright manner, paired with her infectious humor, had endeared her to some and given a distaste for her to others. As a result, despite her willingness to entertain offers from even those potential suitors Lucy would avoid, Vera too spent many dances sitting with the other wallflowers at the side of the ballroom.

Now, they were scurrying to find Lucy's carriage so that they would arrive at Mrs. Clevedon's in time.

"Did you learn anything new today, Lucy?" Not long into their friendship, Lucy had come to recognize that Vera found her relationship to a high-ranking member of the Metropolitan Police to be the most fascinating thing about her. It didn't bother Lucy. If their positions were reversed, Lucy was quite sure she'd have felt the same way. There were so few opportunities for ladies of their station to mix with anyone having to do with crime or, for that matter, newspapers. And thanks to her cousin, Lucy was in close proximity to well-born members of both the police and the press.

"Only that there is yet another constable who cares not whether they ever catch whoever killed a lady of the night." She related the exchange between Eversham and Boddie she'd overheard.

"What a terrible person," Meg said, her lips twisting into an expression of distaste. "The more I learn of men, the fonder I am of my dog."

"That's because Ralph is a darling," Vera said with an indulgent smile. Meg's Pomeranian was a favorite among the Ems, and whenever the club met at Gilford House, he invariably was sick from all the treats bestowed upon him.

"He is, isn't he?" Meg asked with a grin. Then, her expression sobering, she asked, "They still have no idea who killed Mary Crosby?"

All three women had been following the story of the young prostitute, barely fifteen years old, who had been found with her throat slit near the waterfront earlier in the month.

"No," Lucy confirmed with a shake of her head. "And with the sort of attitude Boddie showed toward her, it's no surprise."

"But your cousin is leading the investigation, isn't he?" Vera asked. "He'll find the culprit."

There was a time when Eversham might have been able to devote his time to searching for the man who had murdered Mary, but now that he was in a more senior position, he spent most of his time delegating tasks to the men he managed. So if the case was resolved, it would most likely be done by one of his detectives. To Vera, however, she made a noncommittal sound. Eversham had never expressly forbidden her from speaking about the inner workings of the Met, but she didn't feel right about divulging such things even so.

"He'll try his best," she said with a smile in the other lady's direction. "He always does."

Seeming to accept Lucy's words at face value, Vera changed the subject. "You haven't told her your news, Meg."

Meg pulled a face and rolled her eyes. "It's not anything to be pleased about." To Lucy she said, "My brother is expected home any day now."

Frowning, Lucy asked, "But I should think that's happy news. You're fond of one another, are you not?"

From what she knew of Meg and her brother, Viscount

Gilford, they were quite close. Indeed, Meg always spoke of him and his prolonged sojourn in Europe wistfully.

"It isn't that I am not fond of him," Meg said with a sigh. "It's just that Mama views his arrival as an opportunity to unburden herself with all of her complaints about me and my many sins."

Lucy snorted. "Your mother and mine must do nothing but despair over their disobedient daughters when they encounter one another." Though she spoke the words more as a balm for her friend than anything else. Her own mama was sweetness itself compared to the unpleasant Lady Gilford.

"I suppose I must be grateful my mother is dead," Vera said with a laugh.

At Lucy and Meg's twin expressions of alarm, Vera sighed. "My sense of humor is sometimes too much even for my closest friends. I apologize, ladies."

Though she had been startled by Vera's words, Lucy chided herself for being so sensitive. "Oh, do not apologize, my dear. Meg and I are likely being oversensitive."

But as the carriage rumbled along toward Elise's townhouse, she couldn't stop the sadness that washed over her. How unhappy Vera's childhood must have been. Her mother had died of a fever when the girl was barely more than a baby.

Mindful of that, she gave a bright smile to her companions. "What did you both think of the book?"

Chapter 2

A week later Will was back in London, and to his dismay no new solution to his money problems had occurred to either him or his man of business.

If anything, Mr. Thomas Mayhew had discovered even more bills than he had at first realized. "If I may be so bold, my lord," Mayhew said, his luxurious mustache echoing the frown of the man's lips, "Lady Gilford, despite both our warnings to her about the precariousness of the situation, has continued to spend at the same rate and, in some cases, even higher than she did before she was informed."

Will wanted to drum his head on the surface of the desk in the office that had once been his father's. He knew the issues with the estate's finances had begun while the former Lord Gilford was still alive, but he couldn't help believing that Papa would have prevented matters from becoming this dire long before it was a danger.

He was certain his father would have known better how to manage Lady Gilford.

As difficult as she could be, the one person in the world who was able to curb her behavior had been her husband. His death had left her free to act upon all her worst impulses, and as a result what had begun as a gentle glide down the financial hill had quickly become the unchecked freefall Will now faced.

"I will speak to her again, Mayhew," he told the solicitor. He didn't relish the exchange, but it couldn't be helped. His refusal to take on his responsibilities as the head of the Gilford household—though he would like to place the blame somewhere else—was the root of his current headache, and he must now take his medicine.

Once he had finished signing the letters to creditors Mayhew had brought him, he sent the man off with a gruff farewell.

When the door to the study was shut, he stifled the urge to fortify himself with brandy before he sought out his mother. Taking the stack of bills from dressmakers, drapers, hatmakers, perfumiers, and every other merchant who might be expected to be patronized by ladies of the peerage, he stepped out into the hallway and headed for the morning room.

Even before he reached the landing leading to the second floor, where the public rooms of Gilford House were situated, Will heard the raised voice of his mother wafting toward him, like smoke alerting him to quickly rising flames.

"I have been mistress of this house for nearly thirty years, Mrs. Parker." Lady Gilford's tone was strident, and as Will stepped into the lavishly appointed chamber from which his mother conducted much of the household business, he noted the carefully expressionless face of the housekeeper standing before her. "And I will not stand for such insolence."

Will noticed that his mother was clutching the portfolio—

with white-knuckled hands—the housekeeper used to keep the household accounts.

"Begging your pardon, my lady." Mrs. Parker, who had overseen household domestic matters in the London town-house of the Gilford family since Will was a boy, managed a far calmer tone than he'd have done in her situation. "I mean no disrespect, but his lordship's orders on the matter were that we should try to trim those costs—"

Before she could finish her statement, which would only serve to anger his mother more, Will stepped fully into the room and crossed to where the two women faced one another. "Do not trouble yourself, Mrs. Parker," he told the house-keeper. "I will speak to my mother about the matter. And when she is ready to resume discussion of the household bud-get, she will no doubt summon you."

Yet another reason for him to marry as quickly as possi-ble, he thought as he watched the housekeeper curtsy to them before hurrying out of the room. If this was how Lady Gil-ford treated any servant who attempted to enforce his orders regarding estate spending, then he would need to attend to the matters himself until a new Lady Gilford supplanted her. He certainly wouldn't have the servants treated so harshly. Guiltily he wondered how many such tirades they'd been sub-jected to since he'd decamped to the Continent.

Lady Gilford looked at her only son with a hauteur he rec-ognized all too well. "I never imagined when I welcomed your return last week that I would wish you gone again within days, Gilford. But that is just what has happened."

He took in her still-lovely countenance and had little dif-ficulty understanding what had drawn his father to her. But there was a coldness there he hadn't noticed when he was a child. And in the years since her husband's death, there were lines in her face that seemed to have been wrought not by mirth but by displeasure.

"I have no intention of displeasing you, Mother," he said calmly, not rising to her pettish words. "However, as both Mayhew and I have explained to you more than once, we can no longer afford to spend as freely as we all have done since my father's death. If you will not practice economies on your own, then I shall be forced to take them for you."

"Economies," she spat out as if the word were the vilest of crudities. "When your father was alive, we had no such need to deprive ourselves. This is all due to your gallivanting about the Continent for so many years."

"As we both know, it takes far less to live in Paris than it does in London," he said reasonably. "Though I will take my share of the blame for our current situation. I had no notion of our predicament while I was away and spent accordingly. Now, however, I do know and cannot in good conscience allow the family to live so far beyond our means."

Lady Gilford's mouth tightened in annoyance before she responded. "I suppose you mean to place most of the blame for this nonsense on your sister and me. Though we have only been attempting to present ourselves in society in the manner expected of a viscount's family. Especially given your shameful absence. I am more than certain that your lack of interest in finding Margaret a husband is the reason why she is still unwed at one and twenty."

Will rather thought that the reason why Meg was still unmarried had more to do with her inability to find a man who could meet her stringent criteria for husband. But he did not say so aloud.

"From now on," he said instead, "you will have nothing to quibble at in that regard. I mean to accompany the two of you to any number of events this season. It is time that I began to look for a bride."

At this her eyes widened with the kind of shock and surprise he'd have expected from her if a leopard had suddenly stalked into the room. But instead of pleasure at the news, she gave a huff of annoyance. "I doubt you will find the social engagements we attend to be of any interest. Especially after your time in Paris. It is much better if you spend your evenings at your clubs and the like. You are still young yet. There is no need for you to wed for several years more."

He narrowed his eyes at her, attempting to understand her reasoning. "I thought you would be pleased to learn that I wish to marry." The devil knew every other mother of an unmarried son in the *haut ton* was hell-bent on seeing them leg-shackled.

"Of course I am pleased," she said, belying what she'd just said. "It is only that I had thought I would have more time with my only son before he became some other lady's."

Since she had never expressed a sentiment for either of her children in their lives, Will discounted her words without hesitation. Instead, he considered what instead she might be unwilling to give up.

The answer came to him without much thought. "It is not I you do not wish to give over to some other lady. It is the house. The estates. You are not ready to become the dowager Countess of Gilford." He shook his head with disgust.

Lady Gilford waved away his words as if they were gnats circling in the air. "You can hardly blame me. This estate and its running have been my responsibility for decades now. You cannot expect me to give up everything I have worked for to some empty-headed girl with more hair than wit without a fight."

"I can expect that you would not be surprised at the notion," he said with exasperation. "You've known for those decades that it would happen someday. And the only way I can get the funds needed to refurbish the country estates and to keep us in the style demanded of a viscount's family is to marry an heiress. Do you not wish to continue replenishing your wardrobe at the beginning of every season? And entertaining your friends with the same degree of luxury to which you've become accustomed?"

At that, she made a face. "I do not see why you are making all this fuss about funds. We are well able to continue on credit with London merchants for years to come."

"No, we are not." Will could see now that he would need to keep a firm hand with her. Allowing his mother to argue with him only reinforced her belief that she was entitled to a say in the matter. "I have made my decision and will not be swayed. You had better prepare yourself for your tenure as the dowager Countess of Gilford, whether you wish it or not."

Unwilling to listen to any more of her cajoling or protests, Will strode from the room, ignoring the sound of sputtering protest behind him.

He was donning his hat and coat in the entryway when Parker opened the door to admit Meg and another young lady, who with her hair escaping its pins and her cheeks pink from the still-chill spring air, was pretty but forgettable. So forgettable, in fact, that though he was certain they'd been introduced before he left for Paris, he could not for the life of him recall the chit's name.

"Will," Meg said, a note of warning in her voice, "I think you've met my friend Miss Lucy Penhallow before, have you not?"

Clearly, his sister wished to warn him away from pursuing her friend. Which amused him. In part because he'd just dismissed the chit. And in part because Meg must have forgotten that the surest way to make him do something was to warn him off.

Still, he'd missed his sister enough that he was willing to do her bidding in this matter, at least.

"Indeed, Miss Penhallow and I have met before." Will bowed over the young woman's hand, careful not to do so for too long. A pity, really, he thought as he noticed her nearly lavender-hued eyes. "A pleasure to see you again, Miss Penhallow."

If she'd interpreted his thoughts, Meg's friend gave no sign of it. "My lord," she said, offering him a brief curtsy. "Welcome back to London."

"Are you going out?" Meg asked Will with a frown and a glance upward. "I was hoping you might take some tea with us."

There was no misinterpreting that look. And once again he felt the sting of having left Meg to endure Lady Gilford's temper and histrionics alone for so long.

Unfortunately, he could not put off this meeting with Adrian if he was going to save the family from ruin. And surely having Miss Penhallow at the tea table would curb Lady Gilford's worst impulses.

"An appointment I cannot put off, I'm afraid," he told Meg with a shake of his head. "But I will be sure to do so on another day."

"I shall have to keep you to that promise," his sister said with false gaiety. "Enjoy your errand."

Bidding both young ladies a good afternoon, Will stepped outside and hurried down the front steps of Gilford House and into the hack one of the footmen had summoned for him.

When he was safely inside the hired cab, his thoughts strayed back to Miss Penhallow. She was prettier than he'd remembered.

Her pale blonde hair was unusual in that it was almost white. And there were those eyes. Still, she was obviously one of Meg's dearest friends, and he did not wish to add even more complication to his sister's life. Especially given that he'd not even informed her about the family's precarious financial situation yet. Meg needed stability right now. Not more unrest.

Then, dismissing all thoughts of the winsome Miss Penhallow from his thoughts, he began a mental list of the wealthy young ladies he'd discuss with Adrian once he got to Brooks's.

Chapter 3

"May I fetch you some punch, Miss Penhallow? You must be parched after such a vigorous country dance."

Sir Alton Moncrieff, who was fifty if he was a day, smiled hopefully at Lucy once he'd returned her to a spot at the side of the Leighton-Childes' gaily decorated ballroom.

An aging widower with a dozen children, Sir Alton had already run through the dowries of two wives, both of whom had died presenting him with the aforementioned children. And, to Lucy's frustration, he was impervious to every attempt on her part to dissuade him from pursuing her for the role of the third Lady Moncrieff. Though it was her usual custom to decline all dancing to avoid prolonged exposure to the empty blandishments of gentlemen more interested in her fortune than in herself, Lucy had been unable to say no to the soft-spoken Mr. Barnes.

"I suppose you will do so whether I wish it or not, Sir Alton," she said tartly, wondering how far the man would go to ingratiate himself with her. If she were a different sort of person, she'd have asked him to fetch four glasses, one for herself and then three more for her friends. But despite her annoyance with the man, she was not cruel. "Thank you," she added despite her wish for him to leave her alone.

Once he had disappeared into the crowd, she watched as Meg came toward her on the arm of the handsome Lord Catesby, who was one of her most assiduous admirers, though Lucy was certain neither of them was particularly serious about the other.

Bowing over Meg's hand, Catesby greeted Lucy, then went to search out his next partner.

"I am surprised to find you alone," Meg said with a raised brow as she glanced pointedly at the conversations going on among the ball-goers around them, but none of which included Lucy. "Has even Sir Alton deserted you?"

"Punch." Lucy tilted her head toward where they could see the baronet waiting for a chance to procure her beverage. "But never fear, he will be here again soon enough."

Before they could continue, Elise, Mrs. Clevedon, approached, her cheeks pink from exertion, and looking more elegant than Lucy could ever hope to.

"Here you all are," the widow said with a warm smile. Some five years older than Lucy and ages more worldly, Elise was the sort of lady Lucy would never have imagined would find something like their book club interesting. But from the first meeting she'd attended, the young widow had proved to be clever and witty, and she was now one of Lucy and Meg's dearest friends. "I searched you out when I arrived, but in this crush it was impossible. I did see Vera, however."

Relaxing slightly, Lucy realized she'd been concerned about Vera since that afternoon, when the usually sunny young woman had seemed worried over something. "I wonder where she is now," she said now, scanning the dance floor, then the assembled guests on the edges of it, but there was no sign of Miss Blackwood's bright red hair.

"She'll turn up," said Meg, as if sensing Lucy's disquiet. "Though she usually finds us before the dancing begins. I hope she hasn't been cornered by Lord Exley again."

Lord Exley, a harmless, but persistent gentleman of middle years, was well known for his tendency to corner unmarried young ladies to expound on whichever topic he was obsessed with at the moment. This season it was the dangers of reading on the female constitution, which, for obvious reasons was particularly noisome to the Ems.

"Come to think of it, I haven't seen Lord Exley tonight either." Elise frowned. "If they are together..." While they were all confident that they'd be able to escape from Lord Exley's verbal clutches sooner or later, because of her American plain speaking, Vera was liable to give the man a set-down in such a way that might harm her own social standing.

Lord Exley was married to one of the most influential ladies of the *ton*, unfortunately. And without her approval, a lady in search of a well-born husband—as Vera was—would find it impossible to secure the necessary invitations. Her father might be meeting with impoverished aristocrats through his business dealings, but unless he wished for his wife to be socially ostracized, any potential husbands would not dare marry where Lady Exley did not give her blessing.

Now they were all on alert.

"Why don't we split up and see if we can find her," Lucy

said, unable to get the memory of Vera's troubled expression that afternoon out of her mind. "Meg, you check the retiring room. She could be ill, or resting a twisted ankle—"

"Or having a torn hem stitched up," Meg finished for her.

"Or at the mercy of a gentleman who cannot take no for an answer," Elise added, saying what they were all thinking.

Though they'd begun concerned about Lord Exley's conversational traps, all three ladies were well aware of the dangers posed by other sorts of ballroom pests.

"I'll check the card room and the likely alcoves where an unwanted suitor might take one," Elise, a beautiful widow with experience of such machinations, offered.

"I'll take the library and the terrace," Lucy offered, knowing that any one of them might be found in the library if they went missing at a ball. Especially a library rumored to be as magnificent as this one.

The three friends nodded in agreement, and Lucy continued, "Let's all meet back here after we've searched, whether we find her or not. By then we'll know what other steps we'll need to take."

As she threaded her way through the crowd gathered at the edges of the dance floor, she exchanged greetings with those she knew and asked those with whom she was certain Vera had some acquaintance whether they had seen her that evening. No one had.

She passed a couple of maids and a gentleman whose name she couldn't recall as she went from the ballroom to the corridor, her dancing slippers silent once she reached the thick carpets lining the hallway floor.

Opening door after door, she found only empty rooms. The

one exception was a small parlor where a feverishly embracing couple didn't even hear the door open.

Startled, she shut it hurriedly, and feeling telltale heat creeping over her cheeks, she tried to look innocent as she continued down the hall.

When she reached the library door, which is where she'd expect to find Vera if she had indeed sought refuge from the crowded ballroom, she breathed a sigh of relief as she saw lamplight beaming from the partially open door.

Pushing it open, she was fully expecting to find Vera inside, a novel in her hands as she sat with her feet curled beneath her on an obliging sofa.

It was, instead, the last person she'd been expecting.

Lucy could only stare as the man lifted his glass of what looked like brandy to her.

"Miss Penhallow," said Viscount Gilford. "So we meet again."

Chapter 4

Lord Gilford." Her hand clasped over her bosom like the heroine in a melodrama, Lucy's heart pounded in her chest as she debated what to do. She had the inclination to do as she had when she'd found the kissing couple—to shut the door quickly and hurry away.

Viscount Gilford was Meg's brother, however, and because they'd seen one another only that afternoon, it felt like the height of rudeness to simply mutter an apology and skulk off.

Still, apologize she must.

"I am sorry for disturbing you, my lord," Lucy said with a quick curtsy—the sort that was not so short as to be rude, but not so deep that it would be appropriate for the queen—and continued, "I'll just leave you."

To her surprise, however, the viscount, who had risen on her entry, heaved a great sigh. "You'd better come in if you wish to. Meg will have my hide if she finds out I frightened one of her friends away. And from a library no less."

Torn between her wish to flee and her desire to get a closer look at the Leighton-Childe library, Lucy hesitated only a moment before stepping inside the cozy warmth of the chamber, careful to leave the door ajar.

"We can't have Meg tearing a strip from your hide so soon after your return to England," she said with forced cheerfulness. There was something about his lordship's expression that gave her the impression he was not in the best of moods. "I shall make my inspection of the library so that you do not garner her displeasure, then take myself away."

Even as she spoke, Lucy couldn't stop taking in the magnificence of the chamber. First, there was the brightly colored mural in the classical style depicting Adam and Eve in the Garden of Eden—scandalously unclothed—which covered the domed ceiling in the center of the room. Then there were the various objets d'art the current Lord Leighton-Childe's father had collected on his travels.

But it was the floor-to-ceiling shelves of what looked to be thousands of books that sent a jolt of admiration through her. The Penhallow estate in Essex had its own sizable collection of volumes, but in the same way horse enthusiasts might appreciate rare specimens of equine perfection, so too did Lucy look upon well-stocked libraries.

At Lord Gilford's soft chuckle, she realized she'd made a happy noise as she ran a hand over the spines of a nearby shelf of novels.

While she blushed in embarrassment, the look she turned on him was nevertheless an unrepentant one. "I love books."

"I can tell." In the lamplight, the gold in Gilford's light brown hair glinted and almost made it look as if a halo hovered over him. "My sister is the same way. She wasn't a particularly avid student, but novels and newspapers have always interested her."

"I suppose that's why we are such good friends," Lucy said with a nod. "And why we were first drawn to the Ems."

Frowning, Gilford said, "I don't know of any friends of hers named Emma. They must have moved to town after I left for France. They are also fond of books, I take it?"

Biting back a smile, Lucy corrected him. "The Ems aren't people. Well, we are, but not like you think. The book club Meg and I belong to is named after the newspaper column 'A Lady's Guide to Mischief and Mayhem.' It's the Mischief and Mayhem Book Club, but in its first incarnation it was the M&M club. Later we simply shortened it further by calling it the Ems."

Caressing the arm of the burgundy leather sofa where he lounged, Gilford gave a short laugh. "Ah, that makes sense."

Then, as if the notion had just occurred to him, he asked with what seemed like studied indifference, "I don't suppose there are any wealthy young ladies among the group?"

Perhaps he has a friend who is in need of a fortune, Lucy thought with a mental shrug. It was hardly an unusual situation. Aristocratic families in need of funds had been seeking out alliances with wealthy heiresses for centuries. She wasn't sure whether to be insulted or relieved that he didn't consider her an option. Though maybe that had something to do with her friendship with Meg.

"I don't believe so, no." She watched as he seemed to deflate before her eyes. She felt immediately remorseful since she'd purposely not mentioned Vera. But something within her refused to offer up her American friend to him. She'd examine the reasons why later.

"Forgive me, Miss Penhallow." Gilford ran a hand over his carefully styled hair in agitation, but instead of disordering the locks, it only served to make them more appealing.

"I'd like to blame the brandy," he said with a nod toward where the decanter and several glasses were laid out on a sideboard, "but I haven't had enough to loosen my tongue to that degree. I apologize for my thoughtlessness."

An idea began to worm its way through her mind, but Lucy dismissed the notion as patently absurd. Lady Gilford and Meg didn't seem to be watching their spending. No, Lucy was sure she was mistaken.

Still, there was no denying that Lady Gilford had been very cross since her son's return from the Continent. And there had been no mention of him coming home until a week or so ago. Could it be true? Was the Gilford estate in trouble?

Before she could formulate a way of asking without unpardonable rudeness, he said, "You'll learn the news soon enough, so I may as well tell you. The Gilford fortune has been drained by an unscrupulous steward. We are not penniless, but dam—er, dashed close to it. It's why I came home. To find an heiress to marry."

Despite her already having guessed as much, Lucy felt some shock as his confession. It was one thing to suspect something, but another completely to have one's suspicions confirmed.

She thought about what must have been the small fortune Lady Gilford had spent in the past year or so. She'd refurbished the Gilford townhouse and purchased new wardrobes for herself and Meg for the season—even taking a brief trip to Paris to meet with the renowned House of Worth to have the gowns designed and sewn. She'd bought the servants new livery and had ordered a new coach, despite the fact that the previous one was still in perfectly good working order.

Though she and her own mother were hardly parsimonious, it was no secret that the Viscountess Gilford spent lavishly. Lucy wondered with sudden insight if the news was the reason why Meg's mother had remained home that evening. No doubt Gilford had spoken to her about the matter. Even someone without a taste for luxury would respond to the news that economies must be put into place with unhappiness.

Then, something occurred to her. "You say that *you'll* need to marry a fortune."

The look Gilford raked over her was speculative and sent a frisson of awareness through her.

"That's right. Are you volunteering?"

Chapter 5

"No," she said flatly, ignoring the frisson of awareness that his perusal sent dancing down her spine. "I am not. But I am confused why you say you are the one who will need to marry an heiress. I can name a dozen or more gentlemen who, when faced with this same problem, have sold their unmarried sisters and daughters to the highest bidder without a backward glance."

For the barest moment, anger shone in his eyes. But as quickly as it came, the sentiment was replaced with sardonic amusement. "You have a very poor opinion of gentlemen, Miss Penhallow." He stretched his legs out before him and studied her as if she was some rare creature on display in the Royal Menagerie. "I suppose I should be grateful I have chosen a solution that meets with your approbation."

"It is not for me to approve or disapprove of your actions, my lord," she said, lifting her chin at the challenge in his tone. "Though I will admit to no small degree of relief that you will not make Meg sacrifice herself in such a manner as those others I mentioned."

Before he could respond, a shout rang out from beyond the

open French doors on the far side of the room. Some instinct had her rushing toward where the shout had come from.

"What was that?" Will asked as he followed her.

They both stepped out onto the terrace, and despite the hour, the moonlight served to illuminate the garden. A glance to the left revealed a few couples in conversation outside the doors leading from the ballroom, but they had no reason to look toward where Lucy and Gilford stood.

"I don't know," Lucy said, keeping her voice low so as not to draw attention to them. "It was probably laughter from one of the guests nearer to the ballroom."

A sharp wind brought a tinge of cold that explained, perhaps, why there were so few dancers congregating outside. Even with the stuffiness generated by filling a room with more dancers than it could reasonably hold, there were those who would prefer it to the least bit of chill.

But just as she was about to turn to go back inside, Lucy heard the sound again. This time she was able to determine more clearly what it was. A woman had screamed.

Even before she could fully consider the wisdom of doing so, Lucy was hurrying down the steps of the terrace toward the path leading through the garden.

As she went, she saw a black carriage beyond the gate leading into the mews from the garden. To her horror, she saw a burly man in dark clothing struggling with a red-haired young woman in an evening gown.

Vera.

Her friend's name flitted through Lucy's mind, because it was undoubtedly her friend the man was attempting to subdue.

"You there," she shouted, heedless of who might hear. "Let her go."

Her words must have reached the struggling couple, because the man glanced around as if searching for the voice. Almost immediately his attention turned back to Vera, who had used his distraction to pull away and attempt escape. To Lucy's dismay, he met this bid by striking her friend in the head and tossing her over his shoulder.

As Lucy moved as quickly as she could in her constrictive ball gown, she watched as the man wrenched open the door of the carriage and tossed Vera inside. Without a backward glance, he climbed in after her. He must have rapped on the ceiling of the vehicle, because the horses trotted into motion. Before Lucy's horrified eyes, her friend and her captor were gone.

By the time Lord Gilford reached her side, there was nothing left to see beyond the Leighton-Childes' garden gate.

"They're gone, I take it." It was a statement, not a question.

"Yes."

Lucy blamed herself. If she hadn't lingered in the library with Gilford, she might have reached Vera's side sooner. She would have liked to pretend she'd been there because she was concerned for Meg's family. But that wasn't all it had been. She'd been captivated by her friend's handsome brother. Had wanted to spend more time alone with him.

And now Vera had been taken heavens knew where, and Lucy was at least partly responsible for it.

"You know the lady who was taken?" Gilford asked now, interrupting her guilty thoughts.

"She's a friend. One of the Ems." She continued to stare down the lane, as if against all sense the coach would come racing back any minute. "Vera Blackwood. The daughter of the American industrialist."

An heiress, she almost added, remembering Gilford's question earlier. But her petty decision not to offer up Vera to him on the proverbial silver platter—out of jealousy, she now admitted—was immaterial at the moment. Besides, he could figure it out for himself.

If he recognized the name, Gilford didn't mention it. Instead he simply nodded and said, "No doubt he'll be willing to pay for her safe return."

Before she could respond, a shout from the garden behind them alerted Lucy that the guests on the terrace had heard the shouting.

Turning, she saw both Meg and Elise coming toward them.

"Here you are," Meg said with a purposely wide-eyed look between her friend and her brother. "Lucy, your long absence from the ballroom has been noted, I'm afraid."

Neither Lucy nor Gilford needed more explanation from Meg to interpret the warning embedded in her words.

"We did what we could to downplay things." Elise gave them both a sympathetic wince.

As if conjured, Mrs. Penhallow appeared on the path behind Meg and exclaimed with relief when she saw Lucy, though when she saw Gilford beside her, her relief turned to alarm. "Lucy, what is this?"

Before Lucy could formulate a response, she felt Gilford stand up straighter at her side, and when she glanced over at him, she saw that his expression was grim. "I'm afraid Miss Penhallow and I were too late, ma'am."

Deciding that his apparent decision to brazen out the situation and sound the alarm was the correct one, Lucy nodded. "Lord Gilford is correct, Mama. We were unable to stop them."

"What do you mean, Miss Penhallow?" asked Lady Exley from where she hovered behind Lucy's mother and the other guests, who had begun to gather just far enough away to watch the unfolding drama. "Of whom are you speaking?"

"Miss Vera Blackwood, my lady," said Lucy, hating herself for using Vera in this way, but knowing it could not be helped. "She's been abducted."

Chapter 6

By the time the missing Miss Blackwood's father and the Metropolitan Police had been called and most of the guests at the Leighton-Childes' party had been sent home, the hour was far advanced.

Because they had been the last persons to see Miss Blackwood before she was spirited away, Will and Miss Penhallow had been asked to remain in the townhouse of their hosts so that they could be questioned. First by the constables who responded to the initial summons that had been sent to headquarters. Then by Detective Inspector Cherrywood, who had been assigned to the case because it involved not only someone of high station with a considerable fortune but also an American.

Will stood near the fireplace of the drawing room where he and Lucy, along with her mother and their hosts, had been deposited once they'd told the gathering in the garden what had happened.

The tea tray that had been brought to the ladies what felt like hours ago was now picked over, half-drunk cups and plates of nothing but crumbs partially stacked on one another.

Behind the table where the tray sat, Miss Penhallow and her

mother sat side by side. Both looked to be exhausted, and Will was about to ask Cherrywood if they might be dismissed when the door to the room opened and a couple he knew all too well stepped in.

He'd first met Eversham—Will was dashed if he could remember the fellow's rank now—when he'd investigated the murder of Will's father years ago. The lady with him was the detective's wife, Lady Katherine, who owned one of the most successful newspapers in London. She was also one of the pair who wrote the column that had spawned Lucy's book club.

When Mrs. Penhallow saw her cousin and his wife, she gave a little cry of relief and burst into tears. Beside her, Lucy wrapped an arm about her mother's shoulder and said something soothing that no one else could hear.

Despite the fact that she'd been the one to see her friend abducted, Lucy had proved herself to be made of sterner stuff than either her mother or Lady Leighton-Childe, their hostess.

Through multiple rounds of questions—many of them particularly pointed since Cherrywood had apparently decided that this was some sort of scheme Miss Penhallow and Miss Blackwood had concocted for attention—she had kept her composure. It was remarkable, honestly. Will was certain that even Meg, whom he knew to be as levelheaded a young lady as was to be found in London, would at the very least be angered by Cherrywood's impertinent questions, but she had sat through it all with nary a blush.

It was damned impressive.

Now, however, with Kate having taken the seat on the other side of the teary Mrs. Penhallow, Will watched as Lucy launched herself toward Eversham.

"You will find her, won't you, Cousin Andrew?" she asked the older man as he pulled her to him in a paternal embrace. There was such trust in Lucy's attitude toward the man that Will found himself almost jealous. He'd never inspired such blind confidence before. Not even Meg when she was small.

Silently he added "become someone to be trusted as Lucy trusts Eversham" to his unwritten list of goals for his life back in England.

"I will certainly try, Lucy," Eversham said as he patted Lucy on the back. She pulled away from him and dabbed at her wet eyes with the handkerchief her cousin had given her.

"I simply never imagined such a thing could happen in the middle of Mayfair," she said in a tear-roughened voice. "They were in the mews, but that is hardly hiding. It's obvious they were waiting for Vera. They knew she would be at this ball."

He indicated that she should return to the sofa, where Kate and Mrs. Penhallow sat side by side on one end, leaving the other side free.

"You too, Gilford," Eversham said with a look in Will's direction.

Not wanting to crowd the ladies, Will crossed to the empty chair near Lucy's end of the settee.

Remaining on his feet, Eversham said, "I realize that you two have likely been subjected to multiple rounds of questions already, but I must prevail upon you to go through the details once more. There may be something that one of you remembers in the retelling. And the constable, Cherrywood, and I all have had different experiences in the police force, so we might each pick up some detail in your story that would be missed by the others."

Feeling his own sort of relief that the seasoned detective was here to take control of matters now, Will glanced at Lucy, who had apparently been looking at him, because she hastily looked away.

Interesting.

"Lucy, let's begin with you," Eversham said, gesturing toward her.

Will wasn't sure if it was because she was now telling the story before Kate and Eversham, but twin flags of color appeared on her cheeks.

"Well," she said, sounding firm despite her embarrassment. "Meg, Elise, and I—that is, Miss Margaret Gilford, Mrs. Clevedon, and I—had decided to search out Miss Blackwood because we hadn't seen her in some time and we were afraid she'd been waylaid in some way."

At this, Will saw Eversham's jaw tighten. He'd already listened to Lucy recount the tale multiple times now, and it never got less angry-making in the retelling. He knew—as did every other gentleman who'd ever attended a *ton* party— that there were those among them who would not scruple to take liberties with vulnerable young ladies also in attendance. But he'd thought those sorts were few and far between. He'd never imagined it was such a problem that his own sister and her friends would feel the need to rescue one another.

"We split up to search for her," Lucy was saying when Will returned his attention to them. "Meg to the retiring room, Elise to the secluded alcoves, and me to rooms along the corridor leading to the terrace."

Will wasn't sure whether he should be grateful that Meg, probably because she was the youngest of them, had been sent to the retiring room, where she was unlikely to be harmed, but he was. Damned selfish of him. Especially since he'd been hidden away in the library like a coward instead of protecting his sister from the sort of predation he hadn't even known existed at so-called civilized society entertainments.

"I, um, came across Lord Gilford in the library," Lucy continued, her already heightened color going a shade darker.

"Did you, indeed?" Eversham turned his gaze to Will, and the younger man felt that gimlet gaze in a way he hadn't experienced since his father died. "And what, pray tell, were you doing in the library during a ball, Lord Gilford?"

Fighting the urge to bow his head in the way he and his friends had done when they were called into the headmaster's office back at school, Will instead met the other man's gaze without blinking. "I was *alone*," he said with exaggerated emphasis, "seeking a bit of air in between sets."

He wasn't about to admit he'd been in the library because he couldn't bring himself to ingratiate himself to the heiresses and widows most likely to bring the kind of largesse through marriage that he needed to save his estates.

And the "bit of air" excuse was true enough, since he'd been unable to breathe when he'd stepped into the room and contemplated his task. He'd seen what a marriage made for dynastic or monetary reasons looked like from the time he was a child. His parents might have come to respect one another after a few years, but the fact that they had only two children together served as testament enough that their cordiality only extended so far.

Will wanted the kind of marriage his friend Lord Adrian had with his wife, Meg's former governess, Jane. Even if he chose the most agreeable among the selected heiresses—and there was no guarantee she'd have him—it was unlikely they'd develop what Adrian and Jane had. He wasn't sure why, but he glanced toward where Lucy sat looking his way.

Realizing he'd been caught wool-gathering, he cleared his throat and continued. "I was in the library, chatting with Miss Penhallow," he said calmly, "when we both heard a shout from the open French doors."

"I hurried toward where the sound had come from," Lucy continued, "stepping out onto the terrace and toward the rear of the garden. As I went, I saw a carriage in the lane beyond. And even as I watched, I saw that Vera—that is, Miss Blackwood—was there with a large man in dark clothing. She screamed again and tried to pull away, but he was clearly too strong. I shouted at them—I don't recall what I said—and when I did so, the man got distracted and Vera tried to get away."

Will watched as Lucy's face grew bleak. He chastised himself not for the first time for his lack of attention to what was happening in the mews as he trailed Lucy through the garden.

"He clouted her in the head," Lucy said, "and before I could reach them, he hefted her over his shoulder and tossed her in."

Eversham gave her a nod of approval, "I know how difficult it must have been for you to tell the story again, and I appreciate your strength in doing so."

"You too, my lord," he continued, looking in Will's direction. "I am grateful to both of you for remaining this late to recount the story. Now I think it is time for both of you to go home and get some rest."

Rising with Mrs. Penhallow on her arm, Kate said to Lucy,

"We will take the two of you home in our carriage. Just to ensure you are safe."

Lucy nodded, and as they crossed to the door, she said to Will, "Good night, my lord. Thank you for your assistance."

Before he could reply, she was hurrying out of the room behind her mother and cousin-in-law.

He stared after them for a few seconds before he realized the room was empty except for Eversham and himself.

"Lord Gilford," the detective said to him with a piercing gaze, "what exactly are you playing at?"

Chapter 7

To Lucy's surprise and reluctant pleasure, when she was shown into the drawing room of her friend Jane and her husband Lord Adrian Fielding the next evening, it was only to find Gilford was already there.

But why wouldn't he be there, she reminded herself. Before her marriage to Lord Adrian, and before she became a celebrated author of suspense novels, Jane had served in the Gilford household as Meg's governess. And Lord Adrian had been the late Lord Gilford's right-hand man in the Foreign Office, so would have had a long acquaintance with the siblings.

Before she could speak to Gilford, however, Lucy's hands were gripped in Jane's. "My dear girl," said her hostess, concern in her searching gaze, "Will told us what happened at the Leighton-Childe ball last evening. I am so pleased to see you in person, but you must be exhausted. I thought you might cry off tonight."

"Of course I wouldn't miss it." Lucy squeezed her friend's hands and offered her a grateful smile. "I've been looking forward to this dinner party for weeks."

She knew that Jane, more than anyone, understood just

how upsetting it could be to witness violence in a place where one expected to be safe. She'd been the one to discover the late Lord Gilford's body when he'd been murdered.

Jane slipped her arm through Lucy's and escorted her around the room to present her to those guests she might not have met before now. Lord Adrian's position with the Foreign Office meant that the events they hosted often included visiting dignitaries and colleagues who were rarely in England.

When they reached Gilford, who was in conversation with a handsome American, Lucy noticed that he looked none the worse for wear after last night's contretemps.

"Mr. Woodward," said Jane as that gentleman turned his attention their way, "I believe you and Miss Penhallow have already met?"

"Indeed we have, Lady Adrian," Woodward, whose dark good looks and easy manners made him a favorite at society functions, offered his hostess a smile. Taking Lucy's hand, he bowed over it with a warm smile and said, "Miss Penhallow, I'm so pleased to see you again. You're looking particularly lovely this evening."

Woodward sent a quick glance to Gilford before returning his gaze to hers and continuing in a flirtatious tone, "I hope you will think of me when you wear that particular shade of blue from now on. For I assure you I will think of none but you whenever I see it again."

To Lucy's astonishment, when she turned to greet Gilford his eyes were shooting daggers at his friend. And after he rose from bowing over it, he kept her hand in his.

"Miss Penhallow," the viscount said as he scanned her face, "I hope you are not any the worse for wear after last night's trouble. I know it was distressing for you to witness your friend's abduction."

"I am as well as can be expected, my lord," she told Gilford, wishing they could return to the ease of the way they'd talked in the Leighton-Childe drawing room. "Certainly, in better shape than poor Vera, who must be terrified, wherever she is."

Feeling the eyes of Jane, Woodward, and every other guest in the room on her, Lucy pulled her hand a little. As if he'd only just that moment recalled that her hand was in his, Gilford let go at once. "Have you learned anything new from your cousin? From what he said last night, the police were dispatched to the home of Miss Blackwood's father to inform him of what happened."

"I haven't spoken to him in person," she said, aware that the whole room was listening to her now, "but he did send a note around this morning informing me that he's put his best detectives on the case. Also, that the searches conducted last night of the likeliest places where she might have been taken yielded nothing new. He did promise, however, to update me as soon as there is news."

"If this had happened in my day," said Lord Adrian's grandmother, the dowager Duchess of Langham, from her thronelike chair near the fire, "the fiend would already have been rounded up and put on a ship bound for the Antipodes. I disapprove of this new generation. The entertainments are infinitely duller, and despite this newfangled police force, innocent young ladies are being snatched up in the streets."

To punctuate her disapproval, she brought down her walking stick in a resounding thud on the carpeted floor.

Despite herself, Lucy felt a lift in her spirits. She might not agree with the dowager on everything, but she hoped at Her Grace's age she was half so full of spirit.

Before there could be more discussion, dinner was announced, and to Lucy's pleasure, she saw that she'd been seated between Jane's editor, Mr. Archibald Chase, on one side, and Gilford on the other. After she'd exchanged greetings with the editor, however, Mr. Chase seemed intent upon maintaining a conversation with the lady on his other side.

"You can't take Woodward's flirtation seriously, you know." Gilford watched her from the chair to Lucy's right with all the leashed energy of a caged jungle cat.

Taking a spoonful of the soup that had just been set before her, Lucy glanced over at the viscount. "And why is that?"

She made every effort to maintain her composure under her dinner partner's scrutiny, but there was only so much control she had over her body's response to him. Even when he was being an overbearing ass.

"Because the man is not to be trusted where ladies are concerned."

Lucy waited for some elucidation from him on the matter, but none came.

"That's it?" she asked skeptically. "That is all you will say on the matter?"

She'd heard more fulsome arguments from schoolroom children.

Gilford's only response was a shrug. "You'll simply need to trust me on this. Men discuss things in private that are not fit for feminine ears. And I simply do not want you to get hurt by setting your cap for the fellow."

"And yet, he is welcome in households all across London,"

Lucy said, leaning back so that the footman could remove her soup bowl. "And you count him as a good friend, I believe?"

"What has that to do with anything?" Gilford gave her a disappointed look, as if he'd expected better of her. "Just because I enjoy an evening at the tables with a fellow doesn't mean I'd wish him to court my sister. Or my sister's friend."

This last he said with a pointed look at her from over his wineglass.

"So you fear that I am such an easily influenced ninnyhammer." Lucy spoke with studied politeness that anyone with a longer acquaintance with her would recognize as incipient fury. "That—let me get this right—I will be so overwhelmed with infatuation for Mr. Woodward after his uttering a single line of flattery that I will fall to the floor at his feet and beg him to ravish me on the spot."

She watched in amusement as Viscount Gilford's face gradually transformed from calm smugness to growing alarm. At the word "ravish" Lucy saw the tips of his ears go red, though whether it was embarrassment at having provoked her into saying it or at being made to think of the named activity in polite company she couldn't be sure.

"Oh, come, your lordship," she said, spearing a pea with her fork. "We are both mature enough to have plain speaking between us, are we not?"

Something in her words must have sent Gilford over the edge, however, for he lost all semblance of laziness and sat up straight, leaning toward her so only she could hear him. "You know I meant no such thing, Lucy. I meant only to give you some advice, given how bowled over you appeared in light of Woodward's ham-handed attempt at flirtation. But I suppose there are those who cannot be persuaded to listen to good sense."

Lucy gaped. Of all the arrogant...

"You seem to be in such heated conversation, Miss Penhallow, Lord Gilford, I simply must know the topic," said Lady Fortescue from across the table with a sly smile. She knew full well it was considered rude not only to begin a conversation across the dining table but also to interrupt a private discussion. But the lively widow was, since the death of her elderly husband, no longer beholden to anyone else. And she frequently used that freedom to make mischief.

Gilford, to Lucy's amusement, muttered a low curse before he spoke aloud so that both Lucy and Lady Fortescue could hear him clearly. "It is nothing so fascinating as all that, my lady, I assure you. Miss Penhallow and I have simply been discussing last night's trouble at the Leighton-Childe ball."

As distractions went, Lucy thought with reluctant admiration, it was a good one. After all, the kidnapping had been on the tip of everyone's tongue earlier, and a gossip like Lady Fortescue could not possibly resist adding her own opinion to the talk.

And sure enough, the lady's eyes narrowed with interest. "Oh, excellent," she said with relish. "You must tell me everything about what happened. I read the newspaper accounts, but those are never as satisfying as a description from someone who was actually there. Do you think she'll be rescued?"

"I wouldn't know where to start, my lady, though I have every hope that the police will be successful in their search," said Lucy without really relating the full story.

Before Lady Fortescue could form a response, however, a

male voice rang out. "There is no need for you to tell the tale, Miss Penhallow," said Mr. Chase from Lucy's left side. "I've had the whole story from a friend at the Met. And much as we would all wish that your friend, Miss Blackwood, could be rescued from her captors, I'm afraid that seems a slim possibility indeed."

"No," he continued, looking as grim as any physician delivering a poor prognosis, "I'm afraid it's too late. Miss Blackwood is, in all likelihood, dead."

Chapter 8

There were gasps from all around the table, and Will could have cheerfully leveled the dour Mr. Chase with one punch.

The fellow's proclamation fell in one of those lulls in conversation that happened at every gathering when whoever had the good luck—or in this case, ill fortune—to speak at that moment would have their words heard by everyone.

Beside him, Will saw that Lucy was all but quivering with indignation. Whether at the man's crassness or his pessimism, he couldn't tell. Though knowing her temperament, it was the latter.

But before Lucy could unleash her own criticism on the man, Jane spoke. "Oh, Archie, you promised to be on your best behavior this evening."

Since Chase was Jane's editor, Will guessed that she'd expected some kind of faux pas from him tonight.

"I know I did, Lady Adrian," said Chase, using Jane's formal title, "but that was before I knew there would be talk of Miss Blackwood's abduction."

Jane opened her mouth to offer a response, but before she

could do so, Lucy raised a hand. "I would like to hear what Mr. Chase has to say. My cousin, the detective superintendent, always says that an outside perspective can be helpful in these matters."

There were several murmurs of agreement, and though Jane still seemed reluctant, a speaking look from her husband seemed to make her relent. "Very well, Archie, unleash your analysis."

Chase, who looked a shade uncomfortable now that he was the focus of every eye in the room, cleared his throat but began speaking.

Will felt a reluctant surge of admiration for Chase. Any other man would have succumbed to silence at a chiding from Jane, who had used her governess voice on the editor.

"As I told Miss Penhallow," Chase said carefully, "I had the details of what happened and what she and Lord Gilford witnessed at the ball last night. Having made a study of such abductions, and similar crimes against the wealthy—for my employment as an editor of crime novels—I have observed that the matter rarely ends happily."

"That's nonsense, sirrah," the dowager Duchess of Langham said with a sniff. "There have been many such incidents where the person who was taken captive has been safely returned to their family after the funds were paid."

The dowager sent a reproving look in Jane's direction, as if in chastisement for Jane having invited such a fool to the party in the first place.

Since he'd been one of the only two people to witness Miss Blackwood's abduction, and as Jane's friend, Will spoke up. "Your Grace, perhaps we should hear more about Mr. Chase's investigation of such crimes. Mayhap that will make it clearer how he came to hold such an opinion."

He sent a speaking look in Chase's direction: *Don't make a fool of me as well, Archie.*

Beside him, Lucy sent Will a grateful look, and he felt the power of it down to his toes.

"Well, Lord Gilford, perhaps I should begin with the case of…" And thus Chase began a rather lengthy—at least outside of a lecture hall—speech about the numbers of abductions in the past dozen or so years and how each had concluded. "I'm afraid, if you look at the numbers, it would seem that if there has been no communication from the culprits to her father, then poor Miss Blackwood was very likely done away with sometime today."

By the time he reached the end, Will and, he was certain, most of the others at the table had let their minds wander to more interesting topics. Like the way one perfect coil of Lucy's pale blonde hair brushed at the nape of her neck. Though it was perhaps only Will who was thinking of that.

The object of Will's attention, whose rapt focus had been fixed on Chase all through his monologue, now spoke up. "That was utterly fascinating, Mr. Chase, but we do not know, in fact, whether her family has been contacted with a request for money in exchange for her safe return. Therefore, your conclusion is premature at best."

"Hah!" The dowager gave Lucy an approving look. "Miss Penhallow has an excellent point, Mr. Chase. There has been no mention of a request for ransom, nor for anything in exchange for Miss Blackwood's return. So your prediction of doom cannot be taken seriously."

"Poor Mr. Chase," crooned Lady Fortescue, as if the blow Lucy's comment had leveled had indeed been wounding.

For his part, Chase simply shrugged. "My friend in the police says that if there was going to be a demand for money in exchange for the young lady then it would have happened by now. If ransom was not the reason for the abduction, then Miss Blackwood's chances of survival are not good."

Will thought about what Chase had said. He was sure that if there had been a request for ransom, Lucy would have heard about it by now. It was obvious from the way she and Eversham interacted that her cousin considered her to be trustworthy on such matters.

He glanced over at her, as if to test the truth of what he'd just concluded.

To his surprise, he found that she was looking his way, too.

"What other reason, indeed?" she said for his ears only.

Will's attention for the rest of the meal was taken up by the lady on his other side, who wished to quiz him on the latest fashions in Paris.

Once the ladies had departed the dining room to leave the gentlemen to their port, Will was drawn into a group with Adrian and Woodward, as well as Lord Peregrine Maitland, whom Adrian knew from university.

"I must offer my thanks, Gilford," Adrian said, clapping Will on the shoulder with his free hand—the other held a tumbler of whisky. "I warned Jane that Chase might not be ready for a dinner party with Grandmama in attendance, but she was determined."

"He wasn't so very bad," Woodward said in a low voice so that Chase, who was in conversation with one of the dowager's elderly brothers, wouldn't hear. "And his dissertation on the outcomes of kidnappings among the wealthy of England was interesting."

Sir Peregrine choked on his whisky, Adrian disguised a bark of laughter as a cough, and Will grinned outright.

"Fine," Woodward said, lifting his hands in surrender and offering his own rueful smile. "It was dry as dust. Most statistics are. But you must admit, his conclusion that the Blackwood girl is likely dead by now makes more sense when you consider the information he shared."

"But we don't know whether there has been a request for ransom," Will pointed out, remembering with admiration how Lucy had taken the wind out of Chase's sails. She was proving to be cleverer than he'd expected.

"Yes," Adrian said with a nod. "And though I realize she, as much as anyone, has reason to hope that Chase is wrong, Lucy was right to point out the fact."

"It isn't so difficult to believe that the lovely Miss Penhallow would be the one to point that out, however." Woodward glanced at Will with a smirk, reminding him of his earlier promise to box the American's ears soon. "She has been doing some work for her cousin in his offices at the Met for several months now."

This was the first Will had heard of it, but he saw that Adrian and Perry nodded to Woodward, as if they had been in on the information as well.

It didn't matter, Will told himself. The larger issue was the fact that Eversham was allowing his lovely, unmarried cousin to swan about in such an uncivilized location as Metropolitan Police headquarters.

"I thought Eversham was more sensible than that," he said aloud now, gulping down the last of his whisky.

"I'm not sure what about his allowing her to do a bit of clerical work for him is so objectionable," Adrian said with a shrug. "I suspect she might have been the one to suggest it, but she's a clever lady, and I daresay she enjoys it."

Will shook his head in disappointment. "She very likely does enjoy it, but that's not the point. The point is that she shouldn't be exposed to the sort of unsavory characters who are to be found in such a place."

"Unsavory characters, eh?" Woodward didn't bother hiding his mirth at Will's words.

Perry, who had been watching the byplay among the other men, said with a confused expression, "I rather agree with Gilford on this. Not sure I think police headquarters is the sort of place where any young lady should spend time. Especially not one as pretty as Miss Penhallow."

At Sir Peregrine's words, Will sent a scowl in the man's direction. "Et tu, Perry?"

Adrian and Woodward succumbed to peals of laughter while Will scowled at them and Sir Peregrine just looked more confused.

"I don't understand," Perry said with a bewildered shake of his head. "What was it I said?"

Beside him, Woodward gave the baronet a consoling pat on the arm. "I believe Lord Gilford has developed a partiality for the lovely Miss Penhallow, Perry."

"Don't be absurd," Will growled at his friend. "She is simply my sister's dear friend, and I wish for her to be kept from harm."

"For Margaret's sake," Adrian said with a skeptical nod. "Of course. That is why you looked just now as if you wanted to skewer both Woodward and Perry with the same sword. It's perfectly believable."

"If you are suggesting I am jealous of those two"—Will gestured at the American and now smug Perry—"then you're cracked in the head."

He lifted his chin in the hopes of projecting an air of superiority. "I have no particular attraction to Miss Penhallow. And certainly no reason to be jealous."

Woodward nodded in mock seriousness. "Then you will have no objection if I ask the lady to go riding in the park with me tomorrow."

Will's jaw clenched before he could stop it. "Of course not," he said through his teeth.

"I say, I'm going to do the same." Perry broke into a grin. "Don't know why I hadn't noticed the chit before now, but she's dashed pretty. And smart. Can't resist a clever girl."

And neither, Will admitted silently to himself, could he.

Chapter 9

The next morning when Lucy was in the breakfast room with her mother, she was surprised to be informed by one of the housemaids that several bouquets of flowers had been delivered that morning.

Lucy, who had been about to swallow a forkful of eggs, choked. It took a few moments and several gulps of tea to regain her voice. "Flowers for me, Mabel?"

The maid and Lucy's mother, who had both been looking at her with alarm during her coughing fit, relaxed a little, and Mabel said with a sunny smile, "Of course for you, miss." She glanced over at Mrs. Penhallow and offered an apologetic nod. "Begging your pardon, ma'am, but you being a widow and all…"

But Lucy's mother took no offense. "I understand completely, Mabel. I only wish my daughter would give one of the gentlemen who sent her these flowers a chance."

Now that she'd digested the news, Lucy was feeling a bit less surprised by it. "I do not wish to dash your hopes, Mama, but I suspect these flowers were sent with ulterior motives in mind."

Mrs. Penhallow frowned. "What do you mean?"

Lucy sighed. She'd seen that morning's headline about Vera's kidnapping and had known at once. "It is all over town now that Lord Gilford and I witnessed Vera's abduction. I suspect that all of these gentlemen who sent flowers will also send invitations to drive, dance, or various other entertainments. Anything that might give them an opportunity to get me alone so that they might question me about what I saw."

But Lucy's mother wouldn't be fobbed off so easily. "You have simply become too jaded because of all the attention you've received from fortune hunters over the years. Perhaps this notoriety is just what you needed to bring you to the notice of some gentlemen who will appreciate you for reasons other than your inheritance."

Smiling, Lucy wished she might have just a shred of her mother's optimism. But she'd seen far too many gentlemen be tempted by the latest pretty bit of fluff to believe that multiple men would suddenly conceive a passionate attraction for her.

"If you say so, Mama," she said, finishing her toast before rising from the table. "Perhaps I should go see who the flowers and cards are from before I give up hope altogether."

When she entered the drawing room and began reading through the notes attached to the individual bouquets—which she had to admit, were beautiful—Lucy was pleased to note that one was from Jane's friend Mr. Woodward, who had flirted with her last night when they were introduced.

She smiled, recalling the American's strong features and smiling eyes.

The rest of the flowers were, as Lucy had suspected, from gentlemen she'd had occasion to meet at various *ton* parties since she'd first made her debut, but none had paid her much attention before now.

Being the subject of gossip, it would seem, had an invigorating effect on one's popularity.

She was adjusting the angle of a sprig of snapdragon in one of the arrangements when the butler, Rhodes, appeared in the doorway.

"You have a caller, miss," the rigidly correct servant told her.

Lucy took the card from the silver salver Rhodes proffered. To her surprise, it wasn't one of the importunate acquaintances who'd sent flowers.

"Send him in, Rhodes," she said, wishing she'd chosen one of her more becoming gowns that morning. But it was far too early for a morning call—especially since it was generally understood that when it came to visitors, morning meant early afternoon.

Still, her primrose muslin, a few years out of fashion but still a favorite, would have to do.

When Rhodes showed Lord Gilford in a few moments later, Lucy noted that his dark suit was pristine and his hair—which had a tendency to be a little unruly—was neatly combed.

To her surprise, before he even greeted her, Gilford proffered a posy of light pink roses interspersed with lavender. "These are for you," he said with a short bow. "Meg said they're your favorite."

She accepted the flowers from him and hid her smile behind them as she took in their scent. "They're lovely," she said as she placed them in one of the vases she'd intended for a different posy.

Glancing around the room at the multiple vases of blooms, he said with a raised brow, "I see mine are not the first you've received today."

Having secured his flowers, Lucy turned and gestured for Will to take the chair at an angle from her place on the sofa. "I believe most of them are from curiosity seekers who saw my name in the papers this morning."

At that, Gilford's brows drew together. "They're pursuing you simply because they wish to question you about Miss Blackwood's abduction?"

"I don't know that for certain, of course," Lucy said with a slight shrug. "But it seems the logical reason why I'd be getting such notice from gentlemen who haven't paid me the least attention since I made my debut several years ago."

"I am sorry," Gilford said, looking genuinely troubled by the news. "I hope you won't let their false flattery injure your feelings."

"Of course not," she said with a grin, her heart warmed by his concern. "And not all of them were insincere. I also received flowers from your friend Mr. Woodward, as well as an invitation to drive in the park."

She saw his jaw tighten and remembered his attempts to warn her away from the American the evening before.

"It is a drive in the park, Lord Gilford," she chided him. "Not a marriage proposal."

"I know that," he said grudgingly. "I simply wished to invite you to drive with me today. Now, in fact."

At his words, Lucy perked up. "You did? But it isn't the usual hour for driving in the park."

"I thought we'd go somewhere else," he said with a grin that revealed he'd noticed her pleasure at the invitation.

"Where?"

"I thought we'd go question Miss Blackwood's father to determine whether he's received a demand for money."

How had he known this was a far more interesting invitation to Lucy than a drive in the park could ever be?

Feeling a rush of pleasure at having her dearest wish intuited before she could speak it aloud, she rose. "Let me have my maid fetch my hat and coat."

Chapter 10

Having recognized that his instinctive opposition to Lucy spending time in police headquarters was likely to meet with neither approbation nor thanks from the lady herself, Will had decided on the way to her house that he would instead ask her for more information about her work there.

"I only learned last night that you do some clerical work for your cousin," he said as he steered them in his curricle toward the Blackwood townhouse at the edge of Mayfair. "That is unusual for a young lady, is it not?"

Since his eyes were on the horses and road ahead of them, he only felt her sharp look before she spoke.

"I suppose it is," Lucy said calmly. "But it is only unusual because of my family's status. Girls younger than I am work in factories and offices every day of the year. But I hope that it will become less of an anomaly as more of us begin to take up more interesting tasks than deciding menus and sorting linens."

"That is likely true," Will responded, chancing a look at her, only to find her looking back at him. "But you must admit that deciding menus and the other tasks necessary to keep a household running are important in their own way."

Was he condemning Meg to a life of frustration and boredom if he insisted on a marriage to someone of their own class? He knew his sister was clever and restless with the sorts of tasks his mother had undertaken in the Gilford estates all these years. Was unhappiness at the domestic chores she'd been thrust into as the wife of a viscount the reason his mother was so unpleasant?

It was the first time such a thought had crossed his mind, and Will felt as if his understanding of his world had been upended.

"They are important," Lucy responded, unaware of the turmoil in Will's mind. "But just as some men are more suited to politics, say, or the church, so too are some ladies more suited to running a household."

"And you are not one of those ladies?" he asked, not sure why the idea troubled him, but it did.

"I didn't say that," Lucy responded, a little impatiently if her tone was any indication. "I enjoy my work for my cousin, but it can be tedious when there is nothing else of interest happening."

This got Will's attention. "You mean in the station itself?"

Lucy shrugged. "I will admit that one of the reasons I asked my cousin for the position in the station was out of interest in the cases they investigate."

This didn't surprise him. She was, after all, an aficionado of crime fiction. "And has it been as diverting as you hoped it would be?"

Beside him, Lucy heaved a sigh. "In truth, it's been disheartening. As kind and clever and insightful as Cousin Andrew is, the majority of the policemen I've come into contact with have proven to be incompetent and often willfully obtuse."

Before he could respond, she went on. "They are nothing like the detectives and policemen in novels. Inspector Falcon in Jane's books, for example, is able to see through the lies of murderers with little trouble. He's also willing to listen to women—especially those of the lower classes—when they complain of being mistreated or harmed by the men in their lives."

Will had read all of Jane's detective novels and enjoyed them thoroughly. But that didn't mean he thought they reflected reality. "They are fictional, Miss Penhallow. Even Jane has admitted that Falcon is idealized."

"Of course I know that," Lucy said, waving a dismissive hand. "But I had hoped that exposure to actual police officers would give me some hope for their ability to put aside their own prejudices in order to solve crimes. Instead, the constables and detectives under Uncle Andrew's authority can't even be bothered to investigate a murder if they haven't first been assured of its importance to someone who can further their own careers."

Will hated that Lucy's work with her cousin had disillusioned her like this. But it was common anytime one entered a new arena. When he'd attended his first meeting of the House of Lords, he'd been astonished at how many peers simply didn't show up. Of course, he'd missed three of the past four years himself, he thought ruefully. But that didn't make it right.

"A young prostitute was found murdered in Whitechapel a few weeks ago," Lucy continued, again not waiting for Will to respond. He got the feeling that she'd wanted to complain about this topic for some time.

If he were a different sort of man, perhaps, or if this were Meg he was listening to, he'd have pointed out that she shouldn't use such an improper word—nor should she even know that such women existed. But they were discussing Lucy's work in a police station. The horse had been out of the barn for some time.

"And?" he pressed, when she stopped talking and stared mutely at the opulent houses that lined the cobblestone streets they traversed. He knew without asking that she was seeing something in her mind's eye.

When she turned back to him, he saw there were tears in Lucy's eyes. And he mentally cursed the fact they were in a moving vehicle when he was forced to turn his attention to the horses under his control instead of pulling her into his arms.

"Mary was fifteen years old and had come to London from the country with dreams of factory work, or perhaps a domestic position. But instead she was forced to work on her back." Her voice was grim, and Will again wondered how Eversham could possibly allow her to be exposed to such tales. It wasn't appropriate for anyone, much less a gently bred lady.

"She was beaten to death one night by her pimp when she made some comment he disliked," Lucy continued, the fury evident in her every word. "And we know this because there were witnesses. Her neighbor in the filthy rooming house where she lived informed me when I went to question their landlady that he heard Silas King assaulting her. And now, because of the police not immediately apprehending him, Silas King has gone to ground and will likely go unpunished for this and countless other crimes for which he is responsible."

If Lucy had been familiar with Lord Gilford in a temper,

she'd have known that instead of shouting, he instead became calmly quiet.

"You. Did. What?"

But she was unfamiliar with Will in a temper. And so Lucy waved away his question. "Please don't be tiresome about this. I took my maid with me."

"You took your maid with you," he restated in disbelief. "One of the most dangerous slums in London, and you took your *maid* with you."

"You are missing the point, Gilford," she said impatiently. "The constables who were sent to investigate the murder have done nothing to apprehend the man who killed Mary. Because she has no one to fight for her who might put in a good word for Constable Jenkins with my cousin when it comes time for him to be promoted. Nor does she have a wealthy benefactor to grease their palms."

Getting hold of his temper, Will forced himself to listen to her words. It wasn't his place to read her a scold, after all. But he would have a word with Eversham about her trip into Whitechapel at the soonest opportunity.

"Surely if your cousin's men are so reluctant to do their jobs, then it is his responsibility to see that they do," he said aloud.

"He does what he can, but it does little good when his own superiors don't care about the death of a single prostitute, either."

Unsure of what he should say, Will settled for "I'm sorry, Miss Penhallow."

"You needn't apologize," she said, and there was no mistaking the determination in her voice. "I merely wanted to explain to you why I intend to do my own investigation of Vera's abduction."

"But I thought you said it's crimes against the impoverished that don't get attention from the police," Will said, wondering what he was missing.

"That's true enough," Lucy said, "But I forgot to mention that when it comes to missing women of the upper classes, they are apt to dismiss the cause as nerves or female silliness. I received a note from my cousin this morning informing me that the top brass believe Vera has run home to America because of homesickness."

Chapter 11

As she and Lord Gilford were shown into the drawing room of the Blackwood townhouse, Lucy looked around her avidly. Despite her friendship with Vera for the past several weeks, she'd never been inside the Ashdown Square townhouse Vera's father, a railroad tycoon in their native United States, had let for the family.

"I must admit that these modern houses have appeal," Gilford said, looking almost boyish as he scanned the room's inlaid ceilings and stained glass windows. "If Gilford House weren't entailed—" But he must have recalled at that moment that the estate was nearly bankrupt because he abruptly broke off.

A pang of sympathy for him made Lucy leap into the silence. "Mama and I have considered one of these, as well. What must it be like to have windows that don't stick?"

Thankfully, Mr. Richard Blackwood entered the room at that moment, and both of them focused on their host.

The man looked haggard. Lucy had only met Vera's father a few times, but it was as if Blackwood had aged thirty years in the past three days. There were bags under his eyes that attested to his lack of sleep. And his skin, once marked by healthy color, was now wan.

"Mr. Blackwood," Lucy said, moving toward him with her hands outstretched. "I have come to see if there's been any news of Vera."

Since she'd already heard from her cousin, this was a polite fiction, but Lucy didn't want to inform Vera's father that the Metropolitan Police hierarchy thought his daughter had simply run away. He had enough on his mind at the moment.

"Thank you for coming, Miss Penhallow," Blackwood said in his American accent, with its flat vowels and oddly nasal tone. "I know my daughter would appreciate that you're so concerned about her welfare."

Lucy introduced Gilford, and Mr. Blackwood indicated that his guests should take seats. Lucy and Gilford sat side by side on an overstuffed sofa. Blackwood, meanwhile, remained standing, as if too restless to settle.

"What of you, Mr. Blackwood?" Lucy asked, genuinely concerned for the man's welfare. "I know Vera would not wish for you to neglect your health in her absence."

Blackwood's second wife had died a few years ago, and with his other children—three sons—back in America, Vera had been the one to fuss over her father during their tenure in London.

To Lucy's surprise, a familiar figure swept into the room at that moment, looking as if she was mistress of the house.

"My dear Miss Penhallow," said Lady Evangeline Fortescue, the lovely widow who'd quizzed her about Vera's kidnapping only last evening, as she slipped her arm through

Blackwood's. "And Lord Gilford. How pleasant to see you again. Though the circumstances are dreadful, of course."

Gilford, who had risen on Lady Fortescue's entry, didn't seem to be surprised at her presence here. Then again, he wasn't acquainted with the Blackwood family. "My lady," he said, bowing over her hand with the good manners expected of him. "A pleasure to see you as well, though I must admit to some curiosity. You didn't hint at any connection to the Blackwood family when we spoke last night."

Well done, Lord Gilford.

Perhaps she'd misjudged the viscount's reading of the situation, Lucy thought.

"Blackwood and I have tried to keep our fondness for one another quiet, especially since the news of poor Vera's abduction," Lady Fortescue said with credible dismay. "But this is not a time for Richard to be alone. He's in an unfamiliar city surrounded by strangers. I couldn't possibly leave him to his own devices at such a time."

Vera's father looked upon Lady Fortescue with nothing short of adoration. Though unsure of how sincere the widow's feelings were—Richard Blackwood was, after all, wealthier than most of the lords in Parliament combined—Lucy believed the Americans were sincere at least. And who was to say that Lady Fortescue hadn't fallen head over ears for the man? Perhaps the notoriously fickle lady had finally lost her heart.

"I am glad he has you, then," Lucy said aloud to the widow, who had just cajoled Blackwood to take a seat on the other sofa. Lucy couldn't help exchanging a glance with Gilford, however, and when he returned her look with wide-eyed skepticism of his own, she felt slightly vindicated. "I was just asking Mr. Blackwood whether there was any news of Vera."

"None, I'm afraid." If possible, Blackwood's expression turned even more pinched. "Evangeline, that is, Lady Fortescue, told me what that editor fellow said last night about abduction in exchange for money. That if that's the case, then the abductee is likely to be killed."

"It was just a theory, sir," Gilford said, and Lucy wished she could kiss him. It was such a kindness to give Mr. Blackwood hope, even if there was no rationale for it at this point. "I believe it's far more sensible to listen to what Detective Superintendent Eversham says, given that he has actual experience of such matters. Mr. Chase, the editor chap, seemed sure of himself, but he's got nothing to go on but his own study."

Lucy couldn't help but think of all she'd complained to Gilford about with regard to the Metropolitan Police earlier. Even so, she had a strong belief in Cousin Andrew's competence as a detective. And Gilford was right about Archie Chase.

At Gilford's reassurance, Mr. Blackwood seemed to relax a little. "Do you believe so, Lord Gilford?"

"Of course he does, Richard," said Lady Fortescue with a grateful look in Gilford's direction. "He wouldn't have said so otherwise."

Blackwood nodded, almost like a small child being promised that Father Christmas was, in fact, real.

Deciding she'd better ask the questions she'd come to ask so that she and Gilford could leave the poor man in peace, Lucy leaned forward a little. "Mr. Blackwood, the last time I saw Vera, the afternoon before the Leighton-Childe ball, Vera seemed out of sorts. Do you perhaps know the reason for that?"

Since most unmarried ladies didn't spend a great deal of time with their parents, Lucy wasn't sure he'd know anything, but she had to ask.

At the look on Blackwood's face, however, her heart sank.

"No, Miss Penhallow," he said with a frown. "I wish I had known. Otherwise, I'd have done something to find out. It troubles me to hear that she was unhappy. Perhaps there was something I could have done to make it better."

Like a lioness protecting her cub, Lady Fortescue placed an arm around Blackwood's shoulders. To Lucy and Gilford, she said, "Perhaps the two of you had better go."

Recognizing that they'd likely exhausted whatever Mr. Blackwood might be able to tell them about Vera's state of mind, Lucy rose to her feet. She and Gilford made their farewells to their host and made their own way back to the entrance hall.

They'd just stepped out onto the front steps when the door to the mansion opened to reveal Lady Fortescue. Shutting the door firmly behind her—likely to ensure that none of the servants would overhear her, Lucy surmised—she said, "Richard doesn't know what was troubling Vera that afternoon, but I do. I must have your promises that you won't let this information go any farther than us three."

Lucy wanted to protest that if it was something that might help them find Vera, then she would most certainly tell her cousin at the very least. But before she could say so, Gilford squeezed her hand where it rested on his arm. "I won't make such a promise until I know what it is you mean to say. And neither will Miss Penhallow. We are, after all, intent upon finding her."

Lady Fortescue frowned, but after a moment she nodded. "I suppose if it will help find her, then she'll simply have to face knowing her personal business has been aired."

Lucy clamped her teeth together to keep from urging the woman to speak up.

"On that morning," she said, looking far more troubled than she had in the drawing room, "Vera received a letter that left her agitated. She hurried upstairs and slammed her bedchamber door with such force that it nearly shook the house."

The older woman didn't bother explaining why she'd been in the Blackwood home at such an early hour, but Lucy had no difficulty guessing. She supposed she was glad that Mr. Blackwood had someone to comfort him in his fear and agitation.

"Do you know what was in the letter to overset her so?" Gilford asked, not calling attention to the confirmation that Lady Fortescue was Blackwood's lover, either.

To Lucy's surprise, the widow reached into the pocket of her gown and extended an envelope to her. It looked to have been through a great deal of handling.

"Use what you must to find her," Lady Fortescue said with an intent look at Lucy, who got the feeling the widow cared about Vera's rescue almost as much as Mr. Blackwood. Perhaps she wasn't so self-interested as Lucy had at first thought. "But I must ask you not to tell Richard what this letter reveals. He is not well, and it can do him no good unless it is strictly necessary."

"I give you my word," Lucy said aloud. Then she let Gilford lead her down the steps and hand her into the waiting curricle.

They were barely underway when Lucy had pulled open the writing paper and begun to read.

"Good heavens," she said after scanning a couple of pages. "Vera was engaged to someone back home in America named Christopher Hamilton, and this letter says he's to arrive in London only a couple of days from now. Could it be that the police are right and she has run away back to America?"

Chapter 12

"Miss Blackwood running away doesn't explain what we saw the other night, however."

Will knew that Lucy was hurt by the notion that her friend had kept such important news from her, but he knew what he'd seen with his own eyes that night, and Miss Blackwood—if it had indeed been her—had not gone willingly into that waiting carriage.

He'd guided the curricle to a secluded area of the park so they could discuss the letter before he took her home. And he'd be a liar if he said he didn't enjoy simply sitting close enough to touch her in the shade of the trees.

When in the hell had he ever appreciated such an innocent encounter?

"You're right," Lucy said, oblivious to Will's thoughts that had nothing to do with her friend's disappearance. "Now that I've read the letter more closely, it seems clear he thought she intended to break things off with him. Perhaps putting distance between them was her reason for coming to London with her father. She did tell the other Ems and me that she hoped to meet prospective suitors here. And her father has made no secret of the fact that he is title shopping."

In point of fact, Miss Blackwood had been on the list of eligible heiresses he and Adrian had compiled a few days ago. But he was hardly going to tell Lucy about it. Especially since he'd vetoed Lucy herself from the list once he'd realized she was Meg's close friend. He wasn't quite sure what was happening between them. And the devil knew he could use the infusion of funds a hasty marriage into the Penhallow family would bring the Gilford estates. But Lucy hated fortune hunters. And the idea that she'd ever think he was after her for her money filled him with self-loathing.

Still, the topic of marrying for money sparked an idea. "Perhaps this Hamilton fellow followed Miss Blackwood to London for the simple reason that if she broke their engagement he'd lose access to the money she'd bring by marrying him."

"So Christopher Hamilton was the man we saw hauling her into the carriage?" Lucy's brow furrowed, but she didn't discount the idea. "We don't even know if the man has arrived in London yet."

"That's true, but that seems like something your cousin should be able to find out easily enough." Will realized they'd need to leave soon if he intended to meet Adrian and Woodward for luncheon as they'd planned. Which reminded him of something. "If Eversham can't get the ships' manifests, then Lord Adrian should be able to do so."

Woodward, as a former envoy to England from the United States of America, would have colleagues in the American embassy he could ask, but Will was damned if he'd have Lucy feeling gratitude for that Judas.

Was he being petty? Perhaps. But there was no way he'd let the other man steal Lucy from beneath his nose before he was even clear whether he wanted her or not. That last bit was self-deception of the highest order, since he wanted her more than air. But until he had the chance to examine his feelings for her more closely, he would do what he could to scuttle any plans the American might have for her.

"I don't think it will be necessary to ask Lord Adrian, though the notion is a good one."

The wind had picked up a little, and one of the ribbons of Lucy's bonnet blew up to kiss her cheek. And before Will could stop himself, he reached up to caress the silky soft skin of her face.

Lucy's exquisite lavender eyes locked with his before she lowered her lashes in the age-old sign that a lady wished to be kissed.

Even so, there were rules about that sort of thing.

"Miss Penhallow." Will's voice sounded husky to his own ears, but before he could ask her permission to lower his head to hers, another carriage came clambering by. Lucy's eyes opened wide and she pulled away.

The moment was lost.

Not sure whether to be relieved or annoyed, Will gave the horses the signal to walk on, and they rode in silence until they were almost to Grosvenor Square, where Lucy lived with her mother.

Though his eyes were on the horses in front of him, Will

somehow knew Lucy wasn't looking at him when she spoke up. "I hope you don't think, Lord Gilford, that I—"

"Think nothing of it, Miss Penhallow," Will said before she could finish. "The fault is all mine."

"Fault?"

Will heard the confusion in her tone and knew he'd made a strategic error. Still, he could hardly take back the words at this point. "Yes," he continued, feeling as if his mouth was completely disconnected from his brain in that moment. "It was a mistake. We're simply lucky that carriage came along when it did. We won't speak of it again."

"Won't speak of it again?" Lucy's voice was tight with temper now. And he expected for her to continue with some well-deserved chastisement for him, but instead she gripped his arm and shouted, "Will! Look out!"

He'd chanced a sideways glance at her, but that was all it took for the hansom cab that came barreling toward them from out of nowhere to gain enough of the road to be a danger.

It took all of Will's skill at the reins to get his own equipage out of harm's way.

The driver of the cab was dressed in all black and his face was covered with the sort of mask once favored by highway-men a century ago. But it was from the half-lowered window of the hack that a bundle was tossed with perfect aim into the curricle.

His ears were ringing and his breath was coming in great gulps by the time Will had pulled the carriage to a stop a few doors away yet from the Penhallow townhouse. He tossed the reins to a groom, not even sure to whom the fellow belonged. But one thing he knew for certain was that he didn't give a hang about propriety or his pride or any of the other reasons he'd conjured to be uncertain of Lucy. If it meant prostrating himself before all of London, he'd do it.

When he turned to her, Will had every intention of kissing her senseless. But one look at her sheet-white face and wide eyes told him this wasn't the time.

It was comfort she needed from him now, not his adrenaline-fueled pawing.

Heedless of the fact they were in the middle of a Mayfair street, where anyone might see them, Will pulled her into his arms.

"We might have been killed," she said against his wool-covered shoulder in a wobbly voice. The heat of her body against his—even separated by the many layers of clothing between them—sent Will's senses on alert. Ruthlessly, he brought himself under control, though the scent of roses that wafted up from her skin and hair tempted him nearly beyond bearing.

"We weren't killed, though," he assured her, running a comforting hand over her back as she clung to him. "We're very much alive."

"Who would possibly do such a thing?" she asked, reluctantly pulling away from him. And just as reluctantly, Will let go of his hold on her.

Badly needing to do something with his hands, he ran one over his hair. The other he clenched to keep from reaching for her again.

That was when he remembered whatever it was the passenger of the hansom cab had thrown toward them. Now, however, he *was* mindful of the curious eyes of the residents of Brook Street.

"Let's get you home, then we'll talk about just who it was that came at us like that."

Leaping down to the street, he handed Lucy from the curricle and instructed the groom—who had no doubt been listening intently for the past quarter hour—there would be a handsome tip for him if he'd walk the horses until he returned.

Reaching back into the floor of the coach, he plucked up the bundle-turned-projectile and tucked it inside his coat.

Whatever it was, he thought as he and Lucy made the short walk to the Penhallow townhouse, he hoped the oilcloth-wrapped package would tell them something about either Vera or their near miss. Because he knew one thing for certain.

Whether she liked it or not, he wouldn't let Lucy out of his sight until they had some answers.

Chapter 13

The object inside the oilcloth missile turned out to be a sheet of foolscap wrapped about a stone, and tied securely with a string. Gilford used his pocketknife to cut the strings and unwrapped the page from the rock. He glanced at it and Lucy knew from his expression that its contents infuriated him. Wordlessly, he handed it to her.

"Stop meddling, you nosy—" Lucy broke off without speaking the vulgar word aloud as she read the message scrawled on the page. "Well, I suppose we know for whom this message was intended. Only one of us is appropriate for that particular insult."

She was trying to lighten the mood, but clearly Gilford was unable to be cheered out of this particular mood.

"It isn't amusing, Lucy," he said, looking as if he could chew through steel. "You could have been killed if that cab's driver had miscalculated by a few inches. And it doesn't make me feel any better knowing that I was able to keep us out of the villain's path only by the skin of my teeth. I should have been paying attention to the road rather than—"

Lucy was well aware what he'd been doing at the critical

moment. They'd been arguing over whether that almost-kiss in the park should be forgotten. And Gilford clearly blamed himself for both incidents, which was absurd.

They'd retreated to a small parlor facing the garden, which was used mostly by Lucy for reading and needlework on those rare occasions that she thought to do it. The important reason she'd chosen the parlor instead of the drawing room was that her mother rarely came here, and she'd wanted a few minutes of privacy with Gilford so that they could examine the mysterious parcel.

Now, however, she was glad she'd chosen this room, because it would be easier to ring a peal over his head without an audience.

"You should have paid attention to the road instead of me," she said, drawing herself up to her full, though not particularly impressive, height and putting her fists on her hips. "That is what you are saying, is it not, my lord?"

Gilford looked surprised by her vehemence but didn't back down. "You know it is."

Crossing to where she stood on the far side of the table upon which they'd unwrapped the rock, he hesitated for only a moment before he took one of hands from where it was fisted at her side. Unfisting it gently, he threaded their fingers together, and Lucy felt the warmth of their palms meeting in every sinew of her being.

"Miss Penhallow," he said, looking both abashed and deadly serious. Then correcting himself, he said instead, "Lucy."

She hadn't realized until that very moment that she wanted to hear her given name on his lips with a vehemence she'd not even guessed at.

"It's likely too soon to make any kind of declaration," he said, his warm eyes filled with such sincerity she couldn't doubt him. "In fact, I know it. But I also know this: If you'd been injured this afternoon, I'd never have been able to forgive myself."

"It wasn't your fault," she protested even as he'd begun to shake his head.

"It doesn't matter whose fault it was. The result would have been the same."

Still savoring the feel of his skin on hers, Lucy bit her lip.

"If you intend to continue looking into Vera Blackwood's abduction, then you must promise me that you won't do anything that will put you in danger," Gilford said. "You mustn't do anything without me. We must work together."

Lucy disliked having restrictions put upon her. Especially since there were already so many that were required simply to live as a lady in polite society. Still, she supposed that near-miss this afternoon was reason enough to agree to his terms. And it would be no hardship to conduct an investigation in the company of the most handsome man she'd ever met. If anything, he'd grown even more appealing since their almost-accident.

"Very well," she said with exaggerated reluctance. After all, she couldn't appear to simply bow to his wishes without any protest. Otherwise, he'd think her utterly without a backbone. "But only because I don't want you to fall into a decline."

At her teasing words he broke into a grin. Then, rubbing his thumb over the back of her hand, he said softly, "I have one more request."

Her heart was beating faster, and Lucy asked in a hushed tone, "What is it?"

" 'My lord' and 'Gilford' and 'Lord Gilford' are so formal," he said, his voice almost a caress. "I'd like for you to call me Will."

And this time when their mouths gravitated toward one another, there were no interruptions to stop them.

*   *   *

Will's first sensation when he brushed his lips lightly against Lucy's was one of incredible softness. He'd anticipated she'd be sweet in his arms, but the reality of her lushness against him was better than he'd imagined. And to his surprise and delight, she welcomed the tentative touch of his tongue by opening her sweet mouth.

As a man of five and twenty, he'd kissed any number of women over the years, but there was some corner of his mind that whispered over and over that this particular woman— Lucy—was different. Because *he* felt different.

For what felt like hours but was in actuality only a few intoxicating minutes they held on to each other as if one kept the other from sinking into an imaginary flood surrounding them. Trading caresses with lips, tongues, and mouths.

It wasn't until Lucy's soft gasp when his hand stroked up her side to palm her breast, still chastely covered by her gown, that Will pulled back. He might have come to terms with the fact that he wanted her. But he wasn't going to trap her into a marriage by compromise with him before she'd had an opportunity to decide for herself.

He needed her money, no question, but she deserved better than him, and he damned well knew it.

He stopped, slid his hand back down to rest on her hip, and kissed her eyelids and the tip of her nose, and finally gave her lips a gentle press.

When he pulled away, she looked at him with a slumberous smile.

"Well." Her voice was a little breathy, and he couldn't hide a pang of masculine pride at knowing he'd done that to her.

"Well." He lifted a hand to tuck a wayward lock of hair behind her ear.

"I don't suppose we can cancel our appointments and spend the rest of the afternoon doing that." The disappointment in her voice told him that she already knew the answer, as did he.

Deciding a hasty departure was needed to stop him from reaching for her again, Will stepped back. "I will take the note and the other items to your cousin. He should know that you were threatened today." And he wanted to make sure Eversham knew the severity of what had happened. Will suspected Lucy might downplay things if she thought her cousin might restrict her investigation in any way.

She opened her mouth to object, but Will spoke before she could. "I have reason to be in that area anyway, and I suspect you'll wish to tell your mama about what happened before he can."

Lucy wrinkled her nose adorably at the mention of her mother. "I suppose you're right, but Mama will fly into a pelter no matter who she hears the news of our near crash from."

Mrs. Penhallow was like to be overset by a number of observations her neighbors in Brook Street might relate to her, but Will forbore from mentioning that.

Bowing over Lucy's hand, he secured her consent for the waltzes at the Maitland ball that evening; then, feeling as puffed up as a jaybird despite the danger he and Lucy had nearly been unable to avoid, he collected his hat and walking stick from the Penhallow butler and went to claim his curricle.

Chapter 14

A secret betrothal? Who could have imagined?"
Lucy watched as Meg punctuated her question by taking an enthusiastic bite of a macaroon. The two friends along with Elise were seated around the tea table in the latter's private sitting room. Vera would, under normal circumstances, have been with them, but Lucy knew at this point that these circumstances were a far cry from normal.

"It's hardly such a shock, is it?" At nine and twenty, Elise was older than Lucy and Meg, and she'd either witnessed or read about more scandals in her lifetime than either of the other two could conceive of. "There are as many reasons for concealed engagements as there are hairs on your head, I should imagine, Meg. Especially when there is a sizable dowry involved."

To Lucy's discomfort, Meg looked very like her brother when she furrowed her brow. It made Lucy all too aware that she had her own secrets at the moment—especially the toe-curling kiss that morning with the man in question. Schooling her thoughts, Lucy put all of her focus on the younger of the Gilford siblings.

"It's not so much that I cannot believe in hidden betrothals in general," Meg said with a slight shrug. "I simply can't believe Vera was in one and didn't tell any of us about it."

"When you really think on it," Lucy said thoughtfully, "we only knew Vera for a month or so. How many of us would reveal all of our past friendships and tendres to new acquaintances so soon into the association? We three have been friends for years, and I daresay there are still things we don't know about each other."

Meg frowned. "I've told you both about every gentleman I've ever thought of in a romantic light. Even Lord Skelton, and that particular fondness does me no credit."

At the mention of the Earl of Skelton, whose favorite topic of conversation was an update on the diet of every horse in his enormous racing stable, Lucy and Elise both laughed.

"True," Lucy said with a giggle. "But he is kind, at least, so you shouldn't feel bad about him."

"True," Meg agreed. "But perhaps Vera's intended—and the fact that she didn't go about boasting of him implies this—was not a kind person. Maybe she didn't tell us about him because she intended to break things off with him, so she didn't think he mattered anymore."

"It's also possible that Vera feared that if word got back to her father, he would marry her off to the first impoverished member of the peerage who approached him simply to control her." Elise cradled her teacup in her hands. She'd once explained to her friends that she did this contrary to every etiquette rule of the tea table because she liked to feel the warmth through the porcelain. Especially when she was nervous.

Was she feeling especially troubled at the moment? Lucy wondered.

Though Meg trustingly believed she knew all of her friends' secrets, Lucy knew there were some details of her past that Elise hadn't shared with either of the other two members of their trio. She suspected it was because her friend's marriage hadn't been as uncomplicated as they all believed.

Still, that was for Elise to tell them when she was ready—if at all.

"I wish I could ask more questions of Mr. Blackwood," Lucy said, returning her attention to the matter at hand. "But he did seem to be genuinely troubled by Vera's abduction. And if he knew anything that might give the authorities some idea of where to find her, I have a feeling he would tell them."

"Perhaps he's so devastated because he's the one responsible for her abduction," Elise said with a raised brow.

At Meg's gasp and Lucy's genuine surprise, their friend was unrepentant. "We've already agreed that there are some parents who will stop at nothing to control their children. And we all saw how troubled Vera has been for the past week or so. Maybe she was so upset because of some attempt on Mr. Blackwood's part to coerce her into marriage with someone of his choosing rather than hers."

"And the American fiancé is simply an extraneous detail?" Lucy gave the notion some thought. "We did receive the letter from Blackwood's mistress. Could he have instructed her to chase after us with it with that little story about how much it upset Vera when it arrived?"

"It's possible, I suppose, and it was staged in such a way that it looked natural." Meg lifted another watercress sandwich from the table. "They might not have known you and my brother would pay a call, but once you did, he thought to turn your suspicions away from him and onto Christopher Hamilton by sending Lady Fortescue out to you."

Lucy shook her head. "I was so surprised at learning Lady Fortescue and Mr. Blackwood were in a liaison that it never occurred to me that their performance might be just that—a performance."

"We don't know that it was," Elise reminded her. "It's just a theory at this point. We can't even know if the handwriting on the letter is the same as Christopher Hamilton's because we don't have anything to compare it to."

"I shall need to simply sneak into the Blackwood house and search Vera's bedchamber."

Now it was Elise who gaped at Meg.

Lucy bit back a smile at the byplay.

"Do not look so surprised," Meg said, her shrug echoing Elise's earlier one. "Is Lucy the only one of us who is allowed to be involved in this investigation?"

Looking abashed, Elise said, "No, but we don't know yet whether Mr. Blackwood is to be trusted. And you could be hurt."

"And didn't Lucy and my brother nearly come to danger this morning doing something as simple as driving through Mayfair?"

Wincing, Lucy realized that despite her not telling her friends about what had happened yet, Meg at least had already learned of it.

"I was going to tell you both," she said hastily, feeling her face flame, though whether it was about being caught in a deception or about the kiss that happened not long after their near collision, she wasn't sure. "I just hadn't got to it yet."

"Well, I have no notion of what you're both talking about," Elise said, looking from Lucy to Meg then back to Lucy again. "I take it you and Lord Gilford were set upon while driving in Mayfair?"

Quickly, Lucy recounted what had happened that morning, leaving out the detour to the park and what had happened in the house after their return.

When she mentioned the rock being thrown at them and the moment when Will's curricle and the anonymous driver's cab nearly struck one another, Elise covered her mouth with her hand in shock.

"In broad daylight in Mayfair?" she asked with disbelief. "Whoever this is, he is bold, isn't he?"

Remembering the fear and horror of the moment, Lucy couldn't contradict her friend. "Whoever it is, he's comfortable in Mayfair."

"You think it's one of us?" Meg asked, startled. "Someone from the upper classes?"

Lucy hesitated. She didn't know that for certain, but the thought had occurred to her. "Or employed by a member of the upper classes. Think about it. There are far too many servants and guards on the streets of Mayfair—not to mention the wealthy inhabitants themselves—for someone intent on doing harm there to even make it as far as the far borders of the area. But the fact that this person felt comfortable enough to not only try to ram a viscount's carriage but also throw a large rock at him took either madness or a sense of protection."

"If it is someone from the *ton*," Elise said, her brown eyes narrowed with determination, "then that will make it that much easier for one of us to bring him down."

"I hope so," Lucy said.

Because she wasn't sure whether she could withstand the sort of scare she'd had earlier. At least not unless she knew that she and whomever she experienced it with would come away unscathed.

Chapter 15

Though he'd much rather have found his way to the Maitland ball that evening on his own, Will escorted his mother and sister in the family carriage. This meant that instead of simply jumping down and making his way to the Duke of Maitland's door on foot, he had to wait with his mother and sister in the coach as it crept behind a parade of other vehicles doing the same thing.

"Stop fidgeting, Gilford," his mother snapped at him as if he were a small boy.

He remembered when she'd begun to call him Gilford after his father's death. The change had been unsettling, though in truth he should not have expected his mother to behave any differently. If she was to be relied upon for anything, it was her strict adherence to the rules of etiquette. And it wasn't as if she spoke to him in any casual way. To her, he'd always been William, never Will, as his sister and schoolfriends called him.

Still, he was the sixth Viscount Gilford and was entitled to respect. Even if it was owed to him from his mother.

"I am a grown man, Mother," he said tightly. "Not a boy to be chastised."

If she was cowed by his correction, the viscountess didn't show it. "Very well, then, my lord, please will you calm your fidgets?"

The treacly tone she used was as objectionable as her previous words, but by this point they were nearly to the Maitlands' doorstep, so Will ignored her and gave a knock on the roof before opening the door to the carriage and jumping to the cobblestones.

Lowering the step himself, he reached back inside, and when his mother only looked tightly at him, he offered his hand to Meg, who raised a brow at him but accepted his assistance down.

Once in the ballroom, he glanced toward the corner of the room, where Lucy and her friends were to be found no matter the ballroom. Mrs. Clevedon, another of Lucy and Meg's Ems, was deep in conversation with the son of their hosts, the Marquess of Edgmont.

"Where is she?" he asked his sister, who had been watching him with something like amusement.

"Who?" Meg asked innocently, blinking at him with all the guile of a newborn lamb.

"You know who," Will said impatiently. "Lucy—that is, Miss Penhallow."

On any other day, the cat-that-licked-the-cream look his sister turned on him would have only mildly irritated him. Today, when Lucy had nearly been injured by some unknown villain, Will had no patience for teasing.

Perhaps sensing his mood, Meg touched his arm. "Do not fly into the boughs. She is dancing with Lord Catesby. There." She tilted her head in the direction of a pale-haired lady being promenaded in a country dance by the handsome Catesby, whose estates were on the brink of bankruptcy thanks to his late father's gambling.

Will wanted to swear but contented himself with a feral sound in the back of his throat.

"Did you just growl?" his sister asked, agape.

Ignoring her question, he said, "I thought Miss Penhallow was never asked to dance. She's a wallflower."

He'd seen her with his own eyes at the first two balls he'd attended since his return to London.

"By choice. Not because she's never asked." Meg spoke with no small amount of exasperation at his thickheadedness. "Miss Penhallow chooses not to dance, because if she didn't, her card would be filled with the names of wastrels and fortune hunters at every entertainment of the season."

And didn't that just hit Will right in the solar plexus?

Still, he needed more explanation.

"Then why is she dancing with Catesby?" Will demanded. "Not only does he not have a feather to fly with, but he's a womanizer to boot."

He himself might be a fortune hunter, Will thought grimly, but at least he knew Lucy wasn't in danger of being seduced in his company.

Not much, anyway.

Meg gave him a disgusted look, as if she'd never heard a more crack-brained pronouncement.

"Maybe," she explained to her elder brother as if he were a five-year-old in the schoolroom, "she is dancing with a man she heartily dislikes because she agreed to dance with someone else later in the evening. And since she has to refuse all dances if she refuses one, she is doing that mysterious gentleman the great kindness of agreeing to partner with everyone who asks."

Will listened to his sister's words with growing consternation. It had never occurred to him that by asking Lucy for her waltzes he was consigning her to take to the floor with men she disliked.

"Do not look so alarmed," Meg said with a grin. "At least you know she believes the dances promised to you will be worth it."

Scanning the row of chairs where the other wallflowers lingered, she turned back to him. "If you really wanted to return Lucy's kind gesture, you'd dance with some of the other ladies without partners. There are always plenty of gentlemen at each ball, but they turn their noses up at those girls they deem to be beneath their notice."

He hadn't known this and felt like a churl for not realizing it for himself.

Before he could respond to his sister's rebuke, she was headed toward where Mrs. Clevedon stood on the other side of the room.

Will had just returned Miss Frederica Honeywell to her mother's side after a quadrille when he spotted Adrian and Woodward nearby. After thanking his partner for the dance, he hurried over to where his friends chatted.

"Ah, the man of the hour," said Woodward with a knowing grin. "Were your ears burning?"

Wondering what the American was up to, Will hid his curiosity over the other man's teasing under a veneer of unconcern. "Not particularly," he said with a shrug. "Though your inability to stop thinking about me is your problem, not mine, Woodward."

Adrian hid a laugh behind a cough. And Woodward scowled at him.

When he'd recovered his composure, Adrian said with an apologetic wince, "I believe in this case, Woodward isn't the only one who's been talking about you. There is some gossip working its way around the room that you need to hear about."

At this, Will's gut clenched. Had news of the Gilfords' destitution reached the ears of the *ton* so soon? It had only been a week or so, but he knew that gossip ran rampant when it concerned the peerage.

"You were seen in the middle of Mayfair, man," Woodward said with a shake of his head. "Did you think no one would find out?"

Ah, Will realized. This he had expected.

"Haven't I taught you anything?" Adrian asked with mock disappointment. "Never kiss a lady in a public street. Certainly not in full view of Brook Street."

"I told you what happened with the carriage," Will said, dismissing their teasing. "I was merely comforting Miss Penhallow after she was *rightly* upset by the attack on my curricle. And there was no kissing."

At least not on Brook Street.

"I've had the story from four different people," Woodward said pointedly, "and all of them said you were kissing her. One said she was kissing you, but that was a gentleman who was very likely wishing he'd been the one driving the carriage."

"Are you sure it wasn't you, Woodward?" Will asked with

a scowl. "You seemed awfully intent on impressing her with your own flattery last night."

"Got to you, did it?" he asked, exchanging a sideways glance with Adrian.

"I think you're missing the point," Adrian said with a quelling look at the American. "You were seen with Miss Penhallow in a potentially compromising position. By the end of the evening you'll have been in flagrante delicto. Miss Penhallow's reputation could be in jeopardy."

Will swore. He wanted to convince her of his sincere liking and affection for her before he made an offer. Because that was the only thing that set him apart from the other fortune hunters who flocked around her.

But if circumstances meant he'd need to do so sooner, then so be it. At least he'd be sure she was his.

Still, he wasn't ready to discuss the matter with his friends.

"Thank you for letting me know," he said to them both. "Now, what do you have to report about Christopher Hamilton? Has he entered the country in the past few weeks?"

"He has, indeed," Adrian said, turning serious in a matter of moments. "One Christopher John Hamilton of Philadelphia, Pennsylvania, disembarked from the *Morpho Eugenia* in Portsmouth on the thirtieth of April."

"And Miss Blackwood was kidnapped on May seventeenth," said Will, feeling a stab of excitement at the news. "Hamilton might have been the one to kidnap her, or his appearance on the scene might have prompted either her father or some other of her wannabe suitors to whisk her away. Thank you," he said, clapping Adrian on the shoulder. "This could be just the bit of information we need to find out what became of Miss Blackwood."

"Wait a minute before you run to Miss Penhallow with the news," Woodward interjected just as Will was about to do that very thing.

When he turned a questioning look on Adrian, the other man looked apologetic.

"The thing is, Gilford," said Adrian, "Hamilton didn't come to England on his own."

"No one ever truly travels alone," Will said dismissively. "When I returned from Paris I had my valet, a footman, a cook—"

"Gilford, shut up for a moment and listen to Adrian," Woodward said, breaking into Will's list of his fellow travelers.

"Hamilton didn't come alone," Adrian restated. "He brought his wife."

Chapter 16

She'd forgotten how energetic a country dance could be, Lucy thought as she was escorted off the ballroom floor by one of the Duke and Duchess of Maitland's younger sons, Lord Anthony Maitland. Her determination to refuse all dancing in order to ward off fortune hunters had been a somewhat effective deterrent, but she had to admit she'd missed it.

"I am pleased you chose to dance this evening, Miss Penhallow," said Lord Anthony before bowing over her hand to take his leave of her.

She had to admit he was a handsome young man, with his father's laughing eyes and his mother's honey-colored hair. "I am too, my lord."

Lucy was about to add that she was especially happy to take the floor with such a skilled dancer when as if from out of the clouds painted on the ballroom ceiling, Will appeared.

Perhaps reading the viscount's grim expression as jealousy, Lord Anthony made a swift retreat.

"My dance, I believe." Having barely given her a perfunctory greeting, he then led Lucy onto the floor. His movements were, as always, elegant, but his haste irritated Lucy.

"What has left you in such a mood?" she asked as the musicians played the opening notes of a popular Strauss waltz. Despite her pique, having Will's strong arms around her sent a little thrill through her.

A thrill she hadn't experienced with any of her other partners that evening.

As if he'd needed the rhythm of the dance to calm his mind, Will finally relaxed and looked down at her sheepishly. "I've wanted to speak to you all evening, but every time I tried to make my way to your side, you were dragged off for another dance with some other man."

Lucy bit back a smile at his aggrieved tone. But his next words pleased her in a different way.

"I also spoke to Adrian and Woodward about Christopher Hamilton."

Her pulse picked up. "What did they say?"

Quickly he told her what his friends had found out about Hamilton.

"Married?" Lucy was shocked despite never having heard of the man until that morning. "But why would he pen a letter pleading with Vera not to end their betrothal if he was already married?"

"It's as confounding to me as it is to you," Will said, sweeping her into a turn. "What we do know is that he arrived long before Miss Blackwood was abducted, so it's likely he was responsible."

"It makes no sense," Lucy protested. "It's not as if he can force Vera into marriage. He'd be guilty of bigamy."

They were silent then, and while she enjoyed the intimacy of the dance her grandmother's generation had thought scandalous, Lucy puzzled over the conundrum of Christopher Hamilton.

She'd intended to take the news to Meg and Elise, but as the dance drew to a close, Lucy was approached by an uncomfortable-looking footman.

"I was asked to bring you this, miss," the young man said, handing her a scrap of paper.

There was no way to conceal the interaction from Will even if she'd wished to, Lucy thought with frustration as she searched for somewhere she might read the note out of view of the other guests.

As if guessing her thoughts, Will steered her to an alcove shielded by a pair of ornamental orange trees. Once there, Lucy unfolded the page and read it before handing the note to Will.

I know who has taken Vera Blackwood. Meet me at the fountain during the supper dance. Come alone.

When he was finished Will made a noise of disgust. "As if I'd let you go meet some unidentified note writer without an escort."

Setting aside the fact that he wasn't in any position to "let" her do something or not, Lucy still objected to Will's statement. "This might be our only way of learning where they've taken Vera. I cannot simply ignore that."

"And you can't simply ignore the fact that someone attempted to harm you earlier today," he said tightly. "Whoever this person is, they'll need to find some other way of giving you the information."

She saw at once that one reason for his autocratic words was fear for her safety, and she softened a little. "I'll hardly be in danger in full view of a ballroom full of people."

"The fountain isn't visible from the ballroom," he argued, looking determined. "Though that was a clever attempt on your part."

"The supper dance is about to begin," Lucy said, ignoring his faint praise. "And I'm going to find out whatever this person wants me to know. If you won't let me go alone, then you'd better make yourself invisible."

Not waiting to see what Will's response would be, she slipped out from behind the trees and wended her way along the perimeter of the ballroom toward the bank of four sets of French doors leading out into the opulent gardens of the Maitland townhouse.

Without looking back to see, she instinctively knew Will was not far behind her as she lifted her full skirts so she might navigate the shallow steps leading down to a torchlit sunken garden.

Though she did not wish to call attention to herself, Lucy felt the urge to run through the carefully cultivated trees and flowerbeds laid out in neat rows, fearful the note writer would leave before she had a chance to reach the appointed meeting spot. It took self-control to keep to a sedate pace, so that she might appear to be taking in the admittedly beautiful landscape.

She'd nearly reached the edge of the garden's most magnificent feature, a large stone fountain, when she felt someone step up beside her. She thought it was Will, at first, but the newcomer's patchouli scent alerted her that it was someone else.

"Will you walk with me, Miss Penhallow?" asked the handsome Sir Charles Fleetwood as he threaded her arm through his. "I believe we have much to discuss."

Wondering where Will had gone, and if he would remain out of sight so that she might speak uninterrupted with Sir Charles—who must have written the note—Lucy walked alongside the baronet as he led her to an iron bench on the far side of the fountain.

Politely handing her down so that she might sit, Sir Charles appeared too agitated to sit. As if he needed to calm his thoughts before he could speak, he paced before her in silence for more than a minute.

Finally, when Lucy had been about to press him to say something, he stopped before her and said, "I had hopes of marrying her, you know."

She didn't doubt that it was Vera to whom he referred. Her friend had never mentioned any sort of understanding with Sir Charles, but then again, Vera hadn't said anything about Christopher Hamilton, either. Perhaps their friendship hadn't been as close as Lucy had thought.

Fleetwood, a slenderly built and elegant man, didn't present a particularly formidable impression, but there was something unsettling about the intensity of his gaze.

"I didn't know," Lucy told him in a placating tone. "You must be worried sick since her abduction."

At the mention of Vera's abduction, Fleetwood made a choked sound and turned his face away.

Though she could understand Vera's father reacting to her absence with high emotion, Fleetwood's dramatic actions seemed a bit much given that he'd only known Vera for a few weeks.

When the man turned back toward her, Lucy saw that there were tears in his eyes.

"Come now," she said to him in a soothing voice. "We are all worried about her, but you must not let yourself succumb to despair."

She wished she could glance about to see if Will had indeed followed her into the deepest part of the garden where the fountain lay. Fleetwood was entitled to his feelings about Vera's abduction, but he'd said in his note that he knew where she'd been taken. So far, he'd done nothing but emote.

"You have some idea of what has happened to her?" she prodded gently.

At her question, he turned to face Lucy and she was startled by the coldness in his face. "Yes, I do have some idea, Miss Penhallow. Because I am the one responsible."

Chapter 17

From the nearby cluster of flowering trees where he'd hidden, Will fought the instinct to go to Lucy's side. If Fleetwood was responsible for the abduction of Miss Blackwood, then he was not to be trusted.

But he knew instinctively that Lucy would not thank him for the interruption. Besides, Fleetwood didn't appear to have a weapon, and he was slight enough that Will doubted he could overpower Lucy easily.

Still, he could tell from the tremor in her voice that Lucy didn't feel altogether safe with the man.

"Wh-what do you mean that you are responsible, Sir Charles?" she asked with a composure that gave Will a burst of pride. His Lucy was no coward.

The question hung in the air as Fleetwood appeared to struggle with some inner demon for a moment. Then looking defeated, he said, "I asked you here to give you some sort of Banbury tale about how Miss Blackwood had been spirited away by rookery thieves or some nonsense, Miss Penhallow. But I find that I cannot stand to deceive you any more than I already have."

What the devil was the man nattering on about now? Will wondered. He was beginning to wonder whether Fleetwood didn't suffer a malady of the mind.

Lucy, however, continued to treat the man as if he made perfect sense. "Why don't you simply tell me the truth, then, Sir Charles."

Fleetwood seemed to visibly sag, not unlike a hot air balloon with the air let out Will had once seen as a child.

"Very well, Miss Penhallow," the baronet said. "She wasn't taken by thieves or brigands. She was taken by her American betrothed. And I am the one who arranged it."

Will watched Lucy as she gasped, and he was damned glad he'd not done the same.

"What? How?" Lucy's words echoed Will's thoughts.

Turning to pace again, Fleetwood finally stopped once more to face Lucy. "It is likely not a surprise for you to learn that my estate is badly in need of funds."

This was the first time Will was learning of it, but though he'd received much of the gossip from London while he was away, he hadn't particularly paid attention to the fortunes of any gentlemen unless they were attempting to pay court to his sister. And to his knowledge Fleetwood had never approached Meg.

Sir Charles's words told him, however, that the man might have numbered among the fortune hunters whose dogged pursuit had caused Lucy to give up dancing.

"I have heard something of your ill fortune," Lucy said kindly. "And was this why you pursued Vera?"

As if his legs would no longer hold him up, Fleetwood dropped down onto the bench beside Lucy. Will's jaw tightened, but he let them be.

"I needed her money," Fleetwood said, leaning forward to drop his head in his hands. "But I also cared about her. You must believe that, Miss Penhallow."

"What happened?" Lucy asked.

"I was approached last week by a man, an American, claiming to be Miss Blackwood's betrothed," Sir Charles said with a shake of his head. "You must understand, Miss Penhallow, that I would never have considered his offer if it weren't for the fact that I am in such desperate need of funds. I was willing to wait for Miss Blackwood to make up her mind about me, but my creditors do not care about such things."

"And this American, what was his name?" Lucy asked calmly. She no longer seemed to be unsettled by Fleetwood, only impatient. Will couldn't blame her.

"Hamilton. Christopher Hamilton of Philadelphia."

Well, at least they knew the fellow hadn't lied about being Vera's betrothed, Will thought wryly.

"And he paid you to, what? Lure Vera into the Leighton-Childe mews the night of the ball?"

Fleetwood turned toward Lucy in astonishment, as if she'd just conjured an apple from the air with a snap of her fingers. "How did you guess?"

"Vera must have had some reason to go outside that night," she said with a slight shrug. "And you *did* get me to meet you tonight. I suppose you used an anonymous note with Vera as well?"

At this, Will saw Fleetwood's face flame, even from his relative distance.

"It was not anonymous," Fleetwood said, the shame evident in his voice. "I signed the note with my own name. I told her I was desperate to see her. Her father refused to approve the match, you see. So we'd had to pretend in public that there was nothing between us."

"So, Vera had consented to your suit?" Lucy asked thoughtfully. Will could imagine how hurt she would be if that turned out to be the case. Women cared about sharing such things with their friends.

But Fleetwood looked abashed at the question. "Not precisely," he admitted. "While I do believe she cared for me, she was determined to abide by her father's wishes. But I had every hope of persuading her to go against him."

The man was living in a delusion, Will thought with disgust. It was clear Vera Blackwood had been hiding behind her father's disapproval in order to keep Fleetwood at arm's length, but the man was so desperate for her dowry that he refused to see it.

Lucy still seemed mindful of the need to keep Fleetwood talking, but Will could tell by her pursed lips as she listened to the other man that she was no more impressed with his reasoning than Will had been.

"You must understand, Miss Penhallow, I thought Vera was lost to me." Fleetwood dragged a hand down his face in despair. "This man had a prior claim on her, and though she'd never made mention of a fiancé in America, he knew details of her and her household that he wouldn't have known without some inside knowledge."

And he'd offered Fleetwood a small fortune for simply getting Vera out of the ballroom and into the mews, Will thought cynically. It was clear now that most of Fleetwood's agitation was for himself and his guilt over his own greed.

"Why haven't you gone to the police or Vera's father with this information?" Lucy asked, and this time she did allow some of her scorn for the baronet show. "It's been two days. If they'd known about Christopher Hamilton sooner, the police might have been able to track them down."

Fleetwood responded with his usual histrionics. "No one can chastise me more than I have chastised myself, Miss Penhallow," he said in a wheedling tone. "As soon as I learned what you and Lord Gilford witnessed that night, I realized my mistake. I had hoped that I was playing a role in reuniting separated lovers. But instead, I merely lured poor Miss Blackwood into a predator's trap."

Will rolled his eyes. If this fellow hadn't been born into the gentry, he would have had a promising career on the stage. What he said about luring her into a trap might be true enough, but again, all his chagrin was on his own behalf.

He was inclined to make up some excuse to come blundering into the clearing around the fountain, even if just to remove Lucy from the other man's posturing. But before he could invent something, another man approached from the other direction.

Theodore, Lord Cheswick, Will thought with disgust. He'd been at school with the earl and he'd been a troublemaker even as a boy.

"I might have known you'd find it impossible to keep quiet for long, Fleetwood." Cheswick strode toward Lucy and the baronet, and Will's hands clenched at his sides.

Fleetwood's face went slack at Cheswick's appearance. "What are you doing here?"

"I was invited just as you were, Fleet," said the earl with a little sound of impatience. "Now, tell me what you've been tattling about to the inquisitive Miss Penhallow. She's already proved to be a thorn in my side from the moment she and Gilford wandered outside at just the wrong moment."

To Lucy, the man said with exaggerated sweetness, "You must understand, Miss Penhallow, it's not that I don't find you charming in the normal course of things. But you and Gilford got in the way of what was supposed to be a lucrative enterprise."

Deciding he'd had enough of fearing for Lucy's safety, Will stepped out into the clearing opposite the trio. "If you have a quibble with me, Cheswick, then you can damned well tell me to my face."

If he'd expected Cheswick to be surprised, Will was to be sorely mistaken. Instead, the earl gave a little snort. "Tut tut, Gilford," he chided. "There is a lady present."

"I think you'd better tell us how you were involved with Miss Blackwood's abduction," Will said, ignoring the other man's taunt. Glancing over at Lucy, he extended a hand, and she rushed to his side.

Fleetwood meanwhile looked as if he couldn't decide whether to flee or faint.

"If it's all the same to you, Gilford, I'd prefer not to." Cheswick looked over at his apparent partner in crime. "It is, after all, nothing to do with you."

To Fleetwood he snapped, "Don't look like you're about to have a fit of the vapors, Charlie. You've got the money Hamilton paid you, and the Blackwood chit isn't any concern of yours anymore. Or mine, for that matter."

As if Cheswick's taunts had given him a jolt of backbone, Fleetwood stood up straighter. "You promised that she wouldn't get hurt. You promised."

"I promised that Hamilton would take care of her," the earl retorted, looking bored. "I didn't say *how* he would do that."

"Do you have any idea what they're talking about?" Will asked Lucy in an undertone from where they stood several feet away from the arguing men. "From what Fleetwood said, it sounds like he was the one who turned Vera over to Hamilton."

Before Lucy could respond, though, Fleetwood made a sound of fury. And to Will's astonishment, he pulled a pistol from his coat pocket and aimed it at Cheswick.

"What the devil?" the earl asked in shock. But then he began to laugh, which Will could have told him was the exact last thing one should do when facing a man as prone to emotional outbursts as Fleetwood when he was holding a gun. "What are you doing, Charlie? You don't have the bottle to pull a trigger on me."

Even as he spoke, Will saw Fleetwood's arm tremble, though his grip on the stock seemed steady enough. Still, Cheswick would do himself a kindness by refraining from taunting the other man.

"You don't know what I have the bottle for, Cheswick," Fleetwood said in a surprisingly calm voice. "Especially when it comes to the woman I love."

Cheswick, though his hands were raised now, rolled his eyes at Fleetwood's profession. "The woman you love? You do realize you barely knew the girl. It wasn't her you loved. It was all of her delicious money."

"You take that back, you, you, viper," Fleetwood spat out.

Cheswick might have chosen that moment to issue another taunt, but he didn't get the opportunity.

Because that was when Fleetwood, whether on purpose or by accident, fired the pistol.

Chapter 18

Lucy felt the wind knocked out of her as Will pushed her to the bricks beneath them and covered her with his body.

By the time she'd gotten her bearings back and Will was helping her to her feet, the drama enacted by Fleetwood and Cheswick was over. The pistol, she saw, was lying on the ground, as was Cheswick, who was clutching his arm.

Fleetwood was nowhere to be seen.

"That bloody idiot shot me," the earl said in disbelief.

Immediately, Lucy rushed to the wounded man and knelt by his side. "Let me see, my lord," she told him in a firm tone as she pried his hands off the injury.

Still in shock, Cheswick didn't fight her, and Lucy saw blood oozing from the wound. Over her shoulder, she said to Will, "I need your knife."

He handed it over, and said tightly, "We're drawing a crowd."

Lucy had no time to care. "I must bind up the wound before he loses too much blood. Will you ask one of the servants for some clean cloths? And contact my cousin."

Wordlessly, Will hurried away to do her bidding.

To Cheswick, Lucy said, "You'd better take off your coats unless you wish me to cut through them."

If it were possible, the earl turned even paler at her suggestion. "Do you know how much this coat is worth, Miss Penhallow?"

He began shrugging out of the admittedly well-made suit coat. With Lucy's help it was soon off, and the sight of the blossoming splotch of red on his sleeve made Cheswick swear.

"I knew it was a mistake to bring Fleetwood into contact with Hamilton," Cheswick said as Lucy expertly used the knife to slice through the sleeve.

"You'll need a surgeon to remove bits of cloth, I'm afraid," she told the earl as she gently pulled the fabric away from the singed flesh.

He nodded mutely, but the tautness of the man's jaw told her that he was in pain.

To distract him, she asked, "Why do you say it was a mistake to bring Fleetwood and Hamilton together?"

Cheswick winced as she pressed the wound with a makeshift bandage from the lower half of his sleeve. He looked away from what she was doing as he responded. "Fleetwood has always been a bit high-strung. The sort who falls in love at the drop of a pin and sings the lady's praises to anyone who will listen, only to give her a disgust of him. I should have guessed he'd become prostrate with guilt over taking money from Hamilton."

Will approached then and, crouching beside her, handed Lucy a stack of white cloths.

"How did you become the one who facilitated their meeting in the first place?" he asked Cheswick as he watched her replace the makeshift bandage with a fresh one. "If I recall correctly, you two have never run in the same set."

"You recall correctly," Cheswick said with a touch of asperity. "Fleetwood is a nodcock of the highest order. And I never had much patience with him. But Hamilton I met during a trip several years ago to Philadelphia to visit my maternal aunt's family. We attended many of the same social events during my time there, and when he hailed me in the street near White's a week ago, I immediately recognized him, despite how changed he seemed. Once he told me his reason for coming to London—heartbreak over Miss Blackwood— his haggard condition made sense. He said he was determined to win her back, but as she refused to see him, he needed a way to meet with her. He asked if there was one particular suitor of hers who might lure her into the garden the night of the Leighton-Childe ball."

"He used that word?" Lucy asked sharply. " 'Lure'?"

Cheswick's cheekbones reddened at her question. "I see now that I should have questioned the fellow's motives, but at the time, the man sounded lovesick and desperate. The devil of it—apologies, Miss Penhallow—is that I liked Hamilton. He'd begun his own company with only his own brains and determination. I was impressed. Perhaps overly so, it would seem."

Lucy didn't respond, just waited for him to continue.

Accepting the handkerchief Will handed him, Cheswick mopped his brow. "I thought of Fleetwood as a candidate for Hamilton's little scheme at once. Not only because, despite his pestering, Miss Blackwood still seemed to treat Fleetwood with kindness."

"Probably because she feared a scene," Lucy said with disgust. Men were so slow to recognize bad behavior in their fellows unless it directly touched on them.

Reading her reaction correctly, Cheswick said with self-recrimination, "I admit it, Miss Penhallow. My own actions in this case have been ignorant at best and careless at worst."

With a sigh, Lucy started to rise, but Will was there to offer her an arm. Once she was up, she pulled away and shook out her skirts.

She watched as Will turned to Cheswick and helped him to his feet as well. The earl wobbled a bit, and despite needing the assistance, he pulled away from Will and all but propelled himself onto the nearby bench.

He took a moment to catch his breath, but then said, "One of the other reasons I thought of Fleetwood was the sum Hamilton proposed to offer for performing what was, actually, an easy enough service. I thought by providing Fleetwood with a way to earn enough to keep himself in comfort for a while, I was removing him from Miss Blackwood's cadre of fortune-hunting suitors. At least temporarily."

Seen in that way, it was a sound enough idea, Lucy thought.

"Did Hamilton explain just why he needed to speak to Vera?" she asked aloud. "I have reason to believe she'd broken things off with him. Was that his reason?"

"Something like that," Cheswick agreed bitterly. "He said that he had to plead his case one last time. And that if she still refused him, he'd be on the next ship back to Philadelphia. I suppose I shouldn't be all that surprised he lied. It isn't as if we were anything more than acquaintances. Still, one does expect another gentleman to behave with honor."

Lucy wryly wondered how many ladies of her acquaintance would agree with his lament. Still, when she spoke, it was with kindness. He had paid for his stupidity, after all. "Do you have your own physician you'd wish us to call, Lord Cheswick?"

Before the earl could speak, Will spoke up. "The duchess insisted on sending for their family's doctor."

"I suppose I can't argue with a duchess, can I?" Cheswick said wryly. "I just hope my mother doesn't hear anything about this. She'll stick her own oar in, and I shall be entirely henpecked."

At the mention of the Duchess of Maitland, Lucy gasped. "Oh dear. I got so taken up with treating his lordship's wound, I didn't even think of our hosts and the other guests. My poor mama must be frantic."

Elise, who must have been lurking behind them for several minutes, stepped forward then and pulled Lucy into a hug. "My dear, what a fright you must have had. And don't worry about your mama or the guests. The musicians were playing so loudly no one heard the shot. And as for your mother, I assured both Mrs. Penhallow and the duchess that you were feeling unwell and were waiting for me in my carriage."

"Oh no, I do not wish you to miss the rest of the ball," Lucy said to her friend in dismay.

But Elise waved away her words. "I have danced until there are nearly holes in my slippers. I'm perfectly willing to leave before the end of the ball."

On the bench, Cheswick struggled to his feet. He looked a bit unsteady, but he managed to remain upright. "Mrs. Clevedon," he said with a truncated bow. "I apologize for appearing before you in my shirtsleeves."

Elise turned to him with a raised brow but offered a brief curtsy. "My lord. It's a pity Sir Charles has such a poor aim, my lord. We'd all have been spared a great deal of trouble if he'd aimed a few inches to the left."

Shocked by her friend's rude words, Lucy gave a little gasp. "Elise," she said in a warning tone.

But Cheswick waved away her concern. "Mrs. Clevedon has never been particularly fond of me. We know one another of old."

Some silent communication passed between the earl and Elise before Lucy's friend said with what looked like embarrassment, "His lordship speaks the truth, but that is no excuse for my poor behavior. I apologize."

It was clear to all of them that the apology was meant not for Cheswick but for Lucy.

They were spared further discomfort by the arrival of Detective Superintendent Eversham and Detective Inspector Cherrywood.

Eversham's first concern was for Lucy. He stepped forward and took her by the shoulders, looking her over as if assessing her condition. "You are not hurt?" he asked, as if confirming what he'd already heard from someone else.

Lucy gave him a smile and a quick hug. "I am unharmed. I cannot say the same for Lord Cheswick, however."

At her reassurance, Eversham snapped back into his usual professional manner at the scene of a crime. Turning, he surveyed the area and his eyes landed on the earl, who, to his own shame it was clear, had been forced to resume his seat on the bench.

"I was given to understand by Gilford's note that Fleetwood is the one who delivered the gunshot?"

Lucy nodded and quickly gave her cousin a recounting of what had happened earlier, including her own conversation with Sir Charles and the confrontation between the man and Lord Cheswick.

Eversham took it all in and then turned to Elise with a frown. "What is your role in all of this, Mrs. Clevedon?" Perhaps unconsciously, he glanced toward Cheswick.

As if determined to set the detective superintendent straight, Elise raised her hands as if in denial. "I am here only because I have offered to drive Lucy home."

Lucy's cousin nodded at the widow's words. "Good. That's good. Lucy should get away from this business sooner rather than later."

At his words, Lucy protested. "I am not some wilting flower who must be protected from reality."

But Will spoke up in support of Eversham's proposal. "No one thinks that of you. But this is not your first encounter with violence this week. Not to mention that we have been together during both incidents. There is already talk."

At this last, Lucy blanched. "There is?"

"Your absence from the ballroom has been noted," Elise told her gently, and Lucy felt her face heat. "Though I did my best to correct much of it with the tale of your feeling ill, the fact that Gilford was also missing couldn't be explained away as easily."

Lucy felt her heart sink. She'd never been a particularly punctilious young lady when it came to propriety, but this week she may have ruined her reputation for good.

"You mustn't worry about the gossip," Will told her from where he stood beside her. "I feel sure once news of the shooting comes out, your disappearance from the ball will be forgotten."

Changing the subject, he continued, "I promise to pay a call upon you tomorrow and let you know everything that happens here after you leave." Will's eyes shone with sincerity, and Lucy felt a surge of fondness for this man whom she hadn't even really known until a few days ago.

Glancing over to where Elise stood, as if waiting for her to make a decision, Lucy gave her friend a decisive nod. "Very well. I shall leave. But please make sure that a surgeon looks at Lord Cheswick's arm."

"You may be assured that I will not risk dying of a fever over that sapskull Fleetwood, Miss Penhallow," Cheswick said from the bench.

In a less aggrieved tone, he added, "You have my thanks for your kindness in binding up my wound. If you'd been born a decade or so earlier, you would have made a fine addition to Miss Nightingale's Crimean campaign."

"I was happy to help, my lord," she told the earl.

Turning to the others, she said her goodbyes, and feeling as if she were leaving a play before seeing the end, she and Elise left.

The friends were quiet as they made their way to the line of carriages waiting outside the Maitland townhouse. Once they'd reached the snug interior of Elise's town carriage and she'd given the driver the order to go, Lucy leaned back against the squabs in relief.

Still, before she could fully relax, there was something she needed to speak to her friend about. "Elise, I beg your pardon if this question is impertinent, but I fear I must ask it never-theless. What is between you and the Earl of Cheswick?"

The widow looked at her with a mix of amusement and res-ignation, and Lucy knew that the smoke in this case was most certainly pointing to fire.

Perhaps an inferno.

Chapter 19

It was late by the time Will returned to the Gilford town-house, and despite the excitement earlier, he fell into a hard, dreamless sleep.

He'd asked his valet to awaken him at a far earlier hour than he'd ever have dreamed of during his tenure in Paris. But instead of being groggy, he was alert and eager to start the day. Whether this unusual brightness had anything to do with the fact that he had promised to call on Lucy this morning was not a question he wished to examine too closely at the moment.

Even so, he dressed with special care, and when he rapped on the door of the Penhallows' house in Grosvenor Square a short while later, he was feeling a jolt of excitement at the prospect of seeing her again.

When he was escorted to the Penhallow drawing room, he was greeted not by the sight of the lovely Miss Lucy Penhallow waiting patiently for him.

Well, Lucy was there, of course. But she wasn't alone.

From the leather chair Will had sat in only days before, the Earl of Cheswick rose and bowed.

"My lord, I'm so glad you're here," Lucy said, looking beautiful in a rose-colored muslin morning gown, with her hair arranged in a new style that framed her delicate features in such a way that made his hands itch to replace those tendrils with his hands. "The earl has just been telling me something he forgot to mention in the hubbub last evening."

Remembering his manners, Will stepped forward and bowed over Lucy's hand, holding a little longer than dictated by propriety. And rather than simply allowing his mouth to hover in the air over her ungloved hand, he placed a swift but firm kiss on the back of it.

He must have lingered there with her hand in his for longer than he'd thought because he heard Cheswick cough from somewhere over Will's left shoulder.

Reluctantly, he let Lucy go and gave the other man a brief bow. "Cheswick. What are you doing here?"

Will heard Lucy's sharp intake of breath, but his eyes remained on the earl, who only laughed.

"Lower your weapons, Gilford," the chestnut-haired man, whom even Will had to admit was handsome as the devil himself, sounded placating but his eyes were laughing. "I have no intention of stealing a march on your pursuit of Miss Penhallow."

"His pursuit?" Lucy echoed in astonishment as a blush rose to her already rosy cheeks. "My lord, behave yourself."

Whether the chiding was intended for the viscount or the earl, Will wasn't sure. It would do him no great favors in his courtship of Lucy to call more attention to his absurd jealousy, however, so he didn't argue.

Instead, he took a seat on the settee beside Lucy and asked,

"What was it you were saying about Cheswick forgetting to tell us something last night?"

Looking grateful to move on to a less volatile topic, Lucy gestured to the earl, who still looked amused, damn him.

"Perhaps you'd better be the one to tell, my lord," she said to Cheswick with a smile. "You are, after all, the one to whom Fleetwood confessed his plan."

His patrician features turning serious, Cheswick nodded. "As I was telling Miss Penhallow, in his remorse over the role he'd played in the abduction of Miss Blackwood, Fleetwood told me more of what Hamilton had planned for the lady. It would seem that the American was acquainted with Madame Celestina and intended to have the seer pretend to convey a message to Miss Blackwood from her late mother. The message, of course, would be that her mother wished for Vera to marry no man other than Mr. Hamilton."

Will swore, and Lucy raised a hand to her mouth in horror. Thinking of how much he would have given for one last conversation with his late father, Will was filled with disgust for the kind of man who would stoop to such underhanded schemes. No matter how much Hamilton wished to marry Miss Blackwood, this was beyond the pale.

"However much you might have liked this man during your trip to America, my lord," Lucy said to Cheswick, "I hope that now you recognize that he is horrible."

"Without question, Miss Penhallow," the earl said with a nod. "I should have known better than to trust a fellow on so short an acquaintance, but I was clearly naive. However much Hamilton might need the funds that Miss Blackwood would bring to him through marriage, he has gone about the matter in the worst way."

Will, who felt that the mention of Hamilton needing Vera's dowry hit a little too close to his own situation, still felt compelled to ask, "What do you know of Hamilton's finances?"

"I didn't wish to wait for a reply to my letter to my aunt," the earl said tightly, "so I spoke to another friend who just arrived from Philadelphia—one I would trust with my life— and he said that Hamilton Railroad Company has lost much of its value thanks to a sell-off of its stock. He also said that in the United States the Hamilton name is tarnished now. So, it would seem that a marriage on this side of the Atlantic is his only hope."

"Did you learn from Sir Charles Fleetwood whether or not Mr. Hamilton was able to arrange this sham séance?" Lucy asked, a little line of worry settling into the area between her brows.

Will wanted to know the answer to this question as well. If the séance had happened, then Madame Celestina might be able to tell them how the event had unfolded. If it hadn't, the medium might still have useful information about Hamilton.

"Fleetwood spoke as if the encounter between the two women was still something that had to be arranged," said the earl with a frown. "He spoke very familiarly about the spiritualist. Referred to her by her first name, and slipped up a couple of times by calling her what I suspect is her actual given name: Christina."

Rising to his feet, the earl waited for Lucy and Gilford to do the same before bowing over Lucy's hand. "I thank you for seeing me, Miss Penhallow. Knowing how much you worry for your friend, I thought you needed the information about Madame Celestina at once."

To Will's annoyance, the other man held on to Lucy's hand for longer than necessary, and though he knew that he himself had done the same thing earlier, he was nevertheless glad when Cheswick stepped away. Though the earl's smirk told him just how poorly he'd hidden his jealousy.

For her part, Lucy seemed unfazed by the byplay between the two men. "I am grateful to you for bringing the news," she said as she escorted Cheswick to the door of the drawing room. "And so pleased to learn your wound wasn't as bad as we at first thought."

Bidding Lucy and Gilford a good day, the Earl of Cheswick slipped out the door of the drawing room, closing it behind him.

Since the door had been ajar when Will arrived, he was reluctantly grateful to the other man for closing it. Perhaps Cheswick wasn't so bad after all.

Not doing anything to open the door herself, Lucy instead turned her back to it and said with excitement, "We must speak to this Madame Celestina at once. She might hold the key to where we might find Vera."

"Do you even know where to find her?" Will asked, feeling a little like a whirlwind had just blown through the room.

"Never mind that," she said, waving away his concern as she turned around and—much to his disappointment—opened the drawing room door and gestured for him to follow. "We must go speak to my cousin. I want to know whether the police have apprehended Sir Charles yet."

"Surely you can just send him a no—"

But before he could get the words out, Lucy threw up her hands impatiently. "Of course I could send him a note, but I need to see him in person in his office."

"Why?" he asked with suspicion. After all, the last time he'd blindly followed her, a man had been shot.

As if she were trying desperately to cling to her patience, Lucy said slowly, "Because there is a file there that I wish to look at that might shed some light on Madame Celestina. I should like to read it again before we confront her."

Considering the matter, Will nodded and docilely followed her out the door.

Chapter 20

It was odd entering the offices of the London Metropolitan Police with an escort, Lucy thought wryly as she allowed Will to open the door to the large stone edifice for her. Usually, she was accompanied only by her maid, and even then the other woman didn't generally follow her inside.

She felt the eyes of the policemen of all rank who crowded the main room watching as Will, his hand pressed possessively over hers where it lay on his arm, escorted her through the wide entry hall. As they walked, Lucy felt the discomfort of their stares. Though whether it was because they'd somehow forgotten that she was several rungs higher than they were on the social ladder or because they read some silent message in Gilford's manner or eyes, she couldn't say.

As they neared the corridor leading to her cousin's office, the young man who served as Eversham's assistant hurried forward.

"Miss Penhallow." Constable Stewart, a sturdy-looking Scot who had come to London in search of work several years ago, was a conscientious and quick-witted fellow who kept her cousin on schedule and did any paperwork the detective superintendent required. He'd also been the one to teach Lucy how to do basic clerical tasks like filing and sorting.

"Did I forget that you'd planned on coming in today?" Stewart asked with a worried look. "I had thought that Mr. Eversham said you were—"

Lucy shook her head before the constable could get any further in his question. "No, Mr. Stewart. This is an unplanned visit. I thought I'd bring Lord Gilford to see where I volunteer."

Before she could introduce the two men, Gilford greeted Stewart, who offered the higher-ranking man a deep bow. "A pleasure to meet the man who keeps an eye on Lucy while she's here."

At the choice of words, Geordie Stewart, who had the typical red hair and pale skin of his fellow Scots, turned beet red. "Oh no, your lordship, I would never presume such a thing." The burr of his accent sounded stronger now, perhaps because he was nervous?

"Of course that's not what Lord Gilford means," she said, shooting Will a dampening look. "He only meant that he wishes to thank you for assisting me. Isn't that right, your lordship?"

At her words, Will said with no little show of apology, "Of course, Lucy. I am grateful to you, Stewart. This isn't really the sort of place where I would wish her to spend time, but I trust Mr. Eversham, of course. And it calms me considerably to know that you are here also to keep watch over her."

He glanced over to where a boy who could be no older than ten or twelve swore like a sailor who had been sailing the high seas for scores of years. Lucy winced at the child's language, but she was somewhat inured to it in this environment now.

"I'm happy to be of service, your lordship," Stewart responded to Will. "And as you say, Mr. Eversham is really the one who watches over her while she's in our company."

"I suppose we'd best go pay our respects to him, Mr. Stewart," Lucy said, giving the younger man a sunny smile. "Is he free?"

At the question, Stewart nodded. "He's been ensconced in there for an hour or more. I think he's looking over some documents, but I feel sure he will welcome an interruption from you and his lordship, miss."

With a pleased nod, Lucy held hard to Gilford's arm and led him toward the corridor and the office door just beyond.

Knocking briskly, she stepped inside, followed by Will.

At their appearance in his doorway, Eversham's eyes widened and he rose. "Lucy, my lord, what a pleasure to see you both."

Moving forward, Lucy leaned up to kiss her cousin's cheek, and when she'd done so, she pulled back to look him over.

"That was a look worthy of my wife," Eversham said with a grin. "Though I suppose I shouldn't be surprised, given how alike the two of you are in temperament."

"Someone needs to keep you from working yourself into a decline," Lucy said tartly. "Besides, I am not here today to rake you over the coals. Will and I are here because I need to search out a file I noticed a few weeks ago."

Quickly, she told Eversham what Lord Cheswick had told them that morning, about both Hamilton's financial troubles and the man's plan to use Madame Celestina to manipulate Vera into marrying him.

At Lucy's explanation, the veteran policeman gave a low

whistle. "Every time I think I've seen every way in which one person can wrong another, some clever chap without a conscience finds another. I have to say, however, that using a clairvoyant to give Miss Blackwood a message from her dead mother is a new level of cruelty."

"My thoughts exactly," Lucy said with a shudder. "And the file I'm looking for is about her, I think."

Quickly, she outlined the case she'd seen in the police files when she'd been organizing them a few weeks ago. "I am almost positive I saw the name Madame Celestina there. Though it was listed as only one of the names by which the lady involved was known."

"You're welcome to look for it," Eversham said. "Oh, and by the way, we haven't yet caught up with Fleetwood. He hasn't been back to his rooms. Nor has his family seen him. We plan to keep looking, however. He might believe he cannot be prosecuted for his crime because of his rank, but that is wrong. We cannot simply have peers shooting peers willy-nilly."

Lucy exchanged a look of amusement with Will, who said to Eversham, "I certainly would feel better if you were able to prevent it somehow."

Leaving the detective superintendent to his report writing, Lucy led Will into the corridor just outside her cousin's office where the older files she'd been working on were stored.

Will glanced up and down the hallway, his eyes alight with interest. "When you told me you did some work here, I imagined it to be something akin to the Royal Menagerie. Or at the very least like one of Lady Hathaway's overcrowded routs."

At the mention of the renowned hostess, who always invited far more guests than could comfortably fit in her home, Lucy smiled. "I believe I had something similar in mind as well. But it is really much tamer than one would imagine."

As she spoke, Lucy ran her eyes up and down the rows of cabinets fitted with neat columns of small drawers. After a few false starts, where Lucy pulled open one drawer and flipped through the contents only to make a sound of frustration and close it, she finally gave a little cry. "Yes! I knew it was one of the three."

Turning to wave a sheaf of papers at Will, she shut the drawer she'd found them in and turned to lead him toward a small, empty room with a table in it.

"Is this where they question suspects?" he asked, looking around the room that was almost painfully sparse. "I know that I would be more inclined to tell all my secrets if I were left here for any length of time."

Spreading the pages out on the table in the middle of the chamber, Lucy took a seat in one of the hard chairs. She gestured to Will that he should take the other, and he curbed his gawking long enough to drag the other chair up beside hers and sit.

"This is a case from five years ago in which a traveling theater company was given a citation for remaining in the same location near Hampstead Heath for longer than allowed."

Will frowned, and Lucy was afraid he'd make some dismissive remark about her playing at being a member of the police. But he just indicated that she should continue.

Breathing a mental sigh of relief, she said, "There was a woman in the troupe. At the time, she played mostly ingenue parts—Juliet, Rosalind, Beatrice—roles that are generally acted by young women."

"But what does this have to do with Madame Celestina?" Will scanned the page but saw nothing until Lucy showed him.

"She also performed tarot readings and communicated with the dead," Lucy said, pointing to where the constable had put this particular note.

"Using the name Madame Celestina," Will said with excitement. "You, my dear, are utterly brilliant."

Lucy felt a flush of pride at his words but had to tell him the rest. "Not only that," she said, unable to keep her excitement from her voice, "but look at her actual name just a bit lower on the page."

She watched as Will read the pertinent passage, surprise and shock in his eyes when he raised his head to look at her. "Is that who I think it is?"

"I believe she must be," Lucy said with satisfaction. "Madame Celestina is Miss Christina Fleetwood, Sir Charles Fleetwood's younger sister."

Chapter 21

Though Will and Lucy both wished they could track down Miss Christina Fleetwood as soon as they left police headquarters, they both had engagements they needed to keep. Lucy had promised to visit Applegate's tea shop with Meg and Elise to inform them of everything that had happened last night in the Maitland garden, while Will had agreed to meet with Ben Woodward at Brooks's for much the same purpose.

So, they said their goodbyes and parted ways at the entrance of the Penhallow townhouse, then Will turned his curricle toward home so that he could leave his horses and carriage in the stables he could no longer afford, and took a hansom cab to St. James's Street, where many of London's most fashionable clubs lay.

His memberships at such places were also outside his financial means now, but he was hoping to announce a betrothal soon. The idea of saddling Lucy with his family's debts was repugnant to him, mostly because he feared she would never trust that he wished to marry her for herself alone and not for her fortune. But with every passing day he was more attracted to her. And he was sure she felt the same about him.

He'd simply need to find a way to make her believe his affection was genuine.

When he stepped through the doors of the esteemed gentlemen's club and smelled the familiar scents of leather and cigar smoke, he relaxed a little and went in search of Woodward.

The American was seated at a corner table in the reading room with a whisky in hand and a newspaper spread out on the table before him.

"Oh ho," the American said with a smirk, "the darling of the gossip pages shows himself at last."

Dropping into a chair across from him, Will raised his brows at the quip. He supposed there was likely some talk about his and Lucy's hug in Brook Street yesterday. And it was true they'd disappeared from the Maitland ballroom last night, but that had been explained away, hadn't it?

"What do you mean?" he asked Woodward with a sense of foreboding.

With not a shred of apology, Woodward handed Will a copy of *Town Tattle*. Pointing to a particular column, the American said, "I particularly like the way this anonymous writer refers to you as 'Willing Willie,' though I suppose alliteration is to be expected from a publication named *Town Tattle*."

Scanning the several paragraphs, Will grew increasingly annoyed. "I most certainly did *not* kiss Lucy in broad daylight yesterday."

He had kissed her inside the Penhallow townhouse, where they were shaded from the daylight.

"But that's not the most interesting part," Woodward said, pointing to the paragraph near the end of the column. "Whoever this person is, they certainly have been keeping track of both your and Lucy's movements in the past several days. They actually list out each meeting between you. Including that call to pay your respects to Vera Blackwood's father and how you both disappeared from the Leighton-Childe and Maitland ballrooms together."

Will felt his jaw tighten. "Why can't people mind their own affairs?" he said finally. "My intentions toward Miss Penhallow are entirely honorable, but this reads as if we've been caught in flagrante."

"It is the way of the world, my friend," said Woodward, leaning back in his chair. "Besides, there is only one article about the two of you in *Town Tattle*, while there are seven by my count about the Blackwood kidnapping."

At that Will's eyes widened. Wordlessly, he turned back to the front of the newspaper and began reading the several short pieces related to the Blackwood affair. When he was finished, he told his friend, "Most of this is arrant nonsense. The man who took Miss Blackwood didn't 'grapple' with her for several minutes. It was seconds at most, which concluded when he tossed her over his shoulder."

At that moment, one of the waiters came to bring their beefsteak, and for a bit they were quiet as they tore into their meals.

"So what is the latest on the Blackwood girl's abduction?" Woodward asked once he'd made good work of his food. "A little bird told me you were seen escorting Miss Penhallow to police headquarters this morning."

His slaked hunger having soothed his mood a little, instead of cursing as he'd have done earlier, Will only rolled his eyes now. Quickly, he outlined what they'd learned.

"I hope Fleetwood is found soon," he said in conclusion, "because a man who can fire a gun at a supposed friend isn't to be trusted among civilized people."

Woodward agreed. "Not that I am accepting of dueling as a way of solving one's disagreements, but even in those cases there is a sense of decorum. Firing without warning at another person and then fleeing is barbaric."

Will concurred. But then, he felt that way about most surprise attacks. His father had been stabbed to death by someone he thought was a friend. One of the reasons he was so keen on helping Lucy find her friend was because he didn't want Lucy to suffer the loss of a friend.

"What do you mean to do about Madame Celestina, or rather Miss Christina Fleetwood?" Woodward asked now. "Is her brother hiding with her, do you think?"

"We don't know," Will admitted. "I'd like to think finding Fleetwood would be that simple, but beyond his agreeing to connect Hamilton to Madame Celestina, we don't know what kind of relationship there is between the siblings."

The friends fell silent, each lost in his own thoughts as their full bellies lulled them into a sleepy contentment for the moment.

Will yawned and idly picked up one of the other gossip papers Woodward had cluttered the table with. This one was called *Teacup Tattle* and Will couldn't help but snort at the absurdity of it.

Turning to show Woodward the front page, he said in amusement, "I can't believe you would let yourself be seen reading such a rag."

Woodward shrugged. "In my defense, I chose these particular

gossip sheets with the intention of making you laugh over them with me. That they all had at least one story about you and Miss Penhallow was simply the sugar in the biscuit."

Shaking his head in exasperation at his friend, Will lay the paper back down on the table, but a small advertisement on the back page caught his eye.

Madame Celestina

Readings Given--Fortunes Told--Messages from Beyond Transmitted

Below the ad, an address in Holborn was listed.

Will showed the page to Woodward then rose from the table. "I need to tell Lucy about this," he said hurriedly. "This woman might know where Hamilton has taken Vera Blackwood. We may already be too late to have prevented her from a forced marriage, but at the very least we can get her away from this scoundrel."

As he turned to go, he realized Woodward was following him. "What are you doing?" he asked his friend over his shoulder.

"I'm coming with you," said the American, as if Will were lacking sense. "I'd like to see this Madame Celestina for myself. Besides that, Hamilton is an American, and I'd like the chance to teach him a lesson about giving the rest of us a poor reputation."

Too determined to get to Lucy to give her the news he'd found the medium, Will didn't bother arguing further. Fortunately for him, the porter outside the club had already stopped a hansom for him. Flipping a coin to the man, he told the driver the direction of Applegate's tea shop and climbed into the dank interior of the cab, followed by Woodward.

"Applegate's?" Woodward asked with a raised brow.

"It's a tea shop that Lucy and her friends frequent." Will didn't look away from the dirty window of the carriage. "Owned by a member of their book club. The Ems."

"The Ems?" Woodward asked looking confused. "I've never heard the Mischief and Mayhem Book Club referred to in such a way. Is this a new club?"

"No," Will said, turning back to face the other man. Then he explained how the club members had taken to calling it by the shortened form the Ems Club. The American's expression cleared. "Ah, just so. The original name is a mouthful. I doubt the founders had convenience in mind when they named their column."

Will nodded. "Or that they'd imagined the column would grow to encompass such a wide range of offshoot communities."

"That, too. Though when one considers all the myriad places where men are able to form friendships around shared interests, it's surprising there aren't more such groups for ladies."

The cab was slowing to a stop then, and the two men leapt to the street outside of Applegate's tea shop, then stepped inside.

Chapter 22

The cab ride from Applegate's tea shop to the Holborn address listed in the newspaper advertisement, Lucy thought, under other circumstances should have included only Will and herself.

When Will walked into the tea shop to inform her about finding Madame Celestina's direction, however, he was followed by Mr. Benjamin Woodward. And from the moment the American and Meg saw one another, it was as if some invisible gauntlet had been thrown down between them.

Now the quartet was settled, the two gentlemen in the rear-facing seats, in the confined space of a hansom cab with Lucy glancing every few minutes at the door, wishing there was some way to escape her dearest friend and the handsome American.

"Perhaps you might not be so reliant on my brother to provide entertainment for you, Mr. Woodward," Meg was saying now, "if you had other friends to visit with. Lucy and I, for example, have many other ladies we might call on if we find the other busy."

"And yet," Woodward said, resting a hand on his chin, as if

in thought, "you, too, seem to rely on your brother for enter-tainment in this case. Or am I mistaken in the fact that you asked to come along on this errand only after your brother spoke of it?"

Meg, whose blonde hair had a liberal strawberry threaded through it, narrowed her eyes at Woodward and her cheeks reddened with annoyance. "My friend Lucy invited me along. Though I suppose you have difficulty discerning such niceties of manners. I wonder how you managed to remain employed by the American embassy for so long with such a poor ability to read social cues."

Woodward, whom Lucy had observed over the years of their acquaintance, was normally the most solidly good-natured of men. Not today, however.

"I shouldn't be surprised that you, Miss Gilford, have no idea what it is like to work for a living," Woodward said, his own eyes narrowed in return. "Though you might have need to do so in the near future, and I look forward to seeing how you fare."

At that, Will, who had been watching the verbal fencing match between his best friend and his younger sister with amusement up till now, shot Woodward a glare. "Have a care," he told the other man.

Lucy wasn't surprised that Will had chosen that moment to rein in his friend. Meg's face had lost all color, and Lucy had the impression only her friend's strong self-control had kept her eyes from filling.

As if waking from a trance, Woodward snapped to atten-tion at Will's rebuke and shook his head a little. "My apolo-gies," he said first to Will, and then in a softer voice, "I am sorry, Miss Gilford. Forgive me, please."

Something passed between the two that Lucy couldn't interpret, and judging by Will's puzzled look, nor could he.

When he raised a questioning brow at her, Lucy could only give a little shrug. She hadn't even known Meg and Mr. Woodward were more than casual acquaintances. Whatever was between them seemed to belie that, however.

"I will bid you all good day once we reach Madame Celestina's premises," Woodward said stiffly.

But Meg objected to that. "I am as much at fault as you are. We can certainly behave ourselves for the space of an afternoon, can we not?"

"You are sure?" Woodward's voice was gentle.

Lucy felt all of a sudden as if the pair had forgotten she and Will were present with them in the carriage.

Meg nodded. And before anything else could be said on the matter, the hansom began to slow and Lucy glanced out of the smudged window.

"We're here," she said with a jolt of excitement. "Now remember, if Sir Charles Fleetwood is here, we are not to attempt to apprehend him or anything of the sort. I sent a message to my cousin, and he will send men to question his sister, but who knows when they will arrive."

The others nodded at her, and once the hansom had stopped they descended from the carriage and made their way to number 54 Carey Street where, according to the newspaper listing, Madame Celestina lived.

It was a snug townhouse of neat proportions, and pretty pots of flowers on the front steps gave it a well-cared-for look.

"Not where one would imagine a spiritualist to live," Will said in a low voice close to Lucy's ear and she felt a little shiver run through her. When he tucked her arm into his, she appreciated the feel of his strong body beside her. Though whether because she was fearful what they would find in Miss Fleetwood's house or for her own personal pleasure, she couldn't say.

"The two of you go inside and speak to Madame Celestina," Meg called up to them from the foot of the steps. "There is a small park a little ways down the street I should like to investigate. Will you accompany me, Mr. Woodward?"

Startled, Lucy turned to stare down at her friend, but Meg and Mr. Woodward were already striding arm in arm down the path running along the street.

"What is going on with the two of them?" Will asked her, brows drawn. "Has a romance ignited between the two of them that I don't know about because of my time away?"

But Lucy could only shrug. "I didn't know of anything, but then I suppose Meg and I don't tell one another everything."

When she looked up at Will, she saw he was staring at her mouth. And she felt her face flood with heat.

Before either of them could respond to the pull of heat between them, however, the front door of Miss Fleetwood's house was opened to reveal a woman of middle years wearing the well-made but drab costume of a maid.

"Madame isn't receiving today," the dour woman said before moving to close the door in Lucy and Will's faces.

Chapter 23

Before the heavy door to Miss Fleetwood's house could shut, Will stuffed his boot into the gap between door and frame.

"I beg your pardon, ma'am," he told the maid in a firm voice, "but I am Viscount Gilford and this is Miss Lucy Penhallow. We have business with your mistress that can't wait. It is regarding a matter of some importance, and a lady's safety might be at risk."

But if they'd expected Will's plea to move the maid's finer feelings, they were sorely mistaken.

The woman only rolled her eyes. "Milord, there must be a dozen folk here a week claiming to be quality asking for just one word with my mistress. And I'll tell you just as tell them that she ain't receiving."

"Let them in, Hetty. I'll see them in the parlor." The cultured voice of a lady reached Lucy and Will even from their position just outside the door of the house.

Not turning to face her mistress, Hetty indicated with a sweep of her hand that they should come inside. "Do not overtire her," the maid said as she escorted them through the well-appointed entryway toward a door leading to a pretty, well-lit chamber where a handsome lady bearing a remarkable resemblance to Sir Charles Fleetwood sat in a chair near the fire.

"Bring tea and some of those biscuits you made this morning, please, Hetty," Miss Fleetwood said before turning to Lucy and Will. "My lord, Miss Penhallow, it is a pleasure to meet you. I hope you forgive me for not rising. I am feeling a little unwell today. Please, take a seat."

Not daring to exchange a look with Will, Lucy allowed him to steer her with a gentle hand on her elbow to a settee near the window. Once she was seated, he took his own position beside her.

Lucy only gave herself a moment to take in the finer details of the room. Though the house was in one of the outlying areas near London rather than in one of the more fashionable neighborhoods, the house itself was furnished with care, and unless she missed her guess, despite its small size, no expense had been spared to pay for the appointments.

Turning to their hostess now, she noted that despite having pled illness for just today, Lucy was all but certain that Miss Christina Fleetwood was suffering from some long-term illness. Consumption, if Lucy guessed aright. As if to prove her point, the lady began coughing uncontrollably, and though she quickly hid the handkerchief she'd used to cover her mouth, Lucy spotted a spray of red on the snowy cloth.

During her fit, the maid, Hetty, came hurrying in with a glass of some cloudy liquid, her face tight.

Once Miss Fleetwood's paroxysm had subsided, Hetty pressed the glass into her mistress's hand. And once she'd been sufficiently reassured, the older woman again left the room.

The maid looked as if she would like to object, but must have thought better of it. "Very well," she said with a pointed look at Lucy and Will. "But do not overtire yourself."

"She is very protective of you," Lucy said to their hostess. "You are lucky to have such a loyal servant, Miss Fleetwood."

At the mention of her given name, the woman known as Madame Celestina gave Lucy a wry smile. "It has been some time since I've received a call from someone who knows my true identity, Miss Penhallow, Lord Gilford. To what do I owe the honor?"

"Oh, come now, Miss Fleetwood," said Will with a tilt of his head, "that is not quite true, is it? You have received a call from either your brother or one of his friends in the past little while, have you not?"

At the mention of her brother, Miss Fleetwood sat up a little straighter, though it was clear she didn't possess a great deal of strength. Her lips twisted before she said, "I do not refer to an intrusion from my brother into my home as a 'call,' my lord. Nor one in which he brings unwanted guests along."

At the mention of unwanted guests, Lucy felt her pulse quicken. "Who were these guests?" she asked before she could weigh the wisdom of such a direct question of the woman.

Now it was Miss Fleetwood's turn to ask a direct question. "Why do you wish to know? You have come to me, Miss Penhallow. If I am to answer your questions, I fear you must answer some of mine. It is only fair."

Lucy exchanged a look with Will, wondering how much they dared to tell her. He gave a little shrug, and she took that as a sign that they had little choice.

Turning back to Miss Fleetwood, she gave her a brief

explanation of her friendship with Vera and how Sir Charles and Christopher Hamilton were involved in the young woman's abduction.

At the mention of Hamilton and her brother, Miss Fleetwood's mouth pursed in distaste. "Yes, both my brother and Mr. Hamilton were here—though he didn't give me his name."

"What name did he give?" Lucy asked, curious. Though she supposed it made some degree of sense for Hamilton to wish to keep his identity a secret from someone who could reveal his scheme to trick Vera into marrying him.

"He gave no name," Miss Fleetwood said, accepting a cup of tea from Hetty, who had entered with the tea tray and begun serving them from it. She took a sip before continuing. "Though that doesn't surprise me. He seemed very unsettled as soon as he entered the house. But I suppose that's because his intentions from the first were unsavory."

"What did he want from you, Miss Fleetwood?" asked Will, his voice kind. Lucy could sense that he was trying to make himself seem unintimidating despite his size, and she could have kissed him for it.

As if in response to Will's efforts on her behalf, the spiritualist seemed to relax. "My brother—whom I hadn't seen in a decade or more, mind you—brought him here because he thought I would be amenable to performing a fictional séance for his prospective fiancée, in order to convince the girl that her dead mother was telling her that she must marry this man or her father would be killed."

Lucy gasped. The scheme was even worse than she'd at first imagined.

"Precisely," Miss Fleetwood said with a disgusted expression.

"There have been cases in which I've been approached with a request to twist my gift to fit others' wishes, but never with such a reprehensible aim as this. Of course I told my brother and his friend to leave at once."

"So you never met Miss Blackwood?" Lucy could hear the thread of disappointment running through Will's voice, and she felt the same. They'd had such high hopes that Miss Fleetwood would be able to give them some idea of where they might find Vera.

At this Miss Fleetwood shook her head. "I am sorry to disappoint you, but after I refused them, I never saw my brother or the American again."

"I wonder if you might be able to answer some questions about the man who accompanied your brother?" Lucy asked, well aware that the other woman was tiring and they should leave her soon.

But despite her obvious fatigue, Miss Fleetwood was almost eager to answer their questions. "What this man intended to do was horrible. It is just the sort of chicanery that gives gifts like mine a bad name."

Lucy wanted to know more about her gift but curtailed her curiosity. "Is there anything in particular you remember about the man who accompanied Sir Charles? You say he was an American, but was that all you noticed?"

The medium looked into space for a moment, as if searching her memory. Finally, she said, "He was, as I said, American. Handsome enough with dark, almost black hair. But perhaps the most interesting thing about him was how he reacted to something I said."

Leaning forward in her seat, Lucy somehow knew this was

important. "What was that?" she asked with barely disguised eagerness.

Miss Fleetwood gave Lucy and Will a wry look. "I know the two of you might be skeptical about gifts such as mine, but I can assure you that not all of us are charlatans. I have been able to...sense things...about people from the time I was a small girl."

"And what did you sense about your brother's friend, Miss Fleetwood?" Will asked, and Lucy could tell he was just as interested as she was as the answer to the question.

"I told Mr. Hamilton—for that is the man's name, I'm sure of it—I told him that his cousin would not thank him for what he was doing to his fiancée. And that he, this Mr. Hamilton, would be punished for it."

When the seer spoke, however, Lucy felt nothing but disappointment.

Perhaps sensing her guests' lack of enthusiasm for her revelation, Miss Fleetwood spoke up again. "Perhaps I didn't make myself clear. By fiancée, I mean the absent Mr. Hamilton's fiancée."

At that, Lucy was flummoxed. "Do you mean to say that Christopher Hamilton isn't Miss Blackwood's betrothed?"

"Oh, Christopher Hamilton was at one time assuredly betrothed to Miss Vera Blackwood. But unfortunately, that Mr. Hamilton passed away a few months ago. This Mr. Hamilton is his cousin. And he has been passing himself off as Christopher Hamilton the entire time he's been in England."

Chapter 24

"Don't tell me you believe that spiritualism nonsense, Miss Penhallow," said Woodward once the four of them were back in a hansom cab, only this time it was bound back to Mayfair.

Will had scanned his friend and his sister to see if he could guess what was going on between them, but for the moment his mind was occupied with what Christina Fleetwood had told them. He'd never been inclined to take the performances like those at face value, though he'd attended his fair share of such acts. That the lady had been an actress before turning her talents to giving spiritual readings didn't give her any particular credibility.

Even so, there was something about her revelation about Hamilton that rang true.

Beside him, Lucy responded to Woodward's question. "It is not so much that I believe in spiritualism, Mr. Woodward," she said with a slight shrug. "It is that what she said about the man who calls himself Christopher Hamilton fits in with what Lord Cheswick said about how much he had changed. And it also fits with the way he's gone about attempting a reconciliation with Vera. Because there is no reunion when they were never known to one another in the first place."

"No wonder Vera was so terrified when Hamilton and his thug abducted her." Meg, clearly distressed by what Vera might have gone through, clenched her fists in her lap. At her side, Woodward raised his own hand as if to cover one of Meg's, but when he caught Will's eye the American lowered his hand again.

Oh, he and his friend would definitely be having a little chat, Will thought wryly. It wasn't that he opposed a match between his sister and the former US envoy. Indeed, with Meg's dowry now in question, he would be relieved to have her settled down with someone he trusted. There was simply a code of how these things were carried out. And he would not allow a gentleman, even a friend, to go about courting his sister with anything less than careful attention to her reputation.

All of this, of course, made him a hypocrite, given how he'd been with Lucy this week, but he could live with that.

"Where do we turn to find out whether what Miss Fleetwood—or Madame Celestina or whatever the lady is called—claims is true?" Woodward asked, addressing his question to Lucy, who was clearly less intimidating at the moment than Will.

"I will pass the news on to my cousin first," Lucy said thoughtfully. "I don't know how much stock he will put in such a claim, but he needs to know all the same. Then we may go to Lord Cheswick to ask whether it's possible his friend seemed so changed because he was, in fact, an entirely different person than he'd met years ago."

"Woodward and I can do that," Will said firmly.

The glance Lucy directed his way was a knowing one, and

he had the sense that she knew exactly why he insisted on being the one to interview the handsome earl. But Will could hardly admit that he was jealous of the older, wealthier man.

"It would be improper for you and Meg to visit a bachelor in his home," he added, feeling like his mother at her most officious.

His sister tilted her head as if trying to figure him out. "I supposed that time on the Continent would make you return to London with more liberal views, Gilford. Not making pronouncements about propriety like a society matron."

Before he could respond to the taunt, Lucy spoke up again. "That would be most helpful, my lord. Meg and I can return to the Blackwood house this afternoon to find out if Vera's father knows whether Christopher Hamilton has a cousin."

"I can visit the embassy as well," Woodworth said with what could be an attempt at garnering favor with Meg, but Will was inclined to believe that the man was simply trying to do his bit for the case.

They were back in the heart of Mayfair far sooner than Will would have imagined given how long the earlier drive into Holborn had taken.

In keeping with the division of tasks they'd agreed upon earlier, Will and Woodward left the ladies at their respective homes, where they could refresh themselves before returning to the Blackwood home.

Once they were gone Will gave the hack driver orders to take Woodward and himself to White's, where Cheswick might be found at this hour.

When he'd climbed back inside, he slapped his hands atop his thighs and looked over at his friend. "Well, I suppose I should be surprised, but it seems inevitable, now that I think about it."

But Woodward shook his head. "It's not what you think," he said, raising his hands in protest. "I realize everyone says that when they are caught out in some misdeed or other, but in this case, I tell the truth."

"So you mean to tell me that contrary to everything I've witnessed between the two of you today, you have no ongoing romantic connection to my sister?" Will was disinclined to believe him, but he was open to persuasion.

"That is what I am telling you, yes."

Will had known Woodward since that long-ago time when he'd suffered the greatest loss of his young life. Friendships like that—born of tragedy—were stronger than most. And Will hadn't known the fellow to ever steer him wrong.

There was, however, a first occasion for every action.

"If it isn't what it looks like, then," he said, trying to puzzle it out now, "what is it?"

A long silence fell inside the cab, and Benjamin Woodward stared unseeing at the ceiling, as if looking for answers. Finally he sighed and said, "I cannot tell you."

Will shook his head, as if the motion could clear his ears of the other man's words. "You cannot tell me? About my own sister?"

Woodward ran a hand through his hair in agitation. He obviously didn't like keeping this secret from his friend. But he didn't back down. "I give you my word of honor that nothing between your sister and me is improper."

The cab began to slow in St. James's Street, where the two men had left from earlier. This time, however, their destination was a different club—White's.

Before they climbed out, Will gave his friend a sharp look. "I will take you at your word. But be aware that I will be keeping a close watch over you."

Woodward sighed but only nodded.

Then the two men headed for the entrance of White's club.

Chapter 25

Though the Blackwoods' rented townhouse was not far from Lucy's home on Grosvenor Square, the afternoon was cloudy and a chill was in the air, so Lucy elected to take one of the smaller Penhallow coaches to visit Vera's father once Lucy and Meg had each had a bite of luncheon and then changed into afternoon gowns.

When Meg was handed inside by one of the footmen outside the Gilford townhouse, she and Lucy greeted one another and then commented on the appeal of their respective gowns.

Once those formalities were out of the way, Lucy pinned her friend with a look that would brook no evasions. "What, Miss Margaret Gilford, is going on between yourself and Benjamin Woodward?"

But if she thought her friend would easily be cowed into telling all, Lucy was to be sadly mistaken. If anything, Meg only looked amused.

"You are one to demand answers," she said with a raised brow. "How often have you been in the company of my brother since his return from Paris? You were even seen together looking very cozy indeed in Brook Street yesterday. Care to tell me what is between the two of *you*?"

Lucy narrowed her eyes. "You are more adept at this game than I gave you credit for."

"It comes of having a mama who would pry every last bit of private knowledge out of one if she could." Meg shrugged. "Both Will and I became adept at hiding our true feelings at an early age."

Considering her friend's words, Lucy wondered how this might affect Will now that he was back in London. She hadn't noticed any particular inclination to secrecy on his part, but how well did she really know him? They'd only spent any appreciable time together in the past several days. And even that was hardly what one would call a long time span.

But she'd known Meg for years. They'd been the closest of friends. And though Lucy did know Meg to keep things from her mother, she'd never suspected her friend of hiding things from *her*.

"Do you mean to say," Lucy said aloud, "that there have been things that you've been reluctant to share with me? Because I've never got that sense from you."

Meg quirked her mouth in a half smile. "That's because you've been set about attempting to force me to tell you things. The easiest way to make me resist is to demand something. You know that."

Tapping her finger on her chin, Lucy thought about it. Meg was right. "Very well, though I will just point out that I take it very much as a personal affront that you refuse to tell me about whatever it is between you and Woodward. Especially since he was quite charming to me at Lord and Lady Adrian's dinner party the other evening. I was considering setting my cap for him."

For the barest moment, Meg's eyes narrowed, and Lucy gave a mental cheer. Never say she didn't know the best way to pique her friend's jealousy.

But just as quickly, Meg's expression turned bland, and if Lucy hadn't seen it with her own eyes, she might have suspected she'd imagined that alarm in Meg's eyes.

"I certainly won't stop you," Meg said aloud now, looking as nonchalant as if they were discussing the disposition of a pretty bit of lace. "I don't suppose my brother's heart will be broken. He's said to have had many mistresses during his years in Paris."

Her friend's words were said in such a world-weary manner that Lucy had to stop herself from laughing out loud. Meg Gilford was many things, but there wasn't a cynical bone in that young lady's body.

Still, she could hardly call her to account again. They were friends, after all, and it didn't do to spend all of one's time together bickering. Besides, there were things besides the secrets they were keeping from one another to discuss.

"When Will and I were here, Mr. Blackwood was beside himself with worry over Vera." Lucy thought back in sympathy at the older man's despondency. "I don't believe I've ever seen anyone so afraid for a loved one's safety."

"I suppose Vera and her father are close, considering how young she was when Mrs. Blackwood died." Meg tugged a little at the button on her left glove, then looked up as if something had just occurred to her. "All four of us have lost a parent—or in Elise's case, both parents—in either our childhood or teen years. I hadn't ever thought of it, but perhaps that is why you, Elise, and I were all so instantly drawn to Vera."

Lucy considered it. There had been an almost instant affinity between Vera and the trio of book club members. "I suppose sometimes people are simply meant to be friends. That is how it felt when we met, both of us trying to hide from Lord Xavier behind the same giant topiary."

Meg giggled. "I was certain it could hide both of us, but you insisted that I was making you stand out even more than if you'd simply not attempted to conceal yourself at all. You were right, of course. Lord Xavier managed to sign both of our dance cards at once."

Smiling at the memory, Lucy said, "And then we met Elise at the first book club meeting she attended, when she declared that the heroine of *The Ruby Amulet*—what was her name?— was a ninny, and she'd be shocked if it wasn't written by Lord Xavier, so badly imagined were—Bathsheba! That was her name!—so badly written were Bathsheba's thoughts."

"She was right, wasn't she?" Meg asked with a grin. "I vow Bathsheba spent most of the book admiring herself in the mirror and remarking upon the beauty of her figure."

"Horrid book," Lucy agreed with a shudder. "But it brought us together with Elise, so it had its uses, I suppose."

They were quiet for a moment of comfortable silence, in the way of good friends, and when Meg spoke, it was with a worried voice. "Do you suppose Vera is dead?"

It wasn't as if the thought hadn't occurred to Lucy, but it was the first time either of them had spoken it aloud to one another. "I do worry for her safety," she admitted. "But the one thing keeping her safe—even if her abductor is not

Christopher Hamilton, but his cousin—is that she must be alive if he means to marry her for her fortune."

At that, Meg breathed a relieved sigh. "Of course. I hadn't considered that. But you're right."

Though she was happy to soothe Meg's fears, Lucy wished she had the ability to calm her own. But there were still too many unanswered questions for her to feel sanguine about Vera's chances of survival.

A few minutes later, when she and Meg were shown into the same drawing room where Lucy and Will had been welcomed the day before, Lucy was unhappy to see that far from appearing hopeful, Mr. Blackwood looked even more haggard.

He made an effort to greet them, however, bowing over both their hands and inviting them to sit.

"Feeny, bring some refreshments for our guests," he instructed the butler who had introduced them.

Lucy and Meg demurred, but Vera's father insisted. "For I know how fond my Vera is of the two of you. I will never hear the end of it when she returns if she learns I was rude to you."

He was speaking of his daughter in the present tense, Lucy thought. That was a good sign, at least.

"I am so sorry for what's happened, Mr. Blackwood," Meg said tentatively, clearly wanting to convey her sympathy but also afraid that it would overset the man.

But apparently Vera's father was stronger than he appeared. "Thank you, Miss Gilford. I appreciate that you and Miss Penhallow have been kind enough to stop by."

After they murmured their demurrals, Lucy decided she'd best strike while the iron was hot. "When Lord Gilford and I were here yesterday, sir, Lady Fortescue showed us a letter that came for Vera from her fiancé in Philadelphia, Mr. Christopher Hamilton."

At the mention of Hamilton, Richard Blackwood's countenance hardened. "That scoundrel was not my daughter's betrothed. The two of them may have formed an attachment, but it wasn't one that I condoned. The fellow even had a maid installed in my household to carry notes between them."

Vera's father scowled, apparently still incensed over the incident. "And I'm happy to say that once we arrived in London, I was able to persuade Vera to write to Hamilton and tell him that he wasn't to contact her again."

Lucy wondered how Vera had felt about her father's insistence that she break things off with Christopher Hamilton. From what she'd known of Vera—and she felt safe in saying she and Meg were not nearly as close as they'd thought they were with the American lady—Lucy believed it a little suspicious that she'd simply done as her father demanded. The Vera she'd known, even superficially, was a spirited woman who knew her own mind. If she were set on something, she would only let it go when she was ready.

Even so, there had been the letter from Christopher she and Will had seen. The one that begged her to reconsider.

"I do not wish to upset you further, sir," Lucy went on, "but are you certain that Vera did as you asked?"

"Of course she did," the American snapped. "That is why this fool has taken her. But as soon as the Metropolitan Police find them, he'll be sent on the first ship back to Philadelphia. If I had my way, he'd be on his way to one of your penal colonies, but your cousin, Detective Superintendent Eversham, informs me that it is not possible to simply send someone away like that without getting the courts involved."

Lucy had her own opinions about citizens of other countries coming to Great Britain and trying to manipulate the government into doing their bidding, but she kept those thoughts to herself.

Meg opened her mouth, and Lucy—who knew her friend shared her own views—sent a discreet elbow into the other woman's arm.

"How—oof—frustrating for you." Rubbing at her smarting arm, Meg shot a glare at Lucy.

"It is indeed, Miss Gilford," Blackwood said with a scowl. "It is indeed."

"If you know of Mr. Christopher Hamilton," Lucy said, steering the conversation back on course, "I suppose you also are familiar with his cousin?" She put a finger to her chin. "Now, what was his name again?"

But instead of another outburst, at the mention of Christopher Hamilton's cousin, Mr. Blackwood smiled warmly. "Ah, Jedidiah Hamilton. Now there is a man I would be more than happy for my Vera to wed. A fine, upstanding man, with a sharp head for business as well. It's just a shame that my girl would have nothing to do with him, try though he might to win her over."

At this, Lucy felt her pulse pick up. If Jedidiah Hamilton was intent on persuading Vera to marry him, then would this paragon have crossed an ocean in order to force her into a marriage she didn't want? Some men, however admired by other men, were toads when it came to their treatment of women.

Perhaps whatever Will learned from the American embassy would allow them to view a fuller picture of the Hamilton cousins.

She was about to signal to Meg that they should go now when Lady Fortescue sailed into the room like an angry swan and scowled at Mr. Blackwood's visitors.

"What are you doing here again, Miss Penhallow?" the widow demanded. "I told you yesterday that Richard is unwell. He needs his rest while we wait for Vera to come home."

Lucy exchanged a glance with Meg. She was inclined to argue, since Lady Fortescue wasn't even in a formal arrangement with the industrialist, but they'd gotten what they'd come for and she was eager to give the information about Jedidiah Hamilton to Will and her cousin.

"My apologies, Lady Fortescue," she told the other woman, linking her arm with Meg's. "We were just leaving. As friends of Vera's, we merely wished to give our well wishes to her father."

Lady Fortescue's still-lovely face twisted into a knowing look. "I'm sure you did. Now, please go."

"Thank you, ladies," called Mr. Blackwood after them. But to Lucy, at least, it was clear that his attention was on Lady Fortescue.

Chapter 26

William and Woodward found the Earl of Cheswick in the reading room of White's, drinking coffee and reading *The London Gazette*. His injured arm was in a sling.

He barely looked up when the two other men joined him, Will taking the chair at his right side, Woodward at his left.

"I don't know what else I can tell you about that weasel who shot me or Christopher Hamilton, for that matter, Gilford," drawled Cheswick in an annoyed voice. "I gave you all of it last night. If you wished for Woodward to hear it, you could have told him yourself."

To Woodward, he said with a shrug, "I like you well enough, I suppose, Woodward, but now you have my confirmation of the acquaintance you may leave with your companion. Or remain if you wish, but leave me the hell alone."

"Gilford did tell me, my lord," Woodward said wryly, "but there are some finer details that we need to ask you about."

Cheswick heaved a great sigh and set his paper aside, wincing as if the movement hurt his injury. "Because I hold Hamilton directly responsible for the pain in my damned arm, I will listen to your questions. But after that, you must promise to leave me in peace."

"You have my word as a gentleman," Will assured him, exchanging a glance with Woodward.

"And mine," the American said, placing a hand over his heart.

Still cantankerous, Cheswick waved a hand. "Quickly, please."

Will didn't mince words. "Are you certain that the man you met with here in London was Christopher Hamilton?"

Cheswick opened his mouth, Will was certain to deliver a cutting setdown, but Woodward spoke before the nobleman could.

"We don't ask to annoy you, Lord Cheswick," Woodward explained in an apologetic tone. "But there is a possibility that Christopher Hamilton's cousin, Jedidiah Hamilton, is here in London impersonating him."

"Of course it was Christopher Hamilton I spoke to," Cheswick ground out. "I am hardly so advanced in years that I have become unable to recognize the fellow."

Because he knew that was exactly how he'd react to the same question—after all, no one wished to be accused of being tricked by a charlatan—Will pressed on. "I know you believed the man here in London to be Christopher, but were there any changes to his appearance that you simply attributed to the passage of time?"

"A different hairstyle, for instance," Woodward suggested. "Or maybe he was taller or shorter than you remembered."

Rolling his eyes, Cheswick was clearly disgruntled at their questions, but he looked upward and to the left, as if trying to recall his meeting with Hamilton.

Something must have suggested itself to him, because his

next words were a foul curse. "Yes, damn you. He was taller than I remembered. And he sported a beard, whereas he hadn't when I met him in Philadelphia."

Inwardly, Will cheered. This was precisely what they'd needed to learn from the earl.

"Anything else you remember?" Woodward asked carefully. "So that we needn't bother you again?"

But Cheswick shook his head. "No, though I'll be thinking about it more. I'm annoyed that the man succeeded in pulling the wool over my eyes, of course, but I'm even more incensed that he did so in order to have me introduce him to Fleetwood. Without Fleetwood's involvement, I'd never have been shot."

Will couldn't blame the man for being annoyed at having been caught in the middle, but there were more important things to be angry about, in his own opinion. Like the fact that the impostor had kidnapped a defenseless young woman.

Aloud, however, he said, "We are grateful to you for answering our questions, Cheswick. I hope you continue to recover from your wound."

"And I hope the two of you catch the blackguard," Cheswick said as Will and Woodward rose to take their leave.

"You didn't correct him when he said he wanted *us* to catch Hamilton," Woodward said as they stepped outside. "In point of fact, it will be Eversham and his men who capture him."

Will turned back after requesting the doorman to summon a hansom cab. "At this point I don't give a damn who captures the man, so long as he's off the street and we know where Miss Blackwood can be found."

* * *

That evening Will found himself seated beside Lucy in the Duke and Duchess of Langham's box at the Royal Opera House.

The party had been arranged as soon as the duke and duchess learned he'd returned from Paris. He hadn't even known Lucy was to be a member of the party when he'd accepted. But in light of their current closeness, he was glad of it.

"Never knew you had any particular fondness for the opera, Gilford," said Lord Adrian, who, along with his wife, Jane, was also included in the invitation. "I must admit I find it a bit tedious, though Jane enjoys it, so I came to please her."

Will glanced to where Lucy, Jane, and the duchess were deep in conversation. Knowing them, it had something to do with Vera's disappearance. He was having a difficult time putting the matter out of his own mind, as well. Especially given what they'd learned today. He'd wanted to inform Lucy of what he and Woodward had learned from Cheswick, but there had been no opportunity for privacy. Perhaps he could speak to her at the interval.

She wore a silver-blue gown of satin with a gauzy overlay that showed her creamy shoulders and upper bosom to advantage, and he had difficulty keeping his thoughts to something appropriate for mixed company.

Perhaps they could do… other things… during the interval as well.

He heard Adrian clear his throat and realized he'd been staring at Lucy.

Before he could respond to either Adrian's earlier comment or his amused look, Meg leaned forward from her seat behind them. "Oh, my brother is not an aficionado of the opera per se, Lord Adrian, but like most gentlemen, I believe, he went through a phase in his younger days when he was very interested in watching the dancers—oh, I mean, dancing."

Will felt his ears redden as he glanced back at his sister and gave her a pointed look. "I'm sure I don't know what you mean, Meg. I have always been very fond of hearing a lovely singing voice, however."

"Oh, are we discussing the opera?" asked Lucy as she took her seat beside Will. "I must admit that I have always had a fondness for the theatricality of it. Beautiful costumes, dramatic music, stories of life and death. It is not unlike some of the more colorful novels we read for the book club."

Baron Parkington, Meg's escort for the evening, a bit of a dull dog from what Will recalled of the man from their days at school together, cleared his throat and looked decidedly uncomfortable. "I hope this is not the same book club you were telling me about earlier, Miss Margaret. I must confess I find it shocking that you allow your sister to engage in novel reading, Gilford. A good many physicians have noted that allowing the gentler sex to tax their limited intellects with such activities can have a deleterious effect on their delicate constitutions."

Beside him, Will felt Lucy straighten her backbone. And he heard Meg's sharp intake of breath behind him. Turning to face the marquess, he saw that the fellow appeared oblivious to the hellfire he'd just invited to be rained down upon his head.

Then, to make matters worse, everyone else in the front row of the box turned to look back at his lordship. And Langham, not one to suffer fools, lifted his quizzing glass to imagine the man, as if trying to determine the classification and genus of Parkington's species of nodcock.

Ever the diplomat, however, it was Benjamin Woodward who averted a crisis and said mildly, "Perhaps it's because I'm just a brutish American, but I've always found that the more well-read a lady is, the better she seems as a prospective bride. After all, one must have something to talk about besides household matters and crop yields."

Silence fell in the box as the others waited to see how Parkington would respond.

But the oaf took one look at the escape ladder Woodward had offered him and metaphorically tossed it into the ocean.

"One's wife is not meant to be entertaining," Parkington said, aghast. "She is to be a helpmeet. A precious flower to be sheltered from those worldly things such as novels and the like. One cannot expect the female mind to grapple with the subjects to be found within the pages of a novel. Next you'll be saying ladies belong at university." He gave a little laugh at this last, as if the idea were so absurd as to be laughable.

"As a matter of fact—" Woodward began, but then the curtain opened on the stage below and the singing began.

Parkington had had a narrow escape. And everyone but Parkington knew it.

When the interval came, and Will and Lucy stood, he noticed that the chair beside Meg where Parkington had been sitting was now empty.

"Where did your escort go?" he asked his sister, who was following the other ladies toward the door of the box.

Meg turned to him with a grin. "He was feeling unwell and excused himself. It's just as well, because I know I spent much of the first act composing the ear-blistering tirade I meant to deliver once the curtain came down."

Lucy laughed softly. "As did I."

Beside her, Jane nodded. "I did, too. What a buffoon."

"That's Lord Buffoon to the likes of us," Lucy said wryly. "But honestly, I do not know how to reconcile the fact that ladies are forbidden from attending university but ignorant wretches like Parkington are able to sit in the Lords, on top of being given one of the best educations in the world."

"I understand better now what your book club is up to," Will said, looking from his sister to Lucy and back again. "You're planning a revolution."

Rather than address his words, the ladies gave him twin looks of disappointment and left the box.

"What have I done now?" he asked Adrian and Woodward, who had come to stand beside him.

"My dear fellow," said Adrian with a shake of his head. "The revolution has already begun. The very fact of the book club and all the other activities that have emerged as a result of the newspaper column Kate and Caro write are proof of it. It is not for you or me to question it. We are simply here to ensure that they do not come to harm in the process."

"Come on, Gilford," said Woodward, putting an arm about his friend's shoulders. "Let's go to the smoking room, and you can tell me about your youth misspent ogling opera dancers."

The three men left, and by the time they returned, the curtain had risen once again and the opera had resumed. But to Will's alarm, neither Lucy nor Meg was in their seats. He turned to where Jane sat beside Adrian and asked her, "What happened to Lucy and my sister? Were they not with you?"

Turning to see that neither of the ladies were yet returned, Jane frowned. "I came back before they did and was distracted by my conversation with Lady Heller in the next box. But surely they simply lost track of time and will be here any moment."

But when several more minutes passed with no sign of the missing ladies, he and Woodward, who had been just as alarmed by the ladies' absence as he was, crossed to the door.

Once they stepped out into the hallway, which was largely empty now thanks to the resumption of the performance, the two men exchanged a look.

"We should split up so that we cover more ground," Will said tersely. It might be unfounded, but he couldn't put aside the fact that Lucy had been with him at Miss Fleetwood's today. Could Jedidiah have seen them and decided to do something to harm Lucy? He didn't like to think so, but couldn't forget the sight of Hamilton slinging Vera Blackwood into the waiting coach. "I'll go check the ground floor and the area leading to the entrance. Perhaps they sought out the coach for some reason."

Woodward nodded. "I'll go make sure they aren't in any of the retiring rooms. It won't be the first time I've had to intrude into a space where men aren't allowed, but if I'm lucky, no one will be there to catch me."

At Will's sharp look, the other man rolled his eyes. "You aren't the only man who's had to go in search of a dawdling sister or lady friend in one of those viper's dens."

Grateful to Woodward for the needed bit of levity, he nodded to his friend, and they agreed to meet back at the door to the stairs in five minutes.

But when Will reached the gently sloping entrance area, he saw no sign of Lucy or his sister. Some unexplained impulse made him open the entry door and step out into the chill evening. Out front, he saw that the carriages of the opera-goers were starting to queue up in anticipation of the performance's conclusion.

Here and there, men in evening wear stood chatting and laughing, but Will didn't care about them. He scanned the area for some sight of either Lucy or Meg, but saw neither.

To one side of the theater entrance, he spied a couple of footmen and a coachman engaged in a game of dice to pass the time. He stepped toward them, but as soon as the men saw him they began to get to their feet.

"My lord," said one of the footmen with a guilty look. "We was just…"

"Don't mind me, lads," Will said to them and indicated that they needn't stand upon ceremony with him. "I don't mean to interrupt your game. I'm simply looking for my betrothed and my sister, who seem to have come out for a bit of air. You didn't happen to see them, did you? One is wearing a rose-colored gown, and the other a light blue one."

The footman who'd addressed him exchanged a look with one of the other men—their livery matched, so they were likely from the same household. "Not two of 'em together, my lord. There was a lady by herself, though, who was wearing a gown like you mentioned. Blue it was. And she had hair that was almost white it was so light."

Lucy, Will thought with relief. At least someone had seen her.

"And which way did she go?" he asked.

"She asked us about some gent who'd run past us a couple of minutes before," said the coachman. "He was a tall feller with black hair and a fine beaver hat. Quality from the looks of him. He was in a powerful hurry. All but ran down the lane."

"And she went after him, you say?" Will asked, not liking the sound of this. Knowing Lucy, she wouldn't go haring about after a strange man without good reason. And yet that didn't mean that he wouldn't blister her ears for being so foolhardy when he found her.

If he found her.

"She did," the footman said with a nod. "Would have tried to stop her, of course, but begging your pardon, my lord, it didn't seem our place."

He was about to ask another question when the sound of a scream came from the end of the lane Lucy had disappeared down.

Cursing, Will sprinted toward where the shriek had come from.

Chapter 27

I cannot believe I allowed Mama to persuade me to let Lord Parkington escort me tonight," Meg hissed to Lucy as they followed the throng toward the ladies' withdrawing room at the far end of the corridor. "I knew he was a bit of a stick, but I had no notion he was as bad as all that."

Lucy would have warned her friend if she'd known, but she hadn't been aware of the arrangement until Will had handed her into the carriage to come here. "I've met him many times over the years, I'm afraid. Though thankfully he's spent the past few years sequestered in the country. I suppose since his wife died last year, he's on the hunt for a new one."

"I can only presume that she died of boredom," Meg said grimly. "I know I would if I were unlucky enough to be married off to a man who refused to let me read novels. Or converse about anything of the slightest interest to me."

"A putrid fever, I believe," Lucy said with a stifled laugh. Then, not wanting to sound disloyal, she added, "Though I'm sure she was relieved to take her leave of him."

"Oh, do not be so agreeable when I am being horrid about some poor lady I never even met," Meg chided. "I simply cannot conceive that men such as the marquess still exist. It is a very good thing that I never spoke to him about my work with the suffragists. He would no doubt have had an apoplexy on the spot."

"There are all too many of them, I'm afraid," Lucy said with a note of apology in her voice. "Otherwise there would be no question of women's having the vote or being allowed into university. But even though education is wasted on men like the marquess, the moment there is any hint of allowing ladies to learn beside them, they poker up and begin speaking as if the end of the world is nigh. They are so tiresome."

"At least my brother is not one of their number," Meg said with a genuine smile. "He might be tiresome in other ways, but he is not of that ilk, thank heavens."

Lucy was about to agree, but they'd just reached the door leading into the withdrawing room, and before she could follow Meg inside, she caught a glimpse of a man out of the corner of her eye and turned to look at him.

To her surprise, it was Sir Charles Fleetwood.

What in the world was he thinking showing his face in public? Surely he was well aware that the police were searching all over London for him after his shooting of Lord Cheswick?

Knowing she should tell Meg where she was going, but not wishing to lose sight of the man, she turned and began to follow him as he walked down the corridor away from the stream of operagoers.

As she followed him, she quickly realized that he was walking with purpose. This was a man on his way to some specific location—to a specific person, perhaps? As he went toward the door leading to the staircase, she trailed at a discreet distance.

Was he here in search of Christopher Hamilton—or whatever the man who was posing as Vera's former betrothed was called?

But she soon realized that wherever he was going it was not within the opera house itself, but somewhere outside. He followed the corridor leading from the stairs into the black-and-white-marble-tiled entrance area and made for the doors. Once he'd stepped outside, she followed after him, only to be waylaid by a man who worked for the theater.

"Can I be of service to you, miss?" he asked with an obsequious bow. Then, looking pointedly behind her, as if to call attention to the fact that she had no maid with her, he added, "I'll just send a note to your party, shall I?"

"That won't be necessary," Lucy told the man with her sunniest smile, though in her head she noted that Parkington wasn't the only man to butt his nose in where it wasn't wanted this evening. "My mama is waiting for me in the carriage. She'll worry, so I dare not delay."

And before the man could offer an objection or detain her any longer, she hurried out the door and into the chill night air.

To her relief Fleetwood was at the bottom of the steps leading down to the street below. She watched as he disappeared around the stone wall that separated the opera house from the property next door—a churchyard, from the looks of it. As she neared the corner, she saw a group of servants dicing and rushed past them before they could spot her and try to detain her like the man inside the theater had done. She had enough officious gentlemen to contend with without other people's servants joining in the mix.

As she turned the corner, she saw Fleetwood up ahead and sent a silent prayer of thanks heavenward. As they went farther down the lane, she realized that though there were gas lamps lining the street, the additional lights that had made the area outside the theater relatively easy to navigate were no longer there, and the dimness made it necessary for her to pay closer attention to where she stepped.

Just as Fleetwood neared the overhang of a building that was swathed in darkness, she realized that he'd slowed his steps. Was he meeting someone here? Then, as he reached the far end of the building she saw the figure step out from the other side.

"I don't see why we had to come here," Fleetwood began as he noticed the other person. "But I'm here now, what did you mean by—" But he broke off before he could finish as the other man—for surely it was a man—lifted his arm in the air. Metal glinted in the moonlight, and she heard Fleetwood cry, "No!"

Lucy gave a bloodcurdling scream. Realizing that he and Sir Charles weren't alone, the assailant froze, then sprinted off into the night.

Hoping the man wasn't planning to come back and stab her as well, Lucy rushed to Fleetwood's side and saw blood flowing from a wound in his chest. Nursing another bleeding man soon after seeing to Cheswick's wound after he'd been shot, Lucy felt a sense of unreality. Still, she had to help him. Kneeling down beside him, she withdrew the handkerchief from her pocket and folded it into a pad, which she pressed down hard over the wound. She saw that the injured man was having difficulty breathing and reached down to take his hand. It was clear that this wound was far more serious than the one sustained by Cheswick the other evening. "Don't worry, Sir Charles, I'm sure help is on the way. Just try to stay calm."

"M-m-miss P-p..." he tried to say, but Lucy shushed him.

"Yes, Sir Charles, it's Lucy Penhallow," she said in her most comforting voice. "Do you know who did this to you?"

He seemed grateful for her taking charge and gave a slight nod, though it seemed to take a great deal of his already waning strength. "T-t-tell Christina. S-s-sorry."

But it was clear that the knife must have hit something vital, because Fleetwood's eyes closed then and, as Lucy watched, the life seemed to drain from the man's body. And then he was still.

Sir Charles Fleetwood was dead.

Feeling tears stream down her face, she rose to her feet and took a step away from him.

She was staring down at the blood on her hands when she heard running footsteps coming toward her. But before she could hide she saw that it was Will coming toward her.

"Lucy, my God," he said breathlessly as he reached her, then she realized she must have gotten blood on more than just her hands because he gaped. "Are you hurt? Has someone hurt you?"

"Not my blood," she said in a shaky voice. Only then, it seemed, did Will notice the man lying on the ground behind her.

"Thank God," Will said, pulling her against him, and she was shocked to feel a tremor run through him. "Thank God."

"Sir Charles Fleetwood is dead," she said in a dazed voice. "Someone stabbed him."

Chapter 28

Nearly an hour later, Will watched as Eversham gave orders to Detective Cherrywood. A line of constables held back a growing crowd of gawkers who'd appeared as if out of nowhere to see the dead man.

Not long after he'd found Lucy covered in Fleetwood's blood, Eversham and Kate had arrived, having been summoned by the Duchess of Langham after Meg had returned to the opera box without Lucy.

When he'd found Lucy and seen the dead man behind her, Will couldn't help being reminded of his father's murder. The smell of blood, the sight of the victim lying prostrate on the ground, the overwhelming feeling of dread... It was only the sight of Lucy, trembling and looking shattered, that had brought him back to reality. When Kate had gently taken Lucy in hand and ushered her to the carriage that she and her husband had arrived in, Will had bitten back a protest. He'd wanted to be the one to comfort Lucy. And if he was being entirely honest, he'd needed the comfort of holding her just as badly as she needed him to do it.

Now with the dead man covered in a sheet and Eversham

standing before him, Will felt more himself and only waited for word from Lucy's cousin to escort her home.

"I don't have to tell you how damaging it will be to Lucy's reputation if this gets out," Eversham told him now. "Not only was there no one here to see the perpetrator of the crime, but she was also found covered in the man's blood."

The idea that anyone would think that Lucy Penhallow, who barely came up to Will's shoulder and likely would have difficulty overpowering a lapdog cat, could have had the strength to plunge a knife into a man who outweighed her by five stone at least, was absurd. And yet, absurdity had never been much of a limitation for the gossipmongers when it came to speculation.

"Can't you keep it quiet?" Will asked the other man, running a hand through his hair in frustration. "It's obvious she didn't kill him."

Eversham's mouth tightened. "I will, of course, do what I can to ensure that her identity isn't revealed, but I can't control every last person at the Met who hears her name linked with this case. Plus, they know her because of her work there. It is only to be expected for people to gossip about someone known to them. Not to mention the fact that there is already a crowd of onlookers who have seen her face."

Will uttered the foulest curse he could think of.

"Just so," Eversham said grimly. "I have refrained from asking you about your intentions toward my cousin, because I know you are an honorable man. But the two of you have been involved in three incidents now that required the assistance of the Metropolitan Police. Not to mention the fact that neither of you seems indifferent to the other."

Like the skilled interrogator he was, the detective superintendent let the silence hang between them until Will felt the need to speak.

"Of course my intentions are honorable," he said, feeling strangely calm. "I am very fond of your cousin, and I believe she is fond of me as well. The only thing that has kept me from speaking up thus far is my financial situation."

At this last statement, Eversham gave him a speaking look. "It seems to me that if you had doubts, you should have kept away from her until you were sure. Now it is too late. I am perhaps not as versed in the ways of the *ton*, but I know scandal when I see it. And the two of you are well and truly mired in it. You'd better make your declaration to her tonight so that an announcement can run in the evening papers tomorrow."

For a man who claimed to know little about the ways of the beau monde, Will thought wryly, Eversham seemed to know a great deal about quashing scandal.

"I have been there many times when hasty betrothals have been arranged," the detective said with a shrug, in answer to Will's questioning look. "One learns things."

Thinking back to what he'd heard about the marriages of the Eversham's' friends, as well as his own friends Lord Adrian and his wife, Jane, Will supposed that was the truth.

"Now," Eversham said to him with a clap on the shoulder, "you'd better go get into the carriage and make your offer. The sooner this match is official, the sooner we can shield my cousin from scandal."

Feeling nervous in a way he hadn't since he was a boy, Will strode over to the carriage where Kate had disappeared with Lucy a short time ago.

When he pulled open the door, he exchanged a look with Kate, and she gave him a small nod before saying something he couldn't hear to Lucy, then allowing Will to hand her down. To his surprise, the older woman gave him a quick hug.

"Good luck," she told him with a smile. Then she left him to take her place in the carriage.

The interior of the carriage was much more opulent than those of the cabs he and Lucy had traveled in earlier. He was more familiar with this sort of conveyance, if he was honest. His family had always been wealthy as far back as he could recall.

Of course now, things were different. He wondered whether Lucy would be upset at having to marry a man with a title but no wealth. It was the sort of marriage contracted all the time. A marriage of convenience. He'd come home from Paris with the express purpose of making such a match.

So why was he so nervous now?

Perhaps because the idea of revealing his family's newly discovered loss of wealth filled him with shame? It hadn't been him to lose the money, but that didn't mean he didn't hold some responsibility, if only because of his inattention to the family accounts while he hid away from his duties in Paris.

To his surprise, as soon as he shut the carriage door behind him, Lucy flung herself into his arms and began to sob.

A feeling of protectiveness washed over Will as he cradled her against his chest and pulled her into his lap. He hated that she'd witnessed Fleetwood's murder tonight. This was the second time this week she'd seen one man try to kill another. That she'd been alone when one of the perpetrators had succeeded in murdering his target filled Will with rage.

But he kept his anger to himself, not wanting to frighten her any more than she'd already been this night.

"I don't know why I am so sad," Lucy said after she'd exhausted her store of tears for now. Will had pressed his handkerchief into her hand, and after wiping her face and blowing her nose, she looked up at him with still-shining eyes. "Sir Charles was not a good man. He betrayed Vera in exchange for Hamilton's money. And he tried to convince his sister to trick Vera into believing her dead mother wished her to marry Hamilton immediately. His very ill sister, I might add."

Despite her obvious sorrow, Lucy's vehemence at the despicable nature of Sir Charles Fleetwood's actions remained unchanged. She lay her head against Will's chest, and he stroked a hand down her back in comfort.

"You saw a man stabbed to death," he said, holding her a little tighter when he remembered how close she'd been to a murderer tonight. "You are entitled to feel whatever it is you feel. Even if Fleetwood was not a good man, he didn't deserve to be killed in such a manner."

"He nearly did the same to Lord Cheswick the other night," Lucy said, fiddling with the chain of Will's watch in his coat pocket. "But I suppose the difference is that Sir Charles acted in the heat of the moment. But the man who stabbed *him* seemed to have come with the intention of killing. It was clear from what Sir Charles said that the two had a prior arrangement to meet. And the other man didn't even bother to speak, for as soon as he arrived, he struck."

Will closed his eyes as he gripped her to him. "You're damned lucky the fellow didn't see you. What possessed you to follow Sir Charles like that? You already knew he could be dangerous. What if he'd seen you?"

Lucy sighed, but didn't lift her head. "I didn't think he could possibly do anything to me with so many people about. And since the police had such a difficult time locating him, I thought I should try to at least delay him until he might be apprehended."

"I was terrified when I saw you there," Will said into her hair, remembering that moment when he'd come upon her, covered in blood and crying. "I thought I'd lost you."

At his words, Lucy pulled back a little and looked into his face. "You did?" she asked, reaching up to trace a finger over his cheek.

Unable to stop himself, Will leaned forward and took her mouth.

Chapter 29

At the touch of Will's lips to hers, Lucy made a needy sound and slid her arms around his neck and pulled him down to her.

She'd wanted to kiss him again so many times since their encounter in her family's parlor, but no good opportunity had presented itself. She'd thought of the feel of Will in her arms, his mouth on hers, over and over again.

Now, she took advantage of this moment out of time and gave herself up to the feel of Will Gilford's body pressed against hers.

When he opened his mouth over hers, Lucy didn't hesitate but welcomed his tongue inside her mouth. The contact sent a jolt of heat through her, and she felt the connection as if there were an electric wire running from her mouth to her core.

The sound she made then seemed to bring Will to his senses, though the hand that cupped her breast contracted, as if protesting the fact it couldn't keep going.

Her breath coming in gusts, Lucy dropped her forehead onto Will's chest.

Kissing her softly on the top of her head, Will said, "I am sorry, darling, but there is something I need to speak to you about before that goes any further."

Lucy let his words sink in for a moment before she heaved a sigh and adjusted herself into if not a more decorous position, then at least a more upright one.

The noise Will made when she shifted in his lap made Lucy frown. "Did I hurt you?"

But he shook his head and seemed determined to continue. Which, unfortunately, meant that he needed to place her on the seat opposite, much to Lucy's disappointment.

When she looked up from where he'd set her, she saw that Will's expression was deadly serious. And she feared suddenly that he was going to give her some dire news. Was Meg hurt? Had he learned something about her mother?

"There is something I wish to ask you," Will said, taking her hand in his, stroking his thumb over the back of it.

At his words, Lucy felt her tummy flip. She'd heard enough friends describe the moment when their respective husbands had proposed to know what Will was about to say. She opened her mouth to tell him there was no need to go further, that of course she accepted. But before she could say anything, he held up a staying hand.

"I must tell you something first, however," he said, looking as if he would rather run screaming from the carriage.

Nodding at him, hoping to give him some reassurance, Lucy gestured for him to continue.

Taking a deep breath, he continued. "Nearly two weeks ago, Woodward visited me in Paris and brought an urgent packet from my man of business."

Lucy blinked. Why would he tell her something that didn't pertain to her?

"Inside was the news that the man who acted as steward for the four country houses that comprise the Gilford estates since my father's time had absconded with hundreds of thousands of pounds from the family coffers. And that theft, in combination with the exorbitant amounts of money my mother had spent since my father's death, had left the estate coffers in a woeful state. In short, the Gilford estate was depleted, and I needed to do something to mend things."

"Marry, you mean?" Lucy breathed a sigh of relief. She'd thought he was preparing to tell her something really dire. "I already know all of this, Will."

He was clearly startled, but Lucy wasn't sure if it was because of her pronouncement or her use of his given name.

"You do?" His voice was strained. "How could you possibly know?"

She wanted to pat him on the hand, as men had done to her so many times in her life when explaining something. But Will had never been that sort of man to her. And she wanted only to soothe his obvious nerves over the matter.

"I know because your sister is my dearest friend in the world," she explained simply. "And we tell each other everything."

Though as soon as she spoke the words, Lucy mentally amended them. She still hadn't got the full story on Ben Woodward from Meg. And of course she hadn't told Will's sister about just how skilled he was at kissing.

But what she'd told him was true more or less.

He still looked confused, however. "I never told Meg about the state of the family finances. I didn't want to make her worry. I was hoping to marry soon after returning to London so there would be no need to tell her."

"Do you know nothing about women?" Lucy asked him with affectionate exasperation. "Meg learned of it from your mother, who wasted no time after you informed her of your changed circumstances and poured out her tale of woe to her maid. The maid in turn told Meg's maid, who then told Meg."

Will's eyes were wide with disbelief. And for a few moments he was speechless.

"Will," she told him patiently, "the only people in London who are more fond of gossip than the ladies of the *ton* are their servants. How did you not already know this?"

"I suppose it just never occurred to me that my mother would confide the news to her maid," he said with a shake of his head. "I thought she'd be too ashamed. But of course she probably told the tale in some way that she turned out to be the injured party."

That was true enough, so Lucy just nodded.

Shaking his head as if to clear it, he said, "Then I suppose you know what I intended to say next?"

"Not precisely," Lucy said with a smile. "I know the gist, I believe, but that doesn't mean I don't wish to hear the words."

But instead of looking relieved to know she was expecting his proposal, Will still looked troubled. "Lucy, I was hoping to find some way of repairing the Gilford fortunes before I had the temerity to ask you to marry me."

"But there's no need," she said, feeling as if she was stating the obvious. "I have enough money for all of us. You need to marry an heiress. I am an heiress."

Now it was his turn to sigh. Will looked at her with exasperation. "You must know that it isn't easy on a man's pride to be forced to rely on a bride for funds."

But Lucy thought this was arrant nonsense and didn't bother to hide it. "Marriages have been contracted in order to gain lands, fortunes, jewels, and any number of valuables since before England was even a nation. You can't tell me that you, William, the sixth Viscount Gilford, are too high in the instep to accept my fortune when we marry?"

"When you put it like that," he said, rubbing his nape in embarrassment, "you make me sound foolish."

"Not foolish, darling," she told him, once more flinging herself into his arms. "Merely a little thickheaded."

"Then you'll marry me?" he asked, his deep voice vibrating against her neck where he'd tucked his head.

"Of course I will," she said, turning her head for what was meant to be a brief meeting of lips but turned into a long, languorous kiss that included not only lips, but teeth and tongues.

A brisk knock on the carriage door made them spring apart, though Lucy refused to move back to the seat on the other side of the carriage interior.

Her hand firmly gripped in Will's, she called out for whoever it was to come in.

She'd hoped it would be Kate who looked in on them, but it was Eversham. Her cousin looked faintly amused as he noted her location as well as the couple's linked hands.

The look he leveled on Will seemed to ask a question. Lucy wondered what the older man had said to Gilford when they spoke earlier.

"You may wish us happy, Eversham," her fiancé—her fiancé!—said to the detective superintendent. "Lucy has accepted my proposal of marriage."

Cousin Andrew might have expected the announcement, but that didn't seem to dim his genuine pleasure in it. Lines bracketed his wide smile, and he climbed in to give Lucy a brief hug and to clasp Will's hand in his.

"I could wish that the circumstances were different," he said, and Lucy felt a pang of remorse that she'd forgotten that only a short time ago she'd seen a man murdered. "But that should not dim our joy in the match even so. Such events have a way of telling us in a few hours how suited a pair is to one another. Whereas there are years-long betrothals that could not predict another pair's incompatibility."

"Well said," Lucy told her cousin with a grin. "These are the times when I remember your father was a vicar."

The detective shrugged. "There are worse parental influences."

Changing the subject, he glanced at Will and asked, "Have you brought your own carriage tonight?"

Suddenly thinking of Meg, Lucy's eyes widened. "I forgot all about the others back in the Langhams' box. Do you know if someone has spoken with them?"

"Katherine went to inform them what happened," her cousin said. Then to Will he said, "I believe your sister and mother accepted an escort home from Adrian and Jane."

Will nodded and turned to Lucy. "They brought you tonight, didn't they?"

At her nod, he said to Eversham, "I did bring my own carriage tonight. I can take Lucy to Brook Street."

It would generally be unacceptable for an unmarried young

lady to ride alone in a closed carriage with a gentleman who was not a relative. Lucy waited for Eversham to raise some objection, but her cousin merely nodded.

Before they climbed out of the Evershams' carriage, Will shrugged out of his outer coat and draped it over Lucy's shoulders. She glanced down at her gown, which was covered with Sir Charles Fleetwood's blood, and gave a shudder.

"You'll be home soon," Will told her softly. She thought he was going to kiss her again but he only gave her a look, then climbed out of the carriage.

Fortunately, Will's coachman had managed to get close to the area where Fleetwood had been killed. This despite the crowd of gawkers and journalists who had gathered. Unfortunately, this meant that he and Lucy had to wend their way through the throng in order to get to the vehicle.

"Lord Gilford, is it true that you stopped the killer from attacking Miss Penhallow?"

"Miss Penhallow, did you see the face of the killer? Why were you meeting with Sir Charles? Was it to discuss his attack on Lord Cheswick? Why were you there at both crimes? Are you involved in the disappearance of your friend Miss Vera Blackwood? Miss Penhallow! Miss Penhallow!"

Lucy heard all their questions but answered none. She allowed Will, who had wrapped an arm around her, to hurry her past the shouting journalists and soon they were safe inside the Gilford carriage.

This time, they both climbed in on the same side and their arms went around one another without any awkwardness. And they rode like that the entire way to the Penhallow townhouse.

Chapter 30

Despite his hopes to break the news to his mother himself, the sound of her raised voice emanating from the breakfast room to the corridor outside his bedchamber alerted Will to the fact that she'd learned of his betrothal already.

When he reached the breakfast room itself, he saw that only his mother and sister were there. Clearly the servants had decided to wait until the atmosphere improved.

"Margaret," Lady Gilford said to her daughter, "you can persuade Lucy to break things off with your brother, can you not? I know you have a fondness for her, but you must see that doesn't make her worthy of elevation to Viscountess Gilford."

Will had heard enough. He stepped into the room and said, "That is enough, Mother. I have made my choice, and there is nothing more to be said about it. I will be wed to Miss Lucy Penhallow by special license in the coming weeks."

He hadn't spoken to Lucy about a wedding date last night. She'd fallen asleep on the drive to her house last evening, and he hadn't wanted to bother her with such details. He hoped she wouldn't object to his plan.

Not waiting for Lady Gilford to respond, he went to the

sideboard and loaded a plate with eggs, kippers, and bacon. Behind him, however, he heard his mother continuing on as if he hadn't even spoken.

"Who was her father? He was in some sort of manufacturing, was he not?" the viscountess said with disapproval. "No, not suitable for this family at all. Your brother has lost his senses, Margaret. I mean really. I could have introduced him to any number of eligible ladies from some of the highest-ranked families in the beau monde. But what must he do but become ensnared by a policeman's cousin."

Placing his plate at the head of the table—though there was no set seating for breakfast, he hoped to reinforce his role as head of the family—Will took his seat and accepted coffee Meg poured for him.

Their eyes met and he mouthed "sorry" to her as their mother continued her tirade. But Meg only grinned and mouthed "excellent choice."

At least one member of the household was happy for him, Will thought wryly.

Not allowing his mother to spoil his meal, he methodically worked through his food. Once he was finished, he stood, having ignored most of his mother's complaints.

When he took to his feet, however, he turned his attention to her. "Mother, I should like to see you and Meg in the drawing room in a quarter of an hour."

If he'd expected her to be cowed by the steel in his voice, he was to be disappointed. Instead she sat up straighter and said triumphantly, "I knew you would see reason, Gilford."

Apparently her appetite had been revived by his summons;

she took a new slice of toast from the warmer and spread butter over it.

In the drawing room, Will stood looking out the window into the street below when he heard Meg enter.

Turning, he saw that her grin from earlier remained. "I am so pleased for you both. Though I could wonder why anyone would wish to marry my odious brother. But I have no doubts why you'd want to marry Lucy."

"I am glad you approve of my choice," he told her with a matching grin. Then, his expression turning serious, he told her, "Whatever you can do to reconcile Mother to the match, I beg you to do it. I don't ask on my own behalf but Lucy's."

Meg opened her mouth to reply, but the viscountess sailed into the room and took her customary seat near the window.

When Will and Meg didn't immediately hurry to her, Lady Gilford called out, "Pray, whatever it is you wish to discuss with me, Gilford, please make haste. I have an appointment with Worth himself in a few hours. You know how rare it is to see him in London."

Will stared at her in disbelief. "I told you only days ago that we must curtail spending until I find a way to replenish the family coffers."

Instead of an apology, however, Lady Gilford met her son's words with dismissal. "Oh, I have no doubt you will find a wealthy young lady of good family soon, and we needn't be bothered by such matters. Now, what is it you wish to talk about?"

He would, Will decided, need to be firm with her. He could see now that what he'd considered a firm talking-to about expenses when he first arrived home had been interpreted as a suggestion rather than an order.

He gestured to Meg to have a seat, too, then, choosing to remain on his feet, he turned to them. "I believe you learned of it from someone else before I could tell you," he said, looking from one to the other, "but I have asked Miss Lucy Penhallow to be my wife, and fortunately she has accepted me."

"Oh, not this again," Lady Gilford said with a shake of her head. "I thought we'd agreed that Lucy isn't the right wife for you."

"No," Will returned. "She is not the right wife for *you*, my lady. Which is fortunate, because I am the one who wishes to marry her."

"But her family!" Lady Gilford cried with real agitation. "And not only that, what of her reputation? In the past week she's been involved in a kidnapping and a shooting in the middle of Mayfair."

He waited for her to mention the events of last night, but when none was forthcoming he realized she hadn't yet heard of them. "How did you learn of my betrothal to Miss Penhallow? You clearly haven't seen the papers yet."

At his question, his mother's expression turned sly. "I have my sources. And I refuse to reveal them. There are certain privileges of being Lady Gilford that I simply will not give up."

Since only Kate and Gilford were aware of the betrothal, and he was more than certain that they hadn't been the ones to tell his mother about it, Will suspected someone must have seen his carriage outside Lucy's house last night and had made a deduction that turned out to be right. In all likelihood a servant, since apparently everyone knew how quickly gossip traveled from household to household through the people who served the residents.

Deciding that was a matter for another time, he moved on. "However you learned of it, the betrothal between Miss Penhallow and myself is real, and I will expect you to behave toward her with the utmost courtesy when you see her again. Perhaps you will look more kindly upon her when you consider that she will bring with her to the marriage a sizable fortune, thanks to her late father, whom you were so quick to condemn for his lack of connections." Will watched as his mother seemed to wrestle with the news.

Finally, she said with an inclination of her head—like the queen, Will thought with an inward sigh—"I suppose I must learn to do so, since it seems you have no intention of listening to my advice and will marry the chit whether I approve the match or not."

She clearly meant the words to prompt him to apologize abjectly and beg her forgiveness. Instead, Will simply nodded and said, "I am glad you see reason."

To Meg he asked, "Is there anything you wish to say?"

He had no fear that his sister had complaints like his mother's, but Will thought she deserved to be given a chance to speak.

Glancing over to where her mother was scowling toward the window, Meg rose and hurried toward her brother and threw her arms about his neck and gave him a hard hug. "I am so pleased for you both," she said as she stepped back. "Truly."

Then, as if afraid her mother would somehow manage to trap her into listening to her further complaints, she hurried from the room.

Deciding Meg had the right of it, Will was about to flee as well when he remembered something.

"I checked the safe in my bookroom for my grandmother's rings, but they weren't there. Do you know where I might find them?"

At the mention of the sapphire set his grandmother had worn as her betrothal and wedding set, Lady Gilford's mouth pursed in anger before she sighed. "Am I to keep nothing of the life I had with your father? Soon you will demand I leave this house, where I have lived for the decades since my marriage."

Since he'd heard this same complaint from her already, Will didn't rise to her bait. "You are welcome to choose any of the country houses other than the main one, or I can purchase a townhouse for you in London. I will discuss the matter with Lucy, of course, though."

When she didn't reply, he pressed on. "If the sapphire set is being kept with your jewelry, I would like for you to have your maid bring it, as well as whatever others of the Gilford family jewels you have, to my study within the hour."

He left her then. And seconds after he shut the door behind him, he heard one of the Dresden figurines from the mantel shatter on the other side.

Chapter 31

On the other side of Mayfair, Lucy was telling her mother about her betrothal to Will. Lucy didn't know it, but Mrs. Penhallow's reaction was worlds away from what Lady Gilford's had been.

"Oh, Lucy," Mrs. Penhallow said with a mixture of happiness and exasperation. "I should have known you would not settle for a conventional match."

"But Lord Gilford is entirely conventional, Mama," Lucy said, rising to bring her mother a handkerchief. "He might have lived in Paris for the past few years, but I assure you he is still an English gentleman with all of the attendant behaviors."

"Oh, you will quibble, but you know what I mean," Lucy's mother argued. "What other young lady would accept a betrothal only yards from where a murdered man still lies? Though I must admit I am grateful beyond anything that Gilford was there to save you."

Lucy sighed. She loved her mother, but her inability to ever see Lucy as capable of taking care of herself was frustrating. Not least because at times it seemed that Mrs. Penhallow's views were no different from the gentlemen of the *ton* who claimed women didn't deserve the vote because they were too emotional to make such important decisions.

"Gilford didn't save me, Mama," she said, perching on the settee near her mother's chair. "By the time he arrived, the villain was long gone. And poor Sir Charles was dead."

"Oh, do not argue, Lucy. You know what I mean." Mrs. Penhallow shook her head. "You might not have been in actual danger by that time, but there's no doubt that his lordship's presence kept danger at bay once he arrived."

Knowing it would be impossible to change her mother's mind at this point, Lucy just let her words go without argument.

"I am glad you are pleased with my choice of husband, Mama," she said instead. "He is a good man. I think you will like him."

"But do you love him, my dear?" Her mother's too-keen eyes searched Lucy's, and she gave in to the urge to put her hands over them.

It was too soon for her to know whether she loved Will, she wanted to protest. It had only been a few days. Surely that wasn't long enough to form that kind of attachment.

She liked and respected him, of course. And his kisses made her toes curl and sent zings of sensation through her whole body. But love? That would have to wait until she'd had more time to assess things.

Misinterpreting Lucy's reluctance to answer, Mrs. Penhallow gave a contented sigh. "I felt the same way about your father, though it took me a little while to recognize it for what it was. I thought I'd found a man who was worthy of giving my hand to, of course, but I didn't even think in terms of love. I was happy enough to have a proposal. A love match was beyond my comprehension."

At this, however, Lucy removed her hands from her eyes and looked at her mother. "I never knew you were a spinster, Mama." She'd known her mother was a little older than most young ladies when they married, but that didn't necessarily mean she'd been dismissed as unmarriageable.

"Oh yes," Mrs. Penhallow said with a laugh. "Very much so, but that didn't matter to your papa. It was as if heaven had seen to it that I remain unmarried so that I would be there waiting for him."

Lucy smiled at the notion. Whatever force had ensured that they met, she was grateful for it. She'd not be here otherwise.

They'd been reading through the papers and scandal sheets that mentioned the events surrounding Sir Charles Fleetwood's murder the evening before. More than one of the gossip papers mentioned the fact that Lucy and Will had been seen in a public embrace once again. The insinuations made about what, if any, relationship lay between them were more blatant than the ones the night of the Leighton-Childe and Maitland balls. And a couple wondered when an interesting announcement might be forthcoming from them.

The fact that "interesting announcement" might be referring to a betrothal or, in the more common meaning, a pregnancy, was a nice bit of wordplay. Lucy supposed she'd be subject to the scrutiny of having her waist observed for the next half year, regardless.

The sound of the knocker on the front door carried up to where the two ladies sat.

Since she'd been expecting him to call on her this morning,

Lucy had dressed with care and asked her maid to make sure to leave a few tendrils dangling over her ears. It was her favorite style, and she'd noticed that Will liked to tuck them behind her ears, which she enjoyed as well.

When Rhodes showed Will in, Lucy took a moment while he made his greetings to her mother to soak in the resplendence of him.

He was always handsome and well dressed, and today he had obviously taken great pains with his wardrobe. Or at the very least his valet had.

She was too pleased to see him, however, to pay much attention to his clothing beyond noting that it was attractive on him and fit him splendidly.

When he turned to face her, she couldn't suppress the smile that broke across her face. "Miss Penhallow," Will said, his voice low, which sent a little thrill down her spine. "You are looking lovely this morning."

"As are you," she said, then realizing what she'd said, she blushed. "I mean, that is to say you are—"

But he gave a soft laugh. "I am more than happy to hear that my bride-to-be finds me lovely."

Certain she would either burst into flames or sink into the floor, Lucy was still struggling to regain her composure when her mother walked to the door and then turned to them with an admirably straight face.

"I just remembered I was meant to meet with Mrs. Hughes to go over this week's menus," Mrs. Penhallow said. "Please excuse me."

When the door closed behind her, the betrothed couple turned to one another, and before Lucy knew what had happened, her hands were in Will's hair and his mouth had covered hers.

His short locks were softer than she'd imagined, and as Lucy welcomed the wet heat of his lips on hers, she reveled in the strength of his body against hers. She'd noticed last night, but her mind had been too stunned to truly appreciate it. His sandalwood scent made her want to bury her face in his neck, but that would have meant separating their mouths, and she wouldn't do that for any enticement.

A brisk knock on the door alerted them to the presence of a guest.

"I'll just let them know I'm here, shall I?" boomed Eversham's voice from the hallway, where he was very obviously waiting for them to right themselves.

Inside the drawing room, Lucy smoothed down Will's hair, which was sticking up at odd angles thanks to her hands. Will, meanwhile, was doing his best to adjust Lucy's bodice, which he'd somehow pulled off her shoulder.

"Do come in, Cousin Andrew," Lucy called to her cousin from the chair she'd perched decorously on, holding a book open as if she'd been reading aloud.

Will, meanwhile, was posed with a hand braced against the mantelpiece, staring broodily into the fire. He looked so much like a caricature of a Byronic hero that Lucy almost giggled. As she looked closer, however, she saw that she'd missed some fingermarks near the crown of his head.

When she looked up, Eversham was watching her with a raised brow.

"I apologize for disturbing you," he said blandly, as he watched Will turn to face him, then move to Lucy's side.

"I have some news about Sir Charles Fleetwood's murder, as well as what I was able to learn from the American embassy about Christopher Hamilton."

At the mention of the murder, any amusement Lucy was feeling fled.

She shivered as the memory of Sir Charles's face, twisted in a rictus of pain as he died. Beside her, Will slipped an arm about her waist and held her against him.

With a nod of his head, Eversham indicated that they should sit. And this time, Lucy and Will sat side by side, hands locked together, in an echo of the way they'd been last evening across from Eversham in the carriage.

The detective superintendent took the chair nearest them and said, "I had this information about Hamilton last night, but, as you can probably guess why, it was pushed to the back of my mind by other matters."

Lucy couldn't blame him for forgetting it. A murdered man—a peer no less—was bound to take precedence over a kidnapper. Even when the victim was from a wealthy family.

"I know you asked Woodward to look into the matter," Eversham said with apology, "but I thought we might be able to learn what we wanted to know sooner if I went through proper channels."

"The foreign minister," Will said, and Lucy supposed he knew about such things from observing his father's service as a diplomat. She'd learned a little bit about it through her friendship with Meg, who'd told her some stories.

Eversham nodded, and said, "Thanks to the miracle of transatlantic cables, the embassy was able to query officials in Philadelphia. They learned that Mr. Christopher Hamilton does have a cousin with whom he started a railway business about six or seven years ago. Upon Christopher's death two months ago in an accident near the tracks, his cousin was said to be devastated. And yet, he unselfishly offered to travel to London to give Christopher's betrothed the bad news even before his cousin could be laid to rest."

"She was right." Lucy shook her head in wonder. Turning to Will, she said, "I thought it was all a ruse. But she certainly read Jedidiah Hamilton's deception aright."

"If you mean Miss Christina Fleetwood," Eversham said with a skeptical look, "we haven't ruled out the possibility that Sir Charles's sister was part of Hamilton's plot to force Vera Blackwood into marriage. Perhaps she revealed Hamilton's identity as an impostor to get back at him for some betrayal."

Lucy knew her cousin was right, but she couldn't help but remember how sincere the spiritualist had seemed. "But if she wanted to lead him to the authorities, why didn't she simply contact the police?"

"Perhaps she thought it would sound more believable coming from us," Will said with a shrug. "There are those in the police force who don't believe in talents like Miss Fleetwood's."

He cast a glance to where Eversham stood looking exasperated. Still, Lucy's cousin didn't argue.

"Regardless of her reasons for telling us about Jedidiah Hamilton, given what happened to Sir Charles last night, I am concerned for Miss Fleetwood's safety." Lucy remembered how frail the woman had seemed. She remembered the size and strength of the man who had lifted Vera into the waiting carriage. It would take very little for such a man to overpower

Miss Fleetwood. Especially since her only protection was merely her maid.

"We don't know yet that it was Jedidiah Hamilton who killed Sir Charles Fleetwood," Eversham reminded her with a scowl that seemed to be more about his annoyance that they weren't certain of this yet than any pique at Lucy.

"I don't think we can take that risk," Lucy said, standing to put her fists on her hips. "I propose that we should go warn her."

"And I suppose by 'we' you mean you and I?" Will asked with a raised brow.

"Who else?" Lucy asked, linking her arm in his with a sunny smile.

"Happy betrothal." Eversham clapped Will on the shoulder. "Welcome to the Partners of Clever Ladies League. We meet every Wednesday."

Chapter 32

Rather than waiting for one of the Penhallow carriages to be readied, Lucy's butler summoned a hansom cab for their trip back to Miss Fleetwood's house in Holborn.

There was no question this time of whether they would sit side by side in the vehicle's dank interior. Will told the driver their destination and climbed inside next to Lucy. That hers was the hand that sought out his gave him a warm feeling in the vicinity of his heart, but he wasn't ready to examine it too closely yet.

"I feel sure our mamas would like for us to join the melee in Hyde Park this afternoon to give society a chance to approve our betrothal," Lucy said as the driver set the horses in motion.

Will's mother, he was certain, would prefer for them to stage a very public dissolution of said betrothal, but he wasn't about to tell that to Lucy. There would be more than time enough to discuss what was to be done about the present Lady Gilford. Besides, her friendship with Meg had doubtless given her plenty of glimpses into the less-than-pleasant personality of their mother.

"I daresay they would," he said now, hoping he struck the

carefree tone he was aiming for. "But the announcement will be in the evening papers. That should be opportunity enough for the beau monde to adjust to the notion."

"Already?" Lucy turned to face him. "I thought tomorrow or the next day."

Will was too embarrassed to tell her that the sooner the betrothal was made public, the sooner his creditors would call off their dogs and the repairs to the tenant farms that had been ignored by his erstwhile steward could begin.

Instead, he gave her a half truth. "When your fiancée is the cousin of one of London's most successful newspaper owners and columnists, there is no trouble stopping the presses."

Her eyes widened. "You had Kate stop the presses?"

"I don't know what she did, actually," he admitted. "I just asked Eversham to see to it last night, and Kate sent a note around this morning to congratulate me and to inform me that the notice would run today in the afternoon edition of the *Gazette*."

Looking at their joined hands, Lucy's brow furrowed. "Now that we are betrothed, I have begun to wonder how Vera can have neglected to tell Meg, Elise, and me about her broken engagement back in Philadelphia."

"How do you mean?" Will asked. He'd assumed the friendship between Vera Blackwood and the other Ems was the sort of superficial alliance that seemed to happen every season with different groups of ladies. But Lucy spoke as if they were closer than that.

She thought for a moment, then gave a small sigh. "I suppose I overestimated our closeness. But in my defense, Vera was quite forthcoming about her life back home in the United

States. She described the social season there and compared it to ours. And she spoke of how many suitors presented to her by her father and aunts she'd rejected. Because she said she would settle for nothing less than a love match."

"So, she expected to find a love match here in London?" he asked with a frown. "That seems unlikely when her father was said to be title-shopping for her."

"I realize that now." Lucy fiddled with a bit of ribbon dangling from her pelisse. "But now I wonder if she intended to go along with her father's plans here at all."

"He didn't say anything about her objecting to his attempts to find a match for her," Will argued. Then he shook his head. "I apologize. You know Miss Blackwood and this situation far better than I ever could."

Despite the seriousness of the subject, Lucy gave a snort of laughter. "Did you just say you regret attempting to give your own uninformed opinion precedence over my informed one?"

He met her gaze with his. "Why is that amusing?"

Lucy leaned her head to rest on his shoulder. "I think you may be the perfect man, Viscount Gilford."

Now it was Will's turn to snort. "Hardly."

"Even so," Lucy said, squeezing their joined hands. "I don't discount Vera's preference for a love match, but as for myself, I am very happy to make a match with a gentleman who treats me as if I am not an ignorant ninny."

"No happier than I am to be engaged to a lady who is not an ignorant ninny." Will kissed the top of her head, and they rode on for some minutes in contented silence.

But after a time, Lucy sat bolt upright. "What happened to the wife?"

"What wife?" Will asked before the answer came to him. "You're right," he said. "There was a wife listed on the ship's manifest, but the embassy made no mention of Jedidiah Hamilton being married."

"So where is this alleged wife?" Lucy asked, her blue eyes bright with intelligence.

"Something we will ask your cousin when we return," Will said as the horses began to slow. "We are nearly to Miss Fleetwood's house."

Lucy removed her hand from his and set about doing all those things ladies did to prepare themselves for visiting. She made sure her hair was tidy and the ribbon of her straw bonnet was tied at a jaunty angle beneath her chin.

She must have felt him watching her, because she gave a soft smile. "Will I do?"

"Of course," Will assured her with a half smile. "Though I'm not sure why you bother for Miss Fleetwood and her maid."

This time, Lucy looked disappointed in his answer. "Because everyone deserves respect, Will. Even ladies-turned-actresses-turned-spiritualists and their maids."

It was a similar attitude to the one his father had exhibited. One he'd forgotten in the years since losing him.

"Point taken," he said as the cab came to a stop. "I will try to do better."

Once he was out on the pavement, he reached inside and lifted Lucy down, trying not to respond to the feeling of her breast brushing against his chest. Even through their combined layers of clothes, it was enough to send his imagination on a flight of fancy.

If Lucy's pink cheeks were any indication, her response had been similar.

Will paid the driver and gave him another half crown to wait.

When they got to Miss Fleetwood's door this time, however, it was ajar.

Some prickle of unease stirred the hair on the nape of Will's neck. "Stay out here," he told Lucy in a firm voice.

She didn't argue, only said in as firm a voice, "Take care."

He gave her a hard kiss, then pushed open the door until it was open wide enough for him to go inside. The echo of his boots on the polished wood floors was loud in his ears as he made his way upstairs.

As he went, he called out to the maid who'd let them in the other day. "Hetty!"

When no answer came, he cried, "Miss Fleetwood?"

Nearing the drawing room where they'd met the spiritualist, Will saw that the door was closed. It had been open when he and Lucy were here.

Walking as quietly as he could, Will took a deep breath, and then, hoping he wasn't about to come to harm so soon after finding Lucy, he turned the knob and pushed open the door.

Chapter 33

Despite Will's command for her to stay put, Lucy lasted only a minute or two before she grew too impatient to wait on the front stoop.

Slipping through the gap between the door and the frame as Will had done, she waited for her eyes to adjust to the dimness of the house's interior. When she could make out the familiar forms of the umbrella stand on one side and a boot jack on the other, Lucy noted that nothing seemed amiss in the entryway, at least.

Above her, she heard the floors creak under the weight of someone. She was very still, listening to see if there was the sound of anyone else. But it was only Will. Or so she hoped.

She was about to check the kitchen just off to the left when she heard the sound of footsteps thundering down the stairs.

When Will emerged, his expression relaxed for a brief moment when he saw her. But just as quickly, he gestured to her. "Come, you must tend to her. She's still alive. I'll go down to tell the driver we need the local constable here."

Lucy was already halfway up the stairs when she thought to turn back and ask Will, "Who is it that is still alive? Is there...has one of them died?"

She meant Miss Fleetwood and Hetty, her maid. And fortunately, Will understood her perfectly. His already-grim expression turned even darker.

"Miss Fleetwood is still alive, though I'm not sure for how long."

She knew what his next words would be before he spoke.

"Hetty, her maid, is dead. At least, I believe so."

Unable to find her voice, Lucy nodded. Then, doing what she could to bolster her inner fortitude, she continued climbing until she reached the floor that housed Miss Fleetwood's sitting room.

Will had left the door wide open, and from the landing Lucy could see the bodies of two women on the floor. As she got closer she was able to make out the figure of Hetty lying on her back on the other side of the room. From this vantage point, she looked too still to be alive, but it was clear that Miss Fleetwood was still breathing.

When Lucy knelt beside the spiritualist, it was apparent from the blooms of red on her light green gown that she had been stabbed, and she noted her eyelids fluttering. "Miss Fleetwood?" Lucy asked, wondering where she might find some clean cloths, then deciding she needed to assess the wounds first. "Miss Fleetwood, Christina, can you tell me what happened?"

As efficiently as she could, Lucy began unbuttoning the front of the spiritualist's gown. As she worked, Christina Fleetwood shook her head and reached up to grab Lucy's wrist. "Het-het—"

"Hetty?" Lucy asked, taking the injured woman's hand in hers to calm her.

At Christina's nod, Lucy wondered what to tell her about

her friend. She saw the tears streaming down into Christina's hairline and wished with her entire being that she could tell her something other than the truth.

"S-saved me," Christina murmured with obvious effort. She clung to Lucy with surprising strength. "Y-you s-save her."

At that moment Will returned to the room and moved to Lucy's side. "I found a couple of local lads and sent one of them to fetch the constable and the other to find the nearest physician." In a hushed tone for her ears only, he added, "I also had the one fetching the constable ask for a wagon from the morgue."

At that last, Lucy shook her head, looking down at the pleading gaze of Miss Fleetwood. "You must go check Hetty again, Will."

His brow furrowed, and Lucy was certain he was about to object, so she gave him a glare and gestured with her head toward Miss Fleetwood, whose pale face was still intent on Lucy's.

Understanding what she meant for him to do, Will rose to his feet and went to where the maid, Hetty, lay. She watched as he felt the side of her neck where the blood was said to pump strongest.

Lucy closed her eyes and sent up a quick prayer that she was all but certain would go unanswered.

She was already thinking of how she would break the news of Hetty's death to Miss Fleetwood for the second time when she heard Will mutter something.

Looking down to where Christina Fleetwood lay with her eyes closed but clearly still breathing, Lucy opened her mouth to explain again that Hetty was gone.

Before she could speak, though, Will spoke up in an excited voice, "She's alive! Tell Miss Fleetwood that Hetty is alive!"

Gasping, Lucy turned to face Will, where he was staring down at Hetty with something like wonder. "I must not have checked in the right place, before," he said, shaking his head in what looked like self-derision. "You may believe I'll never forget how to take a pulse again."

"Hetty is alive," Lucy said to her own patient with tears springing into her own eyes. "She is alive, and we will ensure that the two of you stay that way."

Christina's eyes widened and she murmured something that looked like "Thank God." Then, as if she'd been staying awake only long enough to reassure herself of her maid's well-being, she closed her eyes and succumbed to unconsciousness.

The door downstairs opened, and Lucy heard a man's voice identifying himself as Constable Sam Frost. Lucy called down, and when the sturdy man of around thirty (if she didn't miss her guess) hurried into the room, he gaped at the sight of the two bleeding women and Will and Lucy tending to them.

Reaching up as if he wanted to run his hand over his head but then recalling his helmet, Constable Frost simply dropped the hand by his side.

"Lord Gilford?" he asked Will, his voice reedy with alarm.

Will gave the man a brisk nod and had just opened his mouth to speak when a tall, lean man with ginger side whiskers entered carrying a doctor's bag. Then, another man, this one older and clearly related to the first in some way, followed, also carrying a doctor's bag.

They were trailed by a pair of burly men shouldering stretchers.

"Not that I am complaining, Frost," Will said as he allowed the younger of the two men to take over caring for Hetty. "But I only asked for one doctor, and you've brought me two."

"I am Dr. Thwaite, and this is my father, also Dr. Thwaite, as it happens," said the younger man. "Now, unless you plan on assisting, I must ask you all to clear the room so that we might prepare the patients for transport to our surgery."

Lucy didn't want to leave Miss Fleetwood and Hetty.

Slipping an arm about her waist, Will said gently, "You've done all you can for them now. Let the doctors get to work."

He led her toward the door, and after one last glance toward where the physicians tended the injured women, Lucy let Will guide her toward the stairs.

*   *   *

Once outside, Will was startled to see not only Eversham waiting for them, but also a crowd of newspaper reporters only just being kept at bay by a line of bobbies.

Lucy's cousin took one look at her bloodstained clothing and moved forward to usher her toward his carriage, which waited a little way down from the crowd.

Her silence worried Will, but he allowed Eversham to help her into the vehicle before speaking to the detective superintendent.

"This is the third occasion in less than a week where Lucy has had occasion to tend to an injured or dying victim. Why haven't you caught this bastard yet?" His own anger coupled with fear for the lady he was almost certainly in love with made him rail at the older man.

"Because until a few hours ago, I didn't even have the man's real name, much less a viable location to search for him," Eversham snapped. "If you would stop escorting Lucy to crime scenes as some sort of bizarre courting ritual, perhaps she wouldn't be faced with the sight of bullet and stab wounds every other day."

"If your cousin weren't a stubborn, headstrong girl," Will retorted, "then perhaps I could escort her to tamer affairs, but before I can try she is running toward danger as if able to sniff it out."

Neither of them heard the carriage door swing open.

"Would the pair of you kindly lower your voices?" Lucy asked with a scowl. "This is not the way to keep the press away."

Wincing at behaving in such a childish manner, Will glanced over to see that, just as Lucy had said, the newspapermen who'd had all eyes on the door of Miss Fleetwood's house were now focused exclusively on Will and Eversham.

Eversham closed his eyes in frustration. When he opened them, he looked over at Lucy and said simply, "My apologies."

"Apologies," Will echoed. Then, to Eversham, he said, "I am sorry to you as well. I know you've been doing your best to catch Hamilton."

Dragging a hand over his bloodshot eyes, Lucy's cousin sighed. "My best has clearly not been enough. But I will most certainly do whatever it takes to apprehend the fellow. Every time he strikes, he leaves clues behind, but we simply haven't been able to piece them together yet."

This time, it was Will who gave the detective superintendent a comforting clap on the shoulder. "We will find him," he told Eversham firmly. "Because I'm damned if I'll allow him to bring any harm to Lucy or put another injured soul in her path."

And with that, he climbed into the coach and allowed it to take them back to Mayfair.

Chapter 34

At the sound of the carriage door opening to admit Will, Lucy turned from where she'd been staring numbly out the window at nothing. His gilded hair was mussed, and, like hers, his clothing was liberally streaked with blood from tending to the wounded women. He seemed to hesitate for a split second, and then—to her surprise and relief—rather than taking the backward-facing seat across from her, he took the one beside her and gathered her against him, offering the only comfort he could in the aftermath of such horror.

She leaned into him, accepting the assurance of his strong arms holding her. After so many years without her father, she'd come to appreciate the solace of Cousin Andrew's presence in her life. But the support Will offered was different.

He was, for want of a better term, hers. And she was his. Their betrothal, however it might have come about, was a fact now, and unless Lucy wished to spend the rest of her life isolated from the society into which she'd been raised, there was no going back. And if she'd had any doubts about him, Will had erased them all with the way he'd gone into Christine Fleetwood's house alone today with no thought for his own safety.

At that thought, she felt tears well in her eyes and she gripped him tighter.

She wasn't even aware of the sob that broke from her until she heard his words.

"Oh, please Lucy, do not weep," Will said against her hair, rubbing her back with soothing strokes. "I beg of you. I am defenseless against tears. Especially yours."

But once she'd started, it was impossible for her to stop. And despite his pleading, Will seemed to know that.

"All right, sweetheart," he mumured, holding her as she sobbed, "let it all out."

So overcome was she by grief and shock and sadness that she didn't realize the carriage had stopped before her family's townhouse until the carriage door was opened by a footman.

"A moment, please," she heard Will tell the man. Filled with mortification that she'd lost control of her emotions in such a manner, she pulled back and searched her reticule for a handkerchief with one hand while wiping at her eyes with the other.

"Here," Will said, pressing his own into her hand, "you'd better wipe your eyes with this, though I fear there will be no hiding your tears from your mama."

Once she'd dried her eyes and blown her nose, Will's words penetrated her brain and Lucy shook her head. "Cousin Andrew will have notified her of what happened," she said, tucking the soiled handkerchief into her reticule to have laundered before she returned it to him. "And I daresay I wouldn't have been able to hide the matter from Mama in any event. She is always able to tell when I am upset. Even when I don't wish her to know."

He nodded, then opened the carriage door and hopped out so that he might hand her down. Since they were in full view of the servants now, when they said their goodbyes in the entry hall both had to be content with a clasp of their hands.

"I will call later to make sure you are well," Will said, his blue eyes shadowed with concern. Lucy opened her mouth to protest, but he held up a staying hand. "Do not argue for once, Miss Penhallow. We have both been through an ordeal today and my tender sensibilities will need soothing later, I am quite sure."

Despite her somber mood, his words had the intended effect and Lucy laughed in spite of herself. "Very well, my lord," she said with a reluctant smile. Then in a hushed tone, she added, "Now go, before Mama descends upon the both of us and you find yourself the subject of an inquisition."

Later that night, having found herself unable to sleep after she'd indulged in a rare afternoon nap, Lucy sat up in bed reading the next novel slated to be taken up by the book club. It was difficult to concentrate, however. Not least because, despite his insistence earlier, Will hadn't shown up to check on her welfare, nor had he sent a note round.

It hadn't been necessary, she reminded herself, though it was disappointing that he would make a promise then fail to keep it. Especially after the tenderness he'd shown her in the carriage.

But she had seen for herself that witnessing what had been done to Miss Fleetwood and her maid had affected him almost as much as it had her. She knew how gentlemen liked for everyone to believe that they were impervious to the kind of emotions that affected ladies, but she had long suspected that such claims were empty bravado. So perhaps he'd been as exhausted as her and simply gone to sleep, as she had.

Still, she would have liked to see him again so that she might ensure that he was none the worse for wear.

She was reading the same paragraph for the fourth time when she was startled by a knocking sound at her bedchamber window. There was an oak tree just outside of it, and one of the branches often brushed against the glass when the wind was up, but there had been no sign that the weather would be anything but fine tonight. Still, weather had a way of changing from one minute to the next, so she turned back to her book.

Then, to her astonishment, she heard the knocking again, though this time it was accompanied by a male voice. "Lucy," Will hissed, "let me in."

With a gasp, she leapt from her bed and hurried to the window, and when she moved the curtain aside, she saw that, indeed, Viscount Gilford was perched precariously outside her bedchamber window. He had apparently climbed the trellis that rested against the side of the house, but from the way he gripped the ledge, it was clear he wasn't entirely trusting of the trellis.

It took her a couple of tries, but once she managed to raise the window, Will climbed nimbly over the sill and into the room.

"What are you doing here?" Lucy demanded in a hiss, mindful that someone might come investigate if they heard her speaking in her supposedly empty bedchamber.

Turning from where he'd been closing the window behind him, Will frowned at her. "I told you I'd be back to check in on you."

Trying not to allow the way his large frame seemed to fill up her room to affect her, and mindful that she was wearing only her thin nightrail, Lucy crossed her arms over her chest and gave a huff of disbelief at his words. "Which I assumed meant you'd make your presence known in the usual way of things: by presenting yourself at the front door of the house."

Stepping closer, Will reached out to her and, despite her pique, Lucy stepped into his arms and rested her head against his warm chest. "Don't be angry, I had every intention of paying a proper call, but then I fell asleep and it was too late. And I needed to see you."

This last he said after he'd pulled back a little so he could look her in the eye. "If I hadn't seen the light burning from your window I'd have let it wait until tomorrow, but a bit of investigation revealed the trellis and the next thing I knew I was climbing."

She looked into his face, which had become so very dear to her in such a short span of time, and reached up to touch him on the cheek. Turning his head to kiss her palm, he said, "It also occurred to me that whoever it was that attacked Miss Fleetwood and her maid might take it into his head to come here."

At these last words, Lucy gave a start. "Surely not," she said with a frown, though she could tell from his expression that he meant the words.

"Though we saw no sign that Hamilton was still there," Will told her with a calm gravity that was as alarming to her as if he'd shouted the words, "it's entirely possible he was nearby, watching as we entered Miss Fleetwood's house this afternoon. You could be in danger, and I have no intention of allowing anything to happen to you."

"But my cousin—" Lucy began, but Will stopped her mouth with a brief kiss.

"Your cousin has indeed placed men outside the front door of Penhallow House," he said patiently, "but I find I am unable to rest easy unless I am able to watch over you for myself."

In all honesty, Lucy would feel safer with Will here, though she knew that any police officers her cousin had set to watching the house would be trustworthy men.

But aside from safety there was something else that needed to be considered. Without meaning to, she glanced behind Will toward where her bed, its covers mussed from when she'd emerged from it moments ago, sat in the glow of the lamplight.

True to form, this man, who was so easily able to read her, looked down at her now with a raised brow. The warmth in his gaze brought a flush of heat into her cheeks, and Lucy averted her eyes. "Have no fear, little bird," he told her, kissing her on the nose, "I will make a pallet on the floor."

But this was one promise she had no intention of taking him up on. "Do not be foolish," she told him with what she hoped was credible severity. "We are betrothed. And my bed is quite large enough for the two of us."

The look he turned on her was inscrutable, and for a moment she feared he would reject her edict. But after a moment, he nodded. "Far be it from me to turn down such a generous invitation."

* * *

This had been a singularly bad idea, Will thought to himself as he lay staring at the canopy that hung over Lucy's bed.

Once he'd removed his coats, untied his neckcloth, and, with Lucy's help, gotten out of his boots, he accepted the pillow she offered him and tucked it beneath his head. She extinguished the lamp on her bedside table and they lay together in darkness for some minutes in silence.

He wasn't a ravening beast without any ability to control himself. Of course he wasn't, he assured himself. But he'd accepted Lucy's invitation without fully considering the difficulty of sharing a bed with her while the sweet floral scent of her soap against her warm skin enveloped him.

Lying atop the counterpane, a position he'd insisted upon despite her protests, he tried to calm his body's reaction to having her so near and had nearly resigned himself to a sleepless night when he heard her turn on her side.

"Will?" she asked in a soft voice, which he knew was as much from a fear she'd be overheard as it was from hesitation. "Will you... Will you hold me? Like you did this afternoon?"

He didn't answer immediately, and to his shame he heard a quiver of tears in her voice when she spoke again. "Never mind. I thought perhaps because you're here, but—"

Cursing himself as a brute, he interrupted before she could continue. "Of course," he said hoarsely, and ignoring the part of his brain that wanted to believe this was a prelude to anything more than comfort, he slipped beneath the bedclothes and gathered her against him in the dark.

Lucy gave a sigh of contentment against his neck as he tried to ignore just how soft her curves were against his body. "That's better," she said, sliding a hand across his chest and stroking her thumb against the exposed bit of skin where he'd loosened his collar.

Reminding himself that he was here to protect her, not to do any of the myriad things his mind was now suggesting, Will swallowed. She was an innocent, after all, and had no idea what such touches would do to a man.

But he reconsidered his assessment when he felt her lift up on one elbow and bring her lips to his. The kiss was not so untutored as their first had been, but neither was it so self-assured that he thought her anything other than the innocent she was. Even so, the knowledge that this was Lucy—his Lucy—sent a frisson of desire through him the likes of which he'd never known.

She tasted of sweetness and innocence and every bit of the home he'd tried his best to forget during his time in France. It was this he'd come back for, he realized, as he accepted the tentative caress of her tongue into his mouth and then guided her into a deeper kiss while he turned their bodies so that she lay beneath him.

When he lifted his head moments later, they were both breathless and it took a moment for him to realize he'd somehow divested her of her nightdress, and his shirt had joined it on the floor beside the bed.

Far from shrinking away, however, Lucy looked up at him with a trust that he vowed silently never to give her reason to regret. "Is this what you want, sweetheart?" he asked her, reaching up to stroke her cheek. "We can stop if that's what you want. I'm happy to simply sleep with you in my arms if that's what you wish."

"Don't you dare," Lucy said with no little censure in her voice. "I will be very cross if you bring me this close to the brink and then insist upon simply sleeping."

He couldn't stop the soft huff of laughter from escaping him at her words. "Yes, ma'am," he said in a chastened voice.

Then, with as much grace as he could muster, he divested himself of his trousers and crawled back into bed with her. Despite the fact that the room was dark except for the soft glow of moonlight through the windows, he noted that his lady watched him avidly throughout.

When she welcomed him back into her arms, he marveled again at just how good she felt there, and taking her mouth in a hungry kiss he vowed to make her first experience of love-making as pleasurable for her as he possibly could.

This time when he kissed his way down her neck, giving special attention to that spot below her ear she'd seemed to like earlier, he stroked a hand down her body to touch her center.

"Will, please," she said as she shifted her hips restlessly beneath him even as he stroked first one finger, then another inside her and gave her what she wanted. When he touched his thumb to the bud just above where his fingers thrust, she gave a cry that he had to stop with his mouth lest she alert someone to his presence.

"My married friends told me there was pleasure to be had, but I had no notion it would be so much," she said a little breathlessly a moment later, once she'd recovered herself.

Almost lightheaded from the need to be inside her, Will kissed her quickly before guiding himself to her entrance. "This next bit might be a little painful," he warned her, "because it is your first time. But only this once."

She bent her knees and Will uttered a curse, even as he slipped inside her a little. "I do not mind a bit of pain if it means you are mine," she said simply, and he was astonished once again at just how much he felt for this woman he had barely known only last week.

And with one swift thrust he seated himself fully within her.

Beads of sweat broke out over Will's forehead with the concentration it took him to remain still. "All right?" he asked through clenched teeth, thinking that if she said it was not he might weep.

"Yes," she said, her voice a little breathy. "I did wonder if it would work, but though it does feel a little odd, there is no pain."

Even before she finished speaking, Will began to withdraw from her, and when she wrapped her legs around him there was no more conversation as they moved in the dance as old as time.

When he felt the clench of her body around him, he surrendered to his own passion, and burying his face in her neck, he gave a hoarse cry and shuddered against her.

Chapter 35

The next morning, Lucy awoke with an empty bed and an ache between her thighs.

There were no signs that anyone had been in her bedchamber the night before besides her. Somehow Will had even managed to tidy the bedclothes while she slept. If she didn't know better, she'd think the memory of what they shared was some sort of mad fever dream.

Though she'd have liked to remain in bed and revel in the knowledge of just how very thoroughly her fiancé had initiated her into the world of sensuality, she knew her mother would worry if she didn't appear downstairs at her usual time.

She had barely finished her first cup of tea and was debating whether or not to go in search of her cousin to learn if there were any new developments in the search for Miss Fleetwood's attacker or her brother's killer when her mother came rushing into the breakfast room.

"Oh, Lucy," her mother said, her face alight with excitement, "you'll never guess what's happened. It's wonderful! Beyond wonderful!"

Though her mother was hardly as inclined to displeasure as

Viscountess Gilford, Mrs. Winifred Penhallow wasn't given to outbursts of such unrestrained pleasure, either. So whatever had her in such a pelter must be joyful indeed. And Lucy, for one, could use a bit of joy given the events of yesterday.

"What is it, Mama?" she asked, unable to repress a smile. "I haven't seen you this pleased since the dowager Duchess of Langham attended your Venetian breakfast."

Mrs. Penhallow smiled beatifically. "My dear girl, it is even better. And as it happens, this news is somewhat related."

At this, Lucy frowned. "How? I thought you'd decided not to host any entertainments this year."

"I am not," Mama said, her eyes twinkling, "but the Duke and Duchess of Langham are."

Was her mother suffering from an ailment of the mind? Lucy had never known her to be dotty, but she had heard that once they reached a certain age, women were inclined to become forgetful. Eyes narrowed, she scanned Mrs. Penhallow's face for clues.

"Oh, Lucy," Mama said with a shake of her head. "I have not taken leave of my senses. I am perfectly sane. It is just when a mother learns that her daughter's betrothal is to be announced at a ducal ball, she is inclined to become a little excited."

"At a ducal—" Lucy broke off, then put together the clues. "Do you mean to say that they will be announcing my betrothal to Will at the Langhams' ball this evening?"

"That is exactly what I mean, my dear," Mama said, beaming. "I was lamenting to Lady Adrian's mother at the theater last night the fact that it was too late in the season to plan anything as lavish as a ball, and I suppose she must have recounted my words to her daughter. For I just received a note from the duchess offering to announce your betrothal at their celebration this evening."

The Langham ball was an annual event that was usually meant to honor the duke's birthday. That he and his wife had agreed to share the party with Lucy and Will was beyond anything she could ever have imagined. They were dear friends of her cousin and Lady Katherine, but even so, Lucy knew better than to believe such a relationship could simply be transferred from cousin to cousin.

Feeling touched and excited on her own behalf, Lucy smiled back at her mother. "That is truly wonderful news, Mama. I would never have imagined such a thing. Though I suppose it isn't so unusual for Will's family to be honored in this way. His friendship with the duke's brother likely had something to do with it as well."

At that moment, Rhodes announced Will, and a half second later, Gilford himself stepped into the breakfast room. He bowed to both Lucy and her mother, then must have noticed their jubilant moods because he said, "You've had good news, I take it? Do tell me about it. I could use a bit of cheering."

Quickly, Lucy's mother told him about the ball that evening and the betrothal announcement.

When she'd finished, he broke out in a grin. "I wasn't aware Langham and Poppy had agreed to do that," he said, looking pleased. "It is very generous of them."

"It is, indeed," Lucy said with a grin. "Now, I believe Mama has some preparations to make for her gown this evening, so why do we not go into the drawing room?"

But before Mrs. Penhallow could even question Lucy's fib,

Will was shaking his head in apology. "There's no time for that, I'm afraid," he told Lucy. "We must be on the way at once if we are to get there in time."

Lucy felt a stab of fear run through her. "Has something happened?"

"It has," he said hastily. "But there is nothing to be fearful about. In fact, it's good news."

Before she could question him again, Will spoke up. "It's Miss Fleetwood," he told her. "She's awake and she wishes to speak to us."

It was some time before they descended from Will's carriage before a newly renovated establishment not very far from Miss Fleetwood's home. First Lucy had needed to change into something more befitting a sickroom visit. Then, her mother had insisted upon having Mrs. Hughes make up a basket for Miss Fleetwood and Hetty, though Lucy had assured her neither woman was in a fit state for such rich food at the moment. So when they entered the building, Lucy was out of sorts and afraid the physician who had issued the invitation for them to speak to Miss Fleetwood would rescind it.

"It isn't that sort of invitation," Will kept reassuring her, but Lucy couldn't help recalling when her father was in the last stages of the illness that would take him from them forever. She'd allowed her mother to persuade her to go visit a school friend for a couple of days. But when she'd returned, it was to learn she was too late.

There was nothing like that sort of relationship between Lucy and Miss Fleetwood. She barely knew the woman. But ever since that childhood shock, she found herself expecting some kind of bad news when she planned a sickroom visit.

Inside the surgery, however, the mood was one of cool efficiency and competence. When the woman in a nursing sister's uniform greeted them and asked whom they were there to see, Will informed her that they'd been given permission by Detective Superintendent Eversham to see Miss Christina Fleetwood.

At the mention of Eversham, the nurse, who introduced herself as Sister Truman, stood up a little straighter. "Right this way, my lord, Miss Penhallow."

The room she showed them into was small, with room only for a narrow bed and various pieces of equipment that Lucy couldn't even begin to name. But what really made the room seem cramped was the presence of three policemen. Two large constables stood on either side of the bed where Miss Fleetwood lay. The third, standing near the small window, was Eversham.

When they entered, her cousin looked up, and something like relief crossed his face. With a nod, he dismissed the two constables, then pulled a chair near the bed and indicated that Lucy should sit.

But she had questions first. "I thought you said she was better?" To her mind, though Miss Fleetwood had been in the care of the clinic for nearly twenty-four hours, she looked little better than she'd been when Lucy and Will had left her in the care of the Dr. Thwaite and his son.

Her cousin ran a hand over his chin, and Lucy realized he hadn't shaved. He looked more unkempt than she'd ever seen him. "I said she was improved," he corrected her. "But not so improved that she is fully recovered. From what Thwaite the elder told me, though her condition was better than that of Hetty Turner, it was still serious."

At the mention of the maid, Lucy raised a hand to her chest. "Oh, Hetty. I nearly forgot her. Where is she?"

When she'd asked Will about the maid's condition in the carriage on the way here, he'd said Eversham hadn't mentioned her. Lucy wasn't sure whether this meant Hetty was doing so well it wasn't worth mentioning, or if she was doing so poorly he didn't want to discuss her condition until Lucy and Will arrived.

"She's been moved to St. Bartholomew's because of the severity of her wounds," Eversham said with a tight look. "The last report I had from the men I stationed there to protect her said she is doing as well as can be expected."

Before they'd left Christina Fleetwood's house the day before, Lucy had instructed that all of the bills for both women's care be sent to her man of business. Though Will and her cousin had assured her that neither woman had been hurt through any fault of Lucy's, she couldn't help but believe it. If the possibility that Jedidiah Hamilton might wish to harm Miss Fleetwood when he learned she'd spoken to Lucy and Will about him had occurred to her earlier, then both women would be uninjured right now.

Now, the fact that both Christina Fleetwood and her maid were still alive was something to be grateful for. But Lucy would do whatever she could to make sure that the man who had attacked them would be brought to justice.

"It isn't your fault," Will said in a low voice only she could hear. Lucy felt his strong arm around her waist and was grateful for the comfort, even if she didn't quite believe him. To Eversham, he said, "You said when you sent for me that Miss Fleetwood was awake and alert."

Lucy looked down at the sleeping woman and had difficulty imagining it.

"She was," Eversham said to Will. "But that was nearly two hours ago."

Will started to protest, but Lucy placed a hand on his arm. "We are here now. That is the important thing." Glancing over at her cousin, she said, "Perhaps the two of you can go get a cup of tea. I'll remain here by Christina's bedside for a while."

She felt Eversham's questioning gaze on her for a long moment, then he nodded. "My men are just outside the door if you need them."

"We won't be far," Will reassured her.

With a nod to them, Lucy sat down in the chair beside the bed and took Miss Fleetwood's pale hand in hers.

She was startled when at the contact the spiritualist's eyes flew open.

"Miss Fleetwood," Lucy gasped. "Have you been awake the entire time?"

Christina Fleetwood gave a little smile. "Childhood trick," she murmured. "Used to spy on my brothers."

Then, perhaps recalling that one of her brothers was now dead, she made a pained expression.

Her heartbeat having calmed, Lucy patted the other woman's hand. "I am sorry about your brother Charles."

"We hadn't seen one another in a dozen years or more," Christina said, her eyes filled with sadness.

If they'd been estranged for so many years, Lucy thought,

then the other woman must be older than she'd at first thought. Aloud she asked, "And the rest of your family?"

Christina sighed. "Parents dead. Years ago. Another brother. James. Vicar. He'll inherit now, I s'pose."

Making a mental reminder to ask her cousin if James Fleetwood had been contacted about his brother's death, Lucy wondered how he viewed Christina's choice of profession.

Deciding she needed to get answers before the patient drifted off again, Lucy held the other woman's hand lightly, and asked, "Miss Fleetwood, Christina, can you remember what happened yesterday? When you and Hetty were attacked?"

At the mention of Hetty, Christina's eyes filled with tears. "Foolish, loyal Hetty. I told her to run, but she would not. Threw herself between the attacker and me."

Her own eyes burning in sympathetic sadness, Lucy used her handkerchief to dab at Miss Fleetwood's eyes. "Did you recognize him? The man who attacked you both, I mean."

Christina shook her head a little, which Lucy took to mean she hadn't known the man. It was disappointing but hardly unexpected.

"That's all right, dear," she said gently. "Jedidiah Hamilton likely sent someone else to attack you while he remains hidden away with Vera."

But Miss Fleetwood shook her head again, and this time she spoke the word again. "No. It was H-Hamilton."

Already thinking ahead to what she would tell Will and her cousin, Lucy almost didn't hear what Christina said.

Blinking, she stared at the woman in the bed. "I apologize, but did you say that it *was* Jedidiah Hamilton who attacked you?"

Miss Fleetwood looked exhausted but seemed intent on ensuring that Lucy heard what she had to say. "Yes. It was him."

Since Miss Fleetwood had met the man before, Lucy didn't doubt her words.

"Christina," she said in a firm voice, "is there anything else you recall about the attack?"

"Yes," Christina Fleetwood said softly, her eyelids beginning to droop. "He wasn't alone. Was a woman with him."

Chapter 36

That evening, hours after he and Lucy had left Eversham watching over Miss Fleetwood, they'd parted ways and returned to their respective homes in order to rest and ready themselves for the announcement of their betrothal at the Langham ball.

He'd always thought her a lovely young woman, but when he set eyes on Lucy as she and her mother were announced before entering the ballroom, he felt his ears ringing and his palms sweat.

"Easy there, old sport," said Woodward from where he stood beside him. "You look a bit like you've swallowed your own tongue."

That, Will thought, was entirely possible given that he was having difficulty remembering his own name.

He watched Lucy, looking like the embodiment of a fairy princess in one of the storybooks Meg forced him to read her when they children, as she smiled and laughed at something her friend Elise was saying. The gown she'd chosen tonight was such a pale pink that it could almost be mistaken for white. One might have expected that the pale color against her light hair and pale skin might make her look ill or ghostly, but somehow, the gown, a confection of silk and tulle and trimmed in blond satin pieces, made her skin glow. Her cheeks were pink with health, and her hair had been dressed in the style he found most becoming, gathered into some kind of knot in the back with tendrils kissing the skin of her neck.

"A word of warning, Gilford," Adrian said from where he'd come to stand beside him. "It is all well and good to find one's intended beautiful, even desirable. Indeed, it makes marriage much more pleasant. But staring across a crowded ballroom at her as if you mean to throw her over your shoulder and carry her off to your lair is not done."

It took Will a minute to actually comprehend what Lord Adrian had just said. When he did, he turned to give his friend a scowl. "I am not entirely without a sense of decorum. I would not embarrass Lucy in such a manner."

"Oh dear," said Woodward from Will's other side, "I fear you've triggered his protective instincts, Lord Adrian. Soon instead of looking as if he'd like to devour his betrothed, he'll be challenging you to pistols at dawn for besmirching his lady's honor."

Before Will could respond to the teasing, the Duke of Langham came toward him in his usual unhurried manner. When he reached them, he removed his quizzing glass from the small pocket he had sewn into his coats for it, and peered at Will.

"Ah, yes," he said with a shake of his head. "I thought my wife and grandmother were exaggerating, but I see that they were, if anything, understating things."

Will turned from his surveillance of Lucy as she made her

way around the room toward them and gave the duke a cool look. "I can feel you working up to some sort of amusing pronouncement, Duke. If that is the case, then I beg you to say it so that I might go greet my fiancée."

If he'd spoken to the duke in such a way in his younger days, Will would have found himself at the receiving end of a set-down that would have singed the ends of his eyebrows. As it was, Langham, now happily married and head over ears in love with his wife, simply threw back his head and laughed.

To his brother, the duke said, "You've got the right of it. I owe you a hundred pounds."

At this, Will sighed and glanced over at Woodward. "You weren't in on the wager as well?"

His friend shrugged. "Only because I didn't learn about it until this moment." The American sent an aggrieved look toward Adrian.

"My apologies, old friend," Adrian said to the American. "You were not nearby when we arranged it. But I promise to include you the next go round. I feel sure this pair will give us a number of opportunities for creative wagering."

Ignoring his friends' banter, Will glanced once more to where Lucy was surrounded by a gaggle of society's most avid gossips. "Suddenly, I am not quite so eager to rush to my fiancée's side." He was joking, but knowing how cutthroat the ladies of the beau monde—his mother included—could be, he was inclined to stay where he was.

Woodward shuddered. "I'd rather negotiate a high-stakes treaty than face that kind of questioning."

Adrian, who was still employed by the Foreign Office, agreed. "No one is better at winkling out information than the matrons of the *ton*. I hope Lucy was suitably trained to face them."

They hadn't yet discussed the particulars of her upbringing but given how easily she'd managed to move between the different levels of society, Will was reasonably sure she'd also learned how to fend off unwanted questions from prying matrons.

But to his surprise, it was Langham who came to her defense. "My dear chaps, Miss Penhallow is not only a member of the Mischief and Mayhem set, but she is now the co-leader of their book club. I suspect the lady is not only adept at deflecting questions; she is likely well equipped to issue some of her own."

The mention of the book club reminded Will not only of Vera and her disappearance but also of the men's book club Eversham had told him about. "Speaking of the book club," he said aloud, "are any of you aware of a similar group, but for gentlemen? Only Eversham told me about it, and I was wondering who was a member and—"

"Ah, excellent," Adrian said with a grin, clapping Will on the shoulder. "We were going to mention it to you this evening, but Eversham beat us to it. We are all members, of course, and will be happy to welcome you into our number."

Will frowned. "Even, you, Woodward?" Somehow it didn't seem fair that he'd been overlooked while the American had received an invitation. Not that he was going to get his drawers in knots over it.

Woodward looked sheepish. "Adrian and I founded it. And if you are wondering why you were not included, it's because you were off sowing wild oats on the Continent when we started."

Somewhat mollified by the explanation, Will asked, "Do you really meet in order to discuss books? Eversham said you read adventure novels."

"To be perfectly candid," the duke told him, glancing around as if he feared being overheard, "we do a bit more imbibing than book discussion. Not to say we don't discuss books at all. Wrackham brought a very naughty French novel to one meeting, and it was quite interesting indeed."

Will gave a bark of laughter, which he quickly turned into a cough. When he'd recovered himself, he asked with a mix of suspicion and approval, "Is this club simply a way for the husbands of the Mischief and Mayhem set—and Woodward—to meet while the ladies are at their book club meetings, where they actually do discuss books?"

"Do not be absurd," Adrian chided him. "We also meet when they are doing other things together."

"So Eversham lied about the adventure books?" Will wouldn't have expected it of the man, who seemed like such a stickler for the truth.

"Poor fellow," Woodward said with a crooked smile. "He genuinely hoped we'd discuss his favorite adventure stories. So every meeting we do make an attempt to speak about a book. But by the time we get to it, half of us are drunk and the other half are arguing about some philosophical point or other. And a few belong to both groups."

"Who starts a book club where books are not discussed?" Will asked, amused despite himself.

"We intended to read books when we started," Adrian said a bit defensively. "My wife is an author, after all. I'd hoped we could read some of her books. But you know how it is. It is difficult to convince a group of grown men to behave in a certain way. Especially when spirits are involved."

"And one of them is a duke and your own brother," Woodward said under his breath.

Will wondered if the ladies knew of the existence of this club or if the secrecy was one of the appeals. Rather like the Hellfire Club, only for books instead of mock satanic rituals.

He was about to ask when he idly glanced over to where Lucy had been under interrogation from the society matrons and noted that she was no longer with them. The musicians had begun to tune their instruments in preparation for the opening dance, which she'd promised to him.

Scanning the room, he looked for the halo of her light hair among the female heads in the throng on either side of the floor. But he didn't see her. Remembering the story Meg had told him about how the two friends had met, he decided to make a circuit of the room and see if Lucy was perhaps behind one of the large topiary trees that had been brought in to decorate the room.

As he strode away from his friends, he heard one of them—Woodward?—remark something about losing another friend to the graveyard of betrothed and married.

We aren't wed yet.

Though Will had begun to feel a closeness to her that he'd never in his life experienced. They were friends, he realized. Friends who wanted to strip each other naked and proceed from there.

But, he thought as he wended his way through the other guests, he'd need to find her first.

It wasn't lost on him that Vera Blackwood had been taken in the middle of a ball.

The thought sent a stab of fear through him, and his search took on a dark edge.

When he spotted her amid a circle of younger ladies that included his sister, Elise Clevedon, and Jane Fielding, the relief that coursed through him was so intense it almost unmanned him.

From now until they captured Jedidiah Hamilton and his female accomplice, Lucy would have protection. Whether that came from the police or himself, he didn't care. But Hamilton had proved himself capable of abduction and murder, and if he decided Lucy needed to be eliminated, he wouldn't hesitate to harm or even kill her.

His fear and anger at Hamilton must have shown on his face as he approached the group of lively ladies, because once they noticed him, their laughter dimmed.

"Lord Gilford," said Lucy's friend Elise in what sounded to Will's ears like a warning, "I hope you know what a clever, generous, and loyal lady you have asked to wed you."

At her words, Lucy colored, and the other ladies around them, including Meg, Will noted with exasperation, suppressed titters. "Elise," Lucy said with a speaking look, "this really isn't necess—"

But Elise wasn't finished. "Lucy is not without friends, and though you haven't yet shown yourself to be a scoundrel, if at some time in the future you do, then you should expect the wrath of all of us gathered here now to rain down upon you."

The look Elise gave him made Will fear for his bollocks,

and he hadn't even done anything wrong. Still, he didn't want Lucy's friends thinking he meant to mistreat her.

"Ma'am," he said, giving the widow a little bow, "I give you my word that I would not ever wish to cause Miss Penhallow unhappiness. If I do anything to bring down the wrath you spoke of, then I shall be the first to punish myself."

His words must have been, at the very least, adequate, because Elise gave him a look of grudging approval. "Very well," she said, as if this group of ladies—the Ems?—were the arbiters of Lucy's future.

"Are you quite finished threatening my betrothed?" Lucy demanded wryly. "Or is there some other warning you wish to issue him on what is supposed to be a happy occasion?"

At this, Elise gave Lucy a rueful but unapologetic look. "You and I both know how many things can go wrong in a marriage. I simply wanted to make sure he knows that you will not be without friends."

Her face softening, Lucy gave her friend a grateful smile. Will thought she'd never looked more lovely.

"I do know," she said to Elise. "And I am grateful for it."

"I hope you know Elise speaks for all of us," Meg told Will in the silence that descended as Lucy and Elise shared as much of a hug as their evening gowns would allow.

"Et tu, Meg?" he asked his sister with a raised brow.

"I am simply warning you that if you should turn out to be a terrible husband, my loyalties will lie with my friend." His sister raised her own brow right back at him.

"At least I know where I stand," he said to no one in particular.

Finally, Lucy turned to him and said, "I believe this is our dance?"

Around them, the rest of the group split up to search out their own partners, and Will led Lucy onto the floor among the other couples. As the music began, he couldn't help thinking of how much had changed between this and their waltz at the Maitland ball a couple of days before.

For several minutes, they gave themselves up to the rhythm of the dance. And as he looked into her eyes, Will felt something stir within him. Not the sexual attraction he'd come to expect whenever they were together—and sometimes even when they weren't—but something much higher, in the region of his heart.

He reveled in the feel of her in his arms. Her soft rose and lavender scent. Her grace as she allowed him to lead her in the once-scandalous dance.

This is love.

The thought was at once so startling that it made him stumble a little, but also so unsurprising that he wondered why he hadn't realized it before.

"Are you all right?" Lucy asked softly as he regained his balance. "We can go sit somewhere if you wish."

He hid a smile at her solicitude for him—as if he was an elderly gentleman or a recovering invalid. But that was his Lucy. Thoughtful and kind to a fault.

Suddenly, he did want to get out of this ballroom. Away from the eyes of the guests who were watching them to see if the match between them was one of necessity or of something more. Away from their respective groups of friends, who wished them well but also seemed poised to step in if something should go wrong.

"I should like some air." Lucy's voice broke into his thoughts, and he wondered how common the sort of symmetry of thought between them was. It had happened more than once, and he was not yet in a position to be jaded about it.

He nodded, and as they continued to dance, he gradually steered them off the ballroom floor and toward a pair of French doors leading into the gardens.

They'd spent an inordinate amount of time in the gardens of fashionable London this week, but this time, Will vowed, it would be for reasons entirely unrelated to abduction or schemes or murder. They'd been immersed in such darkness since that first night when they'd crossed paths in the Leighton-Childe library; he thought it was time for a little respite for themselves.

As if by unspoken agreement, they walked arm in arm through the French doors and out into the torchlit night air.

They hadn't made it more than a few yards from the terrace and into the thick foliage when Will heard a voice meant only for their ears.

"You'd better come with me, my lord, Miss Penhallow. Otherwise, I'll have to do something that will turn this fine betrothal ball into something tragic."

Will hesitated. He knew that voice. Had heard it only a few days ago when he and Lucy had called at the Blackwoods' townhouse.

How in God's name did she figure into this?

"Lady Fortescue," Lucy said in a cool voice. "How can we help you?"

Chapter 37

Lady Fortescue scowled at them, then to Lucy's surprise and alarm, she leveled a pistol at them. "Come, come. We haven't time to waste. I need to get the two of you across town in a matter of minutes, and we haven't much time."

As she and Will walked side by side in front of the widow, Lucy chided herself for not trusting her instincts when it came to the woman. She'd been suspicious of her the day she and Meg had encountered her at the Blackwood house. She hadn't been able to put her finger on why, but now she realized what it had been. She hadn't seemed at all bothered by the disappearance of her lover's daughter. Not that she had to be fond of Vera, of course, but she could have at least had some real compassion for Mr. Blackwood.

"Might I inquire where it is you're taking us?" Will asked in a casual tone, almost as if he were asking what the soup would be at dinner, or whether he might have another cup of tea.

"You'll see that well enough once we get there," Lady Fortescue said tightly. "Just keep walking. We are headed to the garden gate leading into the mews."

Lucy frowned. "This is the same way that Vera was abducted from the Leighton-Childe ball."

"And it worked well enough, so why should we change things at this late day," the widow snapped.

Lucy was curious as to why the widow was so on edge. It was likely she hadn't ever done anything like this before. From what Lucy knew of her, she'd been married for many years to a man who had left her with a modest fortune, but not enough to live as well as she'd hoped to. That was why Lucy hadn't been too surprised when she saw her with Mr. Blackwood.

"So you were in on Vera Blackwood's abduction?" Lucy asked as she and Will continued down the path through the garden that led to the very back of the property, where the mews ran behind the row of houses. "Why was that?"

"Has anyone ever told you that you ask entirely too many questions, Miss Penhallow?" the widow asked from behind them, and to Lucy's alarm, she felt the prod of the gun's barrel against her back. "Try remaining silent until we get to the carriage, or I'll have to find some way to keep you quiet myself."

Though the words were harsh, the voice that spoke them was trembling a little, as if Lady Fortescue wasn't quite so self-assured as she'd at first seemed.

Curious.

"If you have to hurt someone, my lady," said Will tightly, "then hurt me. I am your greater threat. It makes more sense for you to remove me from the scene first, because I can do the most damage to you."

As Will's words sank in, Lucy wanted to shout at him. Why would he tell Lady Fortescue something like that? He was going to get himself killed, the nodcock.

Rather than acting on his suggestion, however, Lady Fortescue laughed bitterly. "You don't know how much I would love to take you up on your offer, my lord. More than you could ever know. But I've been ordered to bring the two of you to—"

She broke off and it was immediately clear to Lucy that she'd been about to reveal either their intended destination or the name of the person who had sent them here. Though who that could be besides Jedidiah Hamilton, Lucy had no idea.

"I'm confused, my lady," Lucy said aloud now, deciding to ignore the directive to keep silent, since it was obvious the woman was too inexperienced to follow through on her threats. Or so Lucy hoped. "I thought you were in a happy—or at the very least comfortable—relationship with Mr. Blackwood. Why would you risk giving him a disgust of you by doing something like this?"

Apparently, recognizing that Lucy wasn't going to listen to her threats, Lady Fortescue said in a put-upon voice, "Not that it's any of your voice, miss, but I had no choice in the matter."

Lucy and Will exchanged a glance, and she wondered if he was thinking along the same lines as she was. If Lady Fortescue was being forced into this somehow, then perhaps they could make a counteroffer that would persuade the widow to change her allegiance to their side.

At least that was what Lucy hoped Will was thinking.

"Everyone has a choice, my lady," she said to the widow gently. "But if you feel you don't have one, perhaps Lord Gilford or I might be able to offer you something that could make it unnecessary for you to do this other person's bidding. I am quite wealthy, you know. So if it's money that you need—"

She must have struck a nerve, because Lady Fortescue interrupted her and snapped, "I thought I told you to keep quiet."

Before she even realized what was happening, Lucy felt the glance of the pistol's butt against the back of her head. But before Lady Fortescue could bring the full force of the heavy gun down on her skull, Will had been able to capture the woman's wrist with his hand and twist until the widow had no choice but to let go or risk broken bones. They wrestled for a moment, but almost as soon as she realized she'd been defeated, Lady Fortescue seemed to collapse in on herself and slid to the ground in a sobbing heap.

"They will kill him," she said over and over again as she rocked back and forth. "He said if I failed, Richard would die. It's all my fault. It's all my fault."

Will, still slightly breathless from his tussle with the widow, glanced at Lucy with a look of alarm. "Jedidiah Hamilton?" he asked aloud.

Lady Fortescue must have heard him, because her head snapped up and she shook her head. "No, not Jedidiah. His cousin, Christopher."

Chapter 38

After they'd informed the Duke and Duchess of Langham of what had occurred, the duchess settled them into a parlor far from the ballroom, then sent for the tea tray and a physician in that order.

Pulling Lucy aside, Will asked if she was able to remain here alone for a bit while he sent for her cousin and found someone to go with him to check Blackwood's home.

At the mention of going to the Blackwoods', Lucy's eyes widened in alarm. "Shouldn't you wait for Cousin Andrew to send some of his men to do that? They are trained for such things. You are—"

"Not," he finished for her with a smile as he tucked that always-escaping curl behind her ear. "I know I am not, but if Hamilton—whichever of them it is—has taken Blackwood somewhere, as Lady Fortescue suggested, then the townhouse should be safe enough."

"And if for some reason Hamilton has returned to search for something to steal?" Lucy asked, not for one moment falling for his attempt to turn her up sweet.

"Then we will deal with him," Will admitted. "But the

odds of that are very unlikely. Besides, I also want to search Vera's room to see if there are any other letters from Hamilton that might give us some idea which of the cousins it is who has taken both Vera and her father. It's entirely possible that it was Jedidiah who took Blackwood and threatened Lady Fortescue, but he passed himself off as Christopher again."

Lucy looked as if she wanted to argue further but must have realized he wasn't going to be persuaded to her way of thinking. "Fine," she agreed finally. "You may go. But if you are hurt or killed, I will run you through."

She looked adorable, scowling like a thwarted toddler. He wouldn't tell her that, of course. He knew not to endanger his vulnerable bits in such a way. "If I'm dead, then it will do no good to run me through," he reminded her.

"It will do *me* good," she said, throwing her arms around his neck. It was entirely improper to do such a thing in front of other people, even a widow who had just attempted to kidnap them and a duchess who was the soul of discretion.

Deciding if he was in for a penny, he may as well be in for a pound, Will kissed her thoroughly. When he pulled away, he looked down into her slightly dazed expression and said softly, "I love you, you know."

Then before she had a chance to reply, he strode out of the room, shutting the door behind him.

Once back in the ballroom, he went in search of someone who could be trusted to go with him to search the Blackwood home.

He was about to give up and make the trip to the other side of Mayfair alone when he ran into Woodward staring glumly into a glass of what looked like sherry.

Even as distracted as he was by his mission, Will couldn't help noticing his friend's mood. "What's amiss?"

At the sound of his friend's voice, Woodward stood up straighter and threw off the mantle of unhappiness as if it were an ill-fitting coat. "Where have you been? It was supposed to be a ball partly in your honor, and the pair of you snuck out before you finished even a single dance. What kind of rudeness is that?"

Brushing aside the questions, Will said instead, "I'd like you to join me on an errand."

Woodward's brow furrowed. "What kind of errand?"

"The kind where we might need to let ourselves into someone else's house if there is no one there to let us in." Will knew how to bait a hook with the skill of a longtime angler.

As he'd hoped, Woodward was as susceptible to the promise of adventure as any man. "Lead on, MacDuff," he said, gesturing for Will to go ahead of him.

Once they were in a hansom cab, Woodward turned to him expectantly, and Will explained what had happened in as succinct a manner as he was able.

Woodward, who was fairly used to unusual circumstances at this point, gaped. "She tried to abduct the pair of you from your own betrothal ball? The mistress of the last abductee's father?"

"When you put it like that, it does sound suspicious," Will said wryly. "And I still haven't heard the full explanation of why precisely Hamilton wanted us. I understand that he would use Blackwood as leverage to force Lady Fortescue into taking us, but why us?"

Leaning back against the seat with a sigh, Woodward

thought about it. "You and Miss Penhallow have been on this fellow's trail from the moment that Miss Blackwood was taken. Perhaps he needs to know just what it is you've learned about him so that he can determine whether to get rid of you or not."

"That's reassuring." Will shot his friend a scowl, though it was barely visible in the dark of the carriage. "Remind me not to come to you when I am in need of cheering."

"You didn't ask for cheering," Woodward said reasonably. "You asked what the fellow might have wanted with the two of you."

"Touché," Will admitted. "But with that in mind, I have another question. Why is he still here?"

It was Woodward's turn to frown. "What do you mean?"

"If I'm an American who sailed across the Atlantic in order to force a wealthy heiress into marriage so that I might get my hands on her money, then why wouldn't I have gotten married and sailed away by now? Why is he lingering?"

It was something that had been niggling in the back of Will's brain for the past day or so. Ever since the attack on Miss Fleetwood and Hetty. If he was worried about their being able to identify him, then why hadn't he just fled? It wasn't as if their identification of him would matter if he was off living with Vera in New South Wales.

Woodward thought about it. "Perhaps Miss Blackwood's money is in a trust of some kind that isn't available to her until she reaches a certain age?"

Nodding, Will gestured for the other man to continue. "But Hamilton wasn't aware of this. He thought the money was tied up in her dowry. Now he wants to get the money from Blackwood with or without benefit of marriage."

"But that's the odd thing," he said to Woodward. "There's been no ransom demand. If you want money from the father of the lady you've kidnapped, wouldn't sending a demand for money have been your very first action after obtaining the lady?"

"One would think," Woodward agreed. "Every time I think we have a handle on this case, something happens to turn everything we thought we knew on its ear."

Will agreed, and he was getting tired of chasing Hamilton— whichever of the cousins it was who was responsible for all of this.

The coach began to slow then, and as it came to a stop before the house of Richard Blackwood, Will opened the door and jumped to the ground, followed by Woodward.

In the light of the gas lamps lining the street and illuminating the front of the house, Will noticed that it looked as tranquil as any home in the prosperous parts of London. A house a few doors down was entertaining, as was evidenced by the line of coaches disgorging its passengers near where a red carpet had been rolled out. But other than that, the rest of the houses, though well lit, seemed to be quiet for the night.

As the two men jogged up the few steps to the door, a dog began barking somewhere in the distance, and Woodward almost leapt out of his skin.

Hiding a grin, Will asked, "Would you like to go back to the cab before it leaves?"

Woodward made a rude gesture, and Will only laughed harder.

"We just had a serious conversation about a man who has kidnapped one woman, stabbed two, and has allegedly abducted a man with enough money to buy and sell both of us. Forgive me if I am feeling a little jumpy at the moment."

"You're safe with me," Will told him firmly, and he hoped like hell he was right.

Then, raising his hand to the lion's-head knocker, he gave one rap but was unable to knock more because the door swung slowly open with the force of his movement.

Woodward gave Will a sardonic look. "Safe, huh?"

Chapter 39

The next morning, after a sleepless night of tossing and turning and wondering just what Will and Mr. Woodward had found at the Blackwood house, Lucy got up early, dressed, and had her small coach readied so that she might go get the news from the source.

When she arrived at Gilford House, where she had been a frequent visitor ever since she and Meg became friends, she was surprised to find a cart being loaded with trunks, bandboxes, and everything a lady would need for a long trip.

When she was shown in the front door, she saw Lady Gilford directing another of the footmen who was loaded down with yet another trunk from the first landing.

Upon seeing Lucy, the dowager gave a sniff and then turned to follow the servants.

Though her inclination was to let the older woman go to whatever destination she chose without bothering to speak, Lucy knew that if she and Will were indeed going to be married, then she would need to make some sort of peace with the dowager. If only for Will's sake.

"Are you going somewhere, my lady?" she asked pleasantly,

hoping that if she took a friendly tone Lady Gilford would follow suit. "I know Will—that is, Lord Gilford—spoke of your taking a house of your own, but I hadn't realized anything had been formalized."

Once she reached the bottom of the curved staircase, the dowager turned to Lucy, who had stopped a couple of steps from the bottom. "I have decided that given my son's decision to betroth himself to you without a by-your-leave from me, I cannot endure another day in this house. It is clear that neither of you cares one whit for me or my opinions, and I will remove myself from here to go stay elsewhere."

Though Lucy wanted to point out that circumstances had dictated the need for Will to propose to her, not some childish wish to thwart his mother, she stopped herself from saying it. Instead, she told Lady Gilford, "I can assure you that we both care very much about you and your opinions, my lady. I am not sure where Gilford is at the moment, but I am sure he would wish me to tell you how much we both wish you would not leave like this."

"My son is riding in the park, as he does every morning at this hour," the dowager snapped, her still-lovely countenance made less so by her dour expression. "But I suppose you have no way of knowing his habits yet. I can assure you, however, that were I to discuss the matter with him, he would not agree with you. I suppose I must acknowledge that you have asked me to stay, for which I thank you. But I know my son too well."

That the dowager had interpreted Lucy's words as asking the older woman to reconsider her decision to leave was hardly surprising. Ladies like Will's mother often heard what they wanted to hear. And in this case, she wished to hear that someone, even Lucy–whom Lucy herself was quite certain the dowager at the very least disliked heartily–didn't wish for her to go. Still, she had to come to her fiancé's defense.

"My lady, I hope that you do not think that Will—Gilford, that is—does not wish for you to remain here for as long as you need to in order to find a suitable house for yourself."

The dowager sniffed in disdain. "That could take months. I have decided that I will be more comfortable with my friends Lord and Lady Carlyle for the remainder of the season. Perhaps by that time my son will have found a suitable house for me."

Lucy knew from both Jane and her sister-in-law, Poppy, Duchess of Langham, that the Carlyles were cousins of the duke and had treated Jane very badly when she'd been employed as governess for their children. But the dowager counted Lady Carlyle as one of her dearest friends. And if she wished to live with them, then Lucy would not be able to convince her otherwise.

Nodding at the dowager, Lucy stepped closer and went to offer her hand to the other woman. She might be unpleasant and prickly at the best of times, but Lucy had to remember that she had given birth to Will and Meg, whom Lucy loved dearly.

That thought—that she loved Will—gave her a start. Though she liked him a great deal—she would not have given him her body otherwise—she'd thought love was something that one could not feel until some certain amount of time had passed. She wasn't sure how long that amount of time was, mind, but surely it was more than the week or so that she and Lord Gilford had been acquainted.

Realizing that the gentleman in question's mother was staring at her with no little impatience on her face, she extended her hand to Lady Gilford and was surprised when she took it and squeezed. "I suppose I cannot blame you for this, Lucy. We ladies are forever at the mercy of the gentlemen in our lives. And I have no doubt that a surprise betrothal was entirely my son's idea."

Lucy opened her mouth to argue—especially since she didn't think herself at the mercy of Will or *any* man in her life—but her ladyship waved a hand in peremptory dismissal. "Now, I must go. Please tell Meg to seek me out as soon as she awakens."

And with that, the dowager Lady Gilford swanned out the front entrance and was handed into one of the Gilford carriages by a footman. Then the door closed behind her, and Lucy was left wondering what had just happened.

She was still staring at the door when she heard Meg on the landing above. "There you are," she said, hurrying down the stairs toward Lucy. "I was just about to send a note around to you to invite you to luncheon. I missed all the excitement last night and intended to press you for details. Come up and join me for breakfast."

Lucy had to smile at the fact that both of them were in want of information this morning.

As they walked, she related to Meg her conversation with the dowager.

Just outside the breakfast room door, Meg turned to her in amazement. "She simply packed her things and left?"

"It appears that way," Lucy said as she allowed Meg to lead the way to the sideboard, where steaming trays of all variety of breakfast foods had been laid out. Serving herself a healthy portion of eggs and a rasher of bacon, she glanced at Meg, who was doing the same. "I suspect she wished to leave before Will returned from his morning ride."

As Meg followed her to the table, Lucy heard her friend snort. "That is very likely. For all that Mother likes to think of herself as someone who always gets her way, she has not been as adept at manipulating Will into doing her bidding as with Papa. I suspect she wished for him to return and find her gone, in the hopes that he will be so devastated at her removal from the household that he will rush to the Carlyles' and beg for her to return."

Lucy's eyes widened. She couldn't imagine Will begging anyone for anything. Much less his overly dramatic and scheming mother. "Oh dear."

"Exactly," Lucy said as she buttered a piece of toast. "I believe she will be very disappointed by the outcome of her gambit. But at least I will not have to endure another scold from her about how unflattering my gown is, or how the way I've chosen to have Sally dress my hair is not what she would have chosen."

Since the two friends had discussed the dowager's criticism of her only daughter before, Lucy was unsurprised by Meg's words. Still, they reminded her of something. "I suppose this means that once we're wed, Will and I will need to serve as your chaperones now?"

Meg gave a huff of laughter. "Hardly. I am not a green girl in my first season. I should be well able to handle myself."

Lucy was about to reply when Stone came into the breakfast room carrying a note. "Miss Penhallow," he said to Lucy with a deep bow, "this just arrived for you. It was brought by one of the footmen at Penhallow House."

Frowning, Lucy took the missive from the butler and quickly unfolded it.

> *Lucy, I am alive and well, but must see you as soon as possible before I leave England for good. Meet me at the usual place. Come alone, please—my life depends on it.*

As she recognized the handwriting, Lucy was assailed by relief, which was quickly followed by foreboding. That Vera was alive and well enough to write this note gave her the first real burst of hope she'd had since she'd watched her friend being manhandled into a waiting carriage. But in light of everything else that had happened since, including the murder of Sir Charles, the attacks on Miss Fleetwood and Hetty, and Lady Fortescue's attempt to abduct Lucy and Will the night before, there was much that still cried out for explanation.

"I apologize for leaving so soon, but I must go," she said to Meg, rising from the table. "I forgot that I agreed to"—she searched her mind for some errand that Meg would believe plausible mid-morning on a Thursday—"pick up some books from Hatchard's for Jane. She is trying to finish her latest manuscript and wanted them for research."

She had no idea how Jane obtained references for her own writing, but Hatchard's seemed a logical enough place for it. It was also what Lucy thought Vera had meant by "the usual place."

Meg's eyes narrowed. "Jane mostly uses her brother-in-law's library for her research. Or the library at the British Museum.

I've never known her to purchase a book when she can borrow it."

Lucy gave a mental curse. She should have remembered how close Meg was to her former governess. Of course she would be conversant with the way the novelist conducted her investigations.

"What's going on, Lucy?" Meg demanded. "Who is that note from?"

A glance at the clock told Lucy that she had no time to waste. "I will tell you, but you must promise to keep this to yourself."

She handed the note to Meg, who read it and gasped. "She's escaped Hamilton somehow? This is wonderful."

Staring down at Vera's words again, Lucy wondered if there was more to what her friend said than met the eye. "I am not sure what it means," she said truthfully. "But I am bothered by the statement that she's leaving England for good. Does she even know that her father was taken last night—or was thought to have been taken, according to what Lady Fortescue said."

Meg looked crestfallen. "You think she is still being held, then?"

"I don't know," Lucy admitted. "But I am willing to bet that whether she wrote this note of her own accord or was forced to write it by Hamilton, she is still in danger."

Nodding, Meg said, "That makes sense."

"Which," Lucy said firmly, "is why I need to go to her at once. We've waited so long to have contact with her, I can't simply ignore her when she needs my help."

Meg rose from the table as well. "I want to come with you."

Lucy shook her head. "She told me to come alone. I cannot risk having Hamilton, if he's with her, getting spooked. Especially in somewhere like Hatchard's, where there will be any number of innocents for him to harm."

"At least take one of the footmen with you," Meg said, her eyes so much like her brother's, giving Lucy a pang of recognition. "Will would never forgive me if something were to happen to you. He loves you, you know."

Lucy's eyes widened. He'd told her that last night, but she hadn't seen him since to reassure herself of it. She knew that she was in love with him. And the sooner they could put this business behind them, the sooner they could begin their life together.

But she had no time to dwell on Will at the moment. Now, Vera needed her.

"I'm taking the carriage I came here in," Lucy said in a rush of words. "I have to leave now. But I will have my coachman and groom waiting for me. And if you wish, you can tell Will where I've gone when he returns from his ride."

Not waiting to hear what else Meg might have to say, she hurried from the room.

Chapter 40

W here the devil is 'the usual place'?" Will demanded, scanning the note Lucy had left with Meg when she'd set out for God knows where.

He'd been detained in the park by a distant uncle whom he'd not seen in several years and who, unfortunately, was thoroughly enchanted by the sound of his own voice. His father's younger brother had lived in Wales for some years and had clearly saved up a decade's worth of stories that he must have been bursting to tell someone. Will was that unlucky person.

By the time he arrived back at Gilford House he was in a foul mood—especially given that he'd hoped to have learned something from Eversham about the search for Blackwood by now. When he and Woodward had entered the industrialist's house last night, it had been to find the master of the house gone and not a single servant on the premises. And when they'd tried to search Vera Blackwood's bedchamber for some clue as to her relationship with either of the Hamilton cousins, they'd found it cleared of all her possessions. But no message from the detective superintendent had been awaiting him when he handed his hat, coat, and gloves to Stone.

He'd barely gotten past the entry hall when Meg emerged from a nearby sitting room.

He'd known as soon as he saw her face that something was wrong. Once he'd read the note Lucy had received from Vera, his temper had been replaced by fear. Hamilton—whether they were dealing with Jedidiah or Christopher—had already killed one man and attempted to stab to death two women.

And though they'd assumed the woman Christina Fleetwood had identified as one of her and Hetty's attackers was the same one identified as Hamilton's wife on the ship from America, there was a possibility—albeit a small one, in Will's opinion—that the woman had instead been Vera herself.

He didn't want to think that. Both because he knew that Lucy and Meg cared for Vera as a cherished friend, but also because if that was the case, then Lucy was in grave danger at this very moment.

"Where is 'the usual place'?" he asked again, this time with more force, given his escalating fear for Lucy.

"Lucy mentioned Hatchard's book shop," Meg answered, sounding as fearful as he did now. "She and I went there with Vera after a couple of book club meetings."

Will hastily scrawled a message for Eversham, which he instructed Stone to have delivered to Lucy's cousin at once. Hopefully either the detective superintendent or his men would arrive at Hatchard's in time to prevent disaster if his fears for Lucy were well founded.

Then, he took the stairs two at a time to reach the floor above and his study, Meg hard on his heels.

From the cabinet in the far corner, he withdrew a box containing the dueling pistols he'd inherited from his father.

He'd never been much for hunting or shooting, though it was a common enough pastime for most gentlemen of the *ton*. Perhaps because he'd lost his father to violence. The newer pistols were much more efficient and less inclined to misfire, or so he'd heard. But these would have to do.

"Will, you're frightening me," Meg said as she watched her brother load the pistols. "Do you really think that's necessary?"

"I have no idea," he said frankly as he finished loading one of the guns with powder. "But Hamilton has shown himself to be brutal and without remorse. Hopefully Lucy will just have a pleasant meeting with Vera, but I have to be prepared that it will be something worse."

"I knew I shouldn't have let her go alone," Meg said with a note of panic in her voice.

"I sincerely doubt you could have stopped Lucy from leaving if that was her intention," Will said wryly, pocketing the other pistol. Her loyalty and determination were two of her most attractive traits.

The idea that he loved—was madly in love with—his own fiancée was no longer as shocking to Will as it would have been a year ago. He'd seen how happy Adrian had been since his marriage to Jane three years ago—a marriage that had come as a shock to Will, who had seen Adrian as the picture of a man about town—and had, in that place deep within him that he revealed to no one, wished for the same for himself one day. But given how his parents' marriage had been, distant but civil, he wasn't sure it was even possible.

"One day" had arrived on the evening of the Leighton-Childe ball, and Will was certain that, though he'd known Lucy for years, that night had been the first time he'd actually seen her as anything other than his sister's bookish friend. Now he wasn't sure how he'd ever been able to look past her.

"I want to come with you," Meg said, breaking into his thoughts. "I can be discreet. I won't make a scene."

But Will shook his head. "I can't risk it," he said, raising a hand as his sister opened her mouth to offer an objection. "I need you to remain here in case Eversham misses my note. He was supposed to come here this morning to report on whether they've found Blackwood."

At her mulish look, Will said in a softer voice. "Meg, I know you love her, too. I promise you I will do everything in my power to bring her back here. Safe and sound."

Meg rushed forward and gave him a hard hug. Then, brushing at her eyes, she said, "You'd better. And I'm almost certain she loves you too. Though I believe she could have done much better."

Will smiled at the teasing, but silently he agreed with his sister. He'd just have to make sure that Lucy never had reason to regret her promise to wed him, wouldn't he?

Hurrying downstairs, he accepted his hat and coat from Stone and stepped out to climb into the waiting hack.

Chapter 41

Meg listened as the door closed behind Will downstairs, then collapsed into one of the chairs near the fire in the study.

It was hard to believe how much time had passed since her father's murder, and the danger Jane and Adrian had faced only days afterward at the hands of the same perpetrator. She and her mother had been hustled out of London and to the Gilford estate in the country the morning after Papa's death. At the time Meg hadn't understood why, but now she knew it had been because Detective Superintendent Eversham hadn't trusted Lady Gilford's ability to manage the diplomatic party that had been taking place in this very house. All Meg had known was that her beloved father was dead and she'd been separated from the one person in the world whom she felt truly understood by—Jane.

Now, she'd had enough time to make sense of everything that had happened during that chaotic time. And thanks to Jane's friendship, she'd joined the Mischief and Mayhem Book Club and met Lucy and gained more friends than she could have imagined when she was a slip of a girl under the thumb of her overbearing mother.

Lucy was her dearest friend and understood Meg in that easy way that required no explanations or excuses. That she was now in danger, and Meg had done nothing to stop her from racing headlong into it, would press upon her until she learned Lucy and Will were safe.

She wasn't sure what she would do if something were to happen to Lucy or Will. Or, God forbid, to both of them. The very idea made tears spring into her eyes, and she wished she were one of those ladies who always had a handkerchief with her.

Leaning her head against the mantelpiece, she took a deep breath, trying not to cry.

"Miss Gilford, what's happened?"

At the sound of Benjamin Woodward's voice, Meg gave a start and hastily brushed the tears from her eyes before she turned to face him.

"Mr. Woodward," she said in what she hoped was a normal tone of voice. "You startled me. Whyever didn't Stone announce you?"

"I prevailed on Mr. Stone to let me announce myself," the American said with a surprisingly gentle smile. "What's happened, Meg? Where are your brother and mother?"

Meg debated whether to disclose everything that had happened that morning to Ben, but he'd been with Will last night when they'd searched the Blackwood home. And like her, he'd been in on some of the other attempts to gather information about Vera's disappearance. Surely Will could have no objection to her telling his friend what was going on now.

And suddenly, she was telling him everything. The note. Lucy's insistence on going alone. Her own fears that she'd done the wrong thing by not going with her. Will's arrival and the way he'd pocketed the dueling pistols.

"And I'm so afraid that they'll be hurt and it will be all my fault and I'll be alone in the world except for Mother and, well, you know how Mother is, and—"

Tears were streaming down her face at this point, and Meg was certain she should be mortified, but such was the severity of her worry that she simply didn't give a fig about appearing thus before a man she saw as an antagonist at the best of times.

"Hey," Woodward interrupted her and pressed a large handkerchief into her hand. "Hey. Slow down. Take a breath."

He dipped down a little so that he could look her in the eye. "Whatever you might think about your brother, he is not foolish. I'm sure he and Lucy will emerge from this encounter unscathed."

Meg looked up at him and realized she'd never been this close to him before. His eyes, she realized at this angle, were an unusual shade of green with a ring of gold along the outer edge of the iris. She saw the moment he became aware of her, because his pupils widened, and as she watched, the pulse point in his neck quickened.

Unable to look away, she met his gaze and watched almost as if she were someone else as he stood up straighter. Like she'd once seen at a scientific demonstration, their faces moved inexorably closer to one another.

When his lips touched hers, Meg felt the connection throughout her whole body. Almost as if of their own volition, her arms slipped around Ben's neck and pulled him close.

With a groan, he moved his own hands to rest at her waist, and Meg was surprised at how good his hard chest felt against her own softness.

It should have come as a shock when his mouth opened and he touched his tongue against the seam of her lips, but the intimate caress was instead the most natural thing in the world. And when she opened to his gentle invasion, it was as if she'd been waiting for this all her life.

She tentatively touched her own tongue to his, and soon they were engaged in the kind of sparring Meg could never have imagined much less seen as something she herself would participate in. Now she understood why there were so many poems about kissing.

So lost were they in one another that it wasn't until a second round of pounding on the study door that Meg even became aware of a disturbance.

But Woodward must have heard it, because he reluctantly pulled away from her, pressing one last kiss to her lips and then another on her nose. When he stepped back, he looked her over and cursed.

"What's the matter?" she asked, realized belatedly that whoever had been knocking must know what they'd been up to.

"You look exactly as if you'd just been kissed," Woodward said with a scowl. "We're just going to have to brazen it out. And hope whoever it is doesn't guess."

Meg wasn't sure whether to be insulted or not.

But before she had time to do more than smooth back her hair and hope Ben's fingers hadn't done too much damage to her coiffure, the door opened to reveal Eversham.

"Why aren't you with Will and Lucy?" she demanded of

the detective superintendent, who was looking from Meg to Ben and back again.

Still looking suspicious but keeping his thoughts to himself, Eversham said instead, "Where are they? I came as soon as I was able to get away."

Alarm coursing through her, Meg asked, "You didn't get Will's note?"

Eversham blinked. "What note?"

With a growing sense of dread, Meg explained everything again.

Chapter 42

When Lucy climbed out of the carriage in Piccadilly, she scanned the busy street for Vera or anyone who looked suspicious, but there was no sign of her friend.

She hurried toward the entrance of Hatchard's book shop, which had been one of Lucy's favorite haunts since she'd been gifted a three-volume set of *Pride and Prejudice* by Miss Jane Austen from the shop for her fourteenth birthday.

On an ordinary visit, she'd have lingered outside first, scanning the volumes in the window displays on either side of the door, but today she had no time for such things.

But before she could step inside, she heard her name being called. Turning to look behind her, she saw Vera hurrying toward her, looking a bit pale but otherwise well.

"Oh, my dear, you do not know how glad I am to see you," Lucy said, giving her friend an impulsive hug. It was the sort of thing that would scandalize both her mother and the dowager Lady Gilford, especially in such a public locale, but Lucy had spent the better part of a week searching for Vera Blackwood and fearing for her friend's life and she was relieved to see her. "If you only knew how we have been all over London looking for you."

Vera returned the hug but then quickly pulled back. "I wish you had not," she said with a troubled look, which Lucy had difficulty interpreting. "But there's no time for that now. We have to get to the train station at once."

Lucy pulled her into a nearby alley, where they were still within sight of the street, but out of the way of the people walking down the busy sidewalk. "Vera, what's this about? I know you said something about leaving England, but surely you didn't mean today?"

"I do not have time to explain, Lucy," said Vera with a hint of impatience. "You'll understand once we've reached the station. I know this is a little unusual, but you must trust me."

"But Vera," Lucy said, not budging from where she stood, "there are things you need to know. Your father is missing now. I was waiting to learn whether my cousin has had any luck finding him, but I got your note before I could speak to him."

At the mention of Mr. Blackwood, a flash of what could only be hatred flared in Vera's eyes. But just as quickly it was gone.

Had she somehow misunderstood the circumstances of Vera's kidnapping? Lucy wondered. But this was Vera, her friend, whom she'd discussed the plots of any number of books with, and who had clearly been in need of a friend when they'd first met. And Lucy would never forget the sight of Jedidiah Hamilton hauling Vera backward and tossing her into the carriage that night in the mews.

However odd Vera might be acting, Lucy would simply

have to trust her for the moment. If only she could find out what had happened to her since her disappearance.

"All right," she agreed, allowing Vera to take her arm and lead her in the direction of the train station. "But can you not speak to me as we walk?"

Vera gave her an exasperated smile. "You are such an inquisitive soul, Lucy. I've always liked that about you."

They made their way along the increasingly crowded walk, Vera clinging to Lucy's arm as if afraid of losing her.

She had begun to think that Vera would not speak at all, but finally, she said, "You've learned about my betrothal to Christopher Hamilton, I suppose."

"I did hear of it," Lucy admitted, feeling somewhat sheepish about the fact that she'd invaded her friend's privacy in such a way. That Lucy, and indeed her family, had believed her to have been kidnapped and in danger didn't seem quite so strong an excuse now that she was speaking to a seemingly healthy and safe Vera in person. "We intercepted a letter to you from him."

At the mention of the letter, Vera gave a cryptic smile that Lucy couldn't interpret.

"None of us knew you'd been engaged back in Philadelphia," Lucy said, pretending she wasn't beginning to feel uneasy. "Why didn't you tell us?"

"I couldn't tell you, silly," Vera said with a smile. "Then the plan would have been completely ruined."

"What plan?" Lucy asked, feeling as if she was seeing Vera for the first time.

As if Lucy hadn't even spoken, Vera went on. "When I think of how many disgusting fortune hunters I had to let within even an inch of me, Lucy, I completely understand your decision not to dance rather than be pursued by the likes of those scoundrels. I'd have done the same thing, but I had to make Papa believe I was well and truly done with Christopher."

"But the letter we saw said that you had broken things off with him," Lucy said, trying to hide her alarm at what she was realizing from Vera's words. "And then we learned that his cousin had come to London. And that Christopher was dead."

At this, Vera laughed and the sound chilled Lucy to the bone.

"That was Jedidiah," Vera said with roll of her eyes. "He was just a bore, Lucy. You cannot imagine how dull a dog he was. When Christopher came up with the notion of coming to London, I was afraid that if Papa found out, he would cut up rough. So I suggested he come as Jedidiah."

"That was clever," Lucy said, trying to sound admiring despite her fear that Vera might also have suggested that Christopher kill his cousin in order to take his place.

"They looked so much alike, you see," Vera said as chattily as if they were discussing the latest style of sleeve. "And Papa was so fond of Jed. But of course he was. Two peas in a pod, those two. But I tried once more to convince my father when we arrived here that Christopher was just as respectable as Jedidiah, but he would not be moved. So Christopher did what needed to be done. He sent the letter begging me to take him back as if I'd broken things off with him, then he took care of Jed."

By which, Lucy surmised, Vera meant that Christopher had murdered his cousin. Then he'd set out for London.

"But what good did it do to try to make everyone think he was Jedidiah?" Lucy asked, unable to hide her curiosity.

"Because Papa would never allow me to access the money my mother left me if I married Christopher," Vera explained as if she were speaking to a small child. "This way, we staged the abduction to convince everyone that I'd been taken by Jed. And Christopher approached Lord Cheswick, since they'd met when Cheswick was in Philadelphia. It was a risk, of course, because Chris was supposed to be dead, but it worked. And Cheswick introduced Chris to Sir Charles. All of this to hide the fact that Christopher had come for me. Everyone would believe it was his diabolical cousin Jed who took me."

"And then Christopher murdered Sir Charles," Lucy said, stunned at Vera's complete lack of remorse or compassion for anyone but herself.

"Oh please, Lucy. You know as well as I do that Sir Charles was ghastly. His death is no great loss to the world."

Lucy winced.

Reading her expression correctly, Vera gave a soft chuckle. "I have shocked you, haven't I? You have always been the one in our reading group who expressed sympathy even for the most ruthless of villains. You have a soft heart, Lucy."

Lucy wanted to argue, but Vera told the truth. Lucy had always had a facility for placing herself in the metaphorical shoes of other people. And the swiftness and frequent unfairness of the way that the courts in England meted out justice had always bothered her. How was it right for a child of the streets with no other means of putting food in his belly to be hanged for petty thievery when the wealthy man whose watch the boy had stolen made his money by working other children nearly to death in his factories?

"I simply do not believe it can be right for the government to punish murder by committing another murder in turn," she said a little stiffly. "I don't think that makes me a fool." She and Vera had debated the topic a time or two, but Lucy didn't recall the hint of mockery that was present in her friend's voice now.

"Come now," Vera said, gripping Lucy's arm a little more tightly, "you met Sir Charles while you were trying to figure out where I'd gone, didn't you? He was an awful man. Certainly not someone I'd ever consider marrying. Despite what my dear Papa hoped."

At the mention of marriage, Lucy decided to just come out and ask about Vera's marriage. "But why not simply tell your father the truth? It isn't as if he could keep you from your mother's bequest forever."

"I'd have to wait until my twenty-fifth birthday," Vera said with a look of disgust. "I don't want to live until then in poverty. And why should I have to? We thought that if we gave everyone the impression that Jed had forced me into marriage, Papa would relent since he thought him such a paragon. But instead, he still refused to relinquish it."

But Vera simply laughed again. "You should see your face! Don't worry, my kindhearted Lucy. Papa is still alive. He's simply tucked away where he won't be able to tell his banker to stop payment on the draft he wrote for us."

The interior of the station was loud and teeming with people. But all Lucy could think about was how many of them might be harmed if she did anything to overset Vera's good mood. Because without a doubt Lucy knew her former friend would have no compunction about hurting any of them if she thought she needed to.

"Here we are at last," Vera said as they reached one parlor door in particular.

When Lucy tried to let Vera enter first, her friend shook her head. "You first," she said as she pushed Lucy inside.

Lucy looked back as Vera followed her inside, then shut the door behind her and locked it.

"It took you long enough," said a deep voice in the distinct nasal tones of an American accent from the other side of the room, and when Lucy looked up she saw a handsome but somewhat nondescript man standing in the corner. But it was not his looks that made Lucy gasp. It was the pistol he held pointed at her. "You will forgive me if I don't bow, Miss Penhallow, but please allow me to introduce myself. Christopher Hamilton, at your service."

Chapter 43

Will had just alighted from the hackney near Hatchard's when he saw Eversham hurrying toward him. How the devil had the fellow beaten him here?

But the detective superintendent was in no humor for questions, and given the situation, neither was Will.

"I came as soon as your sister and Woodward told me," Eversham said. "I don't believe Lucy is in the bookstore. It's much more likely that Vera has taken her into the station."

Will felt a sense of dread run through him. "Why?" he asked as he followed Lucy's cousin down the street toward the train station, which was one of the busiest in London.

"I had come to Gilford House to tell you what I learned from Richard Blackwood," the detective explained as the two men pushed their way through the crowds covering the sidewalks. "Christopher Hamilton is not dead."

Will swore. "How? Why?"

"Before he left for England, Christopher killed his cousin Jedidiah and made everyone believe it was him," Eversham explained even as he and Will strode forward toward the station's entrance. "He and Vera thought that if they could convince Blackwood that Jed had kidnapped her and forced her to marry him, then Blackwood would release the money left in trust to Vera from her mother to the married couple."

"He and Vera?" Will's mind had stopped trying to comprehend Eversham's words at the mention of Lucy's friend. "So she was the woman who attacked Christina Fleetwood and Hetty. I wish you were joking."

"I wish I were, too," Eversham said with a scowl. "Vera Blackwood has been by Hamilton's side for every crime he's committed since landing on these shores."

"And she's the one who summoned Lucy," Will said to the other man, sidestepping a footman carrying a large trunk.

"I know," Eversham said, "I saw the note. Blackwood says that Hamilton and Vera are planning to flee to South America as soon as they take care of one last detail."

"Lucy," Will said her name on an exhale.

"Yes," Eversham said grimly.

"But why harm Lucy?" Will asked, as he and Eversham finally reached the stately brick building that was one of the crown jewels of England's transportation system. "Why not me? Or you, for that matter?"

Eversham glanced at him as they stepped out of the sunlight and into the busy station. "Because she views Lucy's continued meddling in her disappearance as a betrayal. Vera wanted her abduction to be witnessed, of course, and she knew that if she disappeared from the ballroom her friends would come looking for her. But the investigating Lucy did after that was what Vera believes forced them into the other crimes."

"So she means to teach Lucy a lesson." Will felt the blood chill in his veins. "How?" he asked.

"By pushing her off the platform onto the tracks."

Unsure of where in such a massive structure he would possibly find Lucy, a woman he was now certain he loved with all his heart, Will looked to Eversham.

"Blackwood said that Vera always insists on reserving a private parlor in the station. She is used to all the finer things in life. Including avoiding mixing with the hoi polloi in stations."

With some idea of where to look now, Will broke into a run.

* * *

"But I do not understand," Lucy said for what felt like the hundredth time. "Why can you not wait until your birthday to receive your trust? It is only two years from now. Surely there was no need for such violence and bloodshed."

"Because I could not endure another moment in my father's household, that's why." Vera paced before Lucy, who was bound with her hands behind her. "I should think that you, of all people, would understand that. It was why I found you such a kindred spirit as soon as we met. Like me, you were the target of every fortune hunter in London. Yet your mama insisted you endure season after season. It was clear to anyone with a few moments' acquaintance with you that you are far too clever for the gentlemen of the *ton*. But there you were, paraded before them. 'Like a prize mare' were your exact words, were they not?"

Lucy shook her head in disbelief. She had complained about her mother's insistence that she put herself through the humiliation of a season yet again, but it had been half in jest. She certainly hadn't meant she'd kill to keep from going through it again. If she really wished, she could have put her foot down and refused. But she and her mother had been so close for so long. And Lucy had known that Mrs. Penhallow wished above all things to see her daughter settled. Lucy would certainly never have killed someone over it.

"I did say that, yes," she said in a reasoning tone. "But I would never—"

"Do not become a bore, Lucy," Vera chided. "I told Christopher that you were clever. He'll think I was lying if you continue to be such a spoilsport. Won't you, Christopher?"

Hamilton, who had been peeking out the door to the parlor, as if searching for someone in particular, ignored Vera's question and looked at Lucy. "Your cousin has said nothing about locating Vera's father? You're certain?"

"I haven't spoken to Cousin Andrew since earlier in the day yesterday. We didn't even know Mr. Blackwood was in danger—that is, that he had been taken away to give Vera her inheritance money."

"So you're completely certain that no one knows where Blackwood has been—"

Lucy cut him off. "As far as I know, no one knows where Mr. Blackwood is. But I haven't spoken to my cousin in more than twenty-four hours. It is possible that he's been found, but I'm not a spiritualist like the woman the two of you stabbed."

She had at first spoken in a placating tone so as not to rouse the man's ire, but she was tired of all of this. Of him. Of Vera.

Of being terrified that she'd never see Will or her mother again.

But the anger, instead of coming from Hamilton, was directed at her from her erstwhile friend. She felt the impact of Vera's bare hand on her cheek with all the surprise of a bolt of lightning in a storm.

"I can't have you talking to my husband like that, Lucy," Vera said with a scowl. "I don't care how strong our friendship has been."

Lucy ran her tongue around the inside of her cheek where her teeth had cut into it. "Apologies," she said tightly. She couldn't believe how completely she'd misjudged Vera. She'd thought the American was just what she'd presented herself to be: a lonely, bookish, clever girl in need of friendship outside the restrictive bounds of the ballroom. Instead, she was like a lizard Lucy had once read about—able to change her appearance to suit whatever environment she found herself in. Except Vera changed not only her appearance, but also her personality and manners. It was chilling.

Vera patted Lucy on the head, as if she were a favorite pet. "Apology accepted. Now be a good girl and behave yourself."

Weary beyond belief but determined to keep her wits about her, Lucy tried another tack. "I don't really understand why you must go away, Vera. If you both remained here, then you could continue as a member of the book group. And we could begin our married lives together."

"Lucy, my dear friend," Vera said, sitting down on a chair nearby, "your naivete is astounding sometimes. Of course we must leave England altogether because of my father's whore and her inability to keep her mouth closed."

Lucy had wondered what Vera thought of her father's relationship with Lady Fortescue, and now she had her answer.

But Vera wasn't finished. "Then there is the murder and the stabbings, of course."

This last she said in such an offhand way that Lucy had to keep herself from gasping aloud. Instead she tried to match Vera's manner, saying, "I suppose you are referring to Sir Charles and his sister and her maid?"

"Your father isn't the only one with an inability to keep his mouth shut," Hamilton said sharply, looking at Vera over his shoulder. "You need to stop telling her everything if you want me to release her."

But if Vera was frightened by her husband's warning, she didn't show it. "I haven't told her anything she didn't already know. I told you that Lucy is as clever as they come. I wouldn't have been able to endure her wide-eyed innocence otherwise."

Despite what Lucy now knew about Vera's character, the insult still made her wince. If you'd asked her two weeks ago whom she trusted more—Vera or Will—she'd have said Vera without question. But now...

"Do not look so sad, Lucy," Vera said with a trill of laughter. "I did offer you a compliment, after all. And besides, you have figured out that it was Christopher you saw that night in the street behind the opera house, have you not?"

A glance at Christopher Hamilton told her that he was indeed the same build as the masked man she'd seen plunge his knife into Fleetwood's chest. But the mention of it reminded Lucy of something. "Christina Fleetwood said there was a woman with Christopher when he attacked them. It was you, wasn't it?"

Vera gave her a bright smile. "I knew you'd figure it out, clever girl. See there, Chris. I told you she is smarter that most ladies."

"I hated to do it," Vera told her. "But it had to be done. She'd seen his face, you see. Never mind that she'd somehow guessed that he wasn't who he pretended to be. She might have got it wrong in thinking that he was Jed pretending to be Chris and not the other way around, but she was close enough to be a threat. It was just too bad we didn't manage to finish them off."

Before Lucy could respond, Hamilton pulled the door to the parlor closed and turned to them. "Eversham and Gilford are going from parlor to parlor looking for us. We need to get out of here before they reach this one."

"That wasn't the plan," Vera said hotly. "We were going to wait here for—"

"I don't give a damn what the plan was, Vera," he snarled. "I said we are going to get out of here."

To Lucy's surprise, the bravado that had marked Vera's attitude from the moment they'd reached the station disappeared and she seemed to deflate. "All right. Just give me a moment to untie Lucy and—"

"There's no time," Hamilton said. "We have to get out of here. Just leave her."

Vera gave a glance in Lucy's direction, and she must have seen something there that gave her pause because she turned back to Christopher and said, "I said wait for me to untie Lucy. You have been ordering me about since you came from America, and I'm tired of it. This marriage was supposed to be a chance for me to get free, not to simply switch jailers."

Hamilton swore and came over to where Vera stood with her arms akimbo. "We don't have time for this, Vera. And if I've been ordering you around it's because you've been acting like such a little fool. Now do as I said, grab your valise, and let's go."

It happened so quickly that at first Lucy wasn't sure she could believe the evidence of her eyes. One minute, Christopher Hamilton had been scolding Vera, and the next, Vera had pulled a knife from the valise in her hand and had plunged it into Hamilton's chest.

The piercing scream Lucy heard then was her own.

Chapter 44

Will and Eversham were three parlors down when he heard the unmistakable sound of Lucy's scream.

Will took off at a run, and when he pushed open the door to the compartment the noise had come from, the door was blocked by the bulk of a man's body on the floor. He had a gaping wound in his chest that appeared to have killed him instantly. Right through the heart, he'd guess.

Shouldering his way in, he found Lucy comforting a sobbing Vera Blackwood. The knife Vera had used to kill Hamilton was still lodged in the body, thank God.

"You can't know how cruel he could be, Lucy," the other woman said in a watery voice. "I loved him. Of course I did. But he would have made a terrible husband. I should have seen it sooner."

Will should have been surprised at the murderess's complete lack of self-awareness, but at this point nothing about Vera Blackwood would surprise him.

He wanted to pry her arms from around Lucy's neck, but before he could even get to them, Lucy said something into Vera's ear.

The other woman stiffened, and then, pulling away from Lucy, she nodded and began dabbing at her eyes with a handkerchief and smoothing down her hair. When she moved to sit on a chair near Lucy's, Will saw what he hadn't been able to see before.

Lucy's hands and feet were bound to the chair.

Fortunately, Eversham entered before Will could get close enough to show Vera Blackwood what he thought of her brand of friendship.

And the detective superintendent was followed by a pair of constables who set about moving Hamilton's corpse so that the door could be opened properly.

While Eversham directed two more constables to arrest Vera Blackwood, Will began cutting through the ropes that bound Lucy to the chair.

When she was freed, he began to massage her hands and the ugly red marks that had been left there by the bindings, but she pushed his hands away and threw her arms around his neck and squeezed him as if she'd never let him go.

Will clutched her to him and breathed in the now-familiar scent of her and felt the warmth of her body against his and the soft silk of her hair against his cheek. To think that he'd almost lost her today to a woman with no more conscience than an animal in the wild terrified him in a way he'd never been afraid of anything in his life.

"Promise me you will never ever do something so foolish again," he said even as he stroked his hands down her back as if assuring himself that she was really here in his arms.

"It's an easy promise to make," Lucy said against his neck. "I thought maybe she'd been present when Hamilton tried to kill Christina and Hetty. And that she'd just gone along with him on the rest of the plans. Never did I once imagine that the woman whom I counted as a dear friend, who laughed, cried, and gossiped with the rest of us like any other lady, would be the one who suggested Christopher Hamilton kill his own cousin in cold blood, or attempt to murder two innocent women, or any of the other things we now know she's responsible for."

"When Meg told me you'd gone to meet her," he said, feeling once again the jolt of fear that had coursed through him, "Lucy, I was so afraid for you. For us. I only just found the woman I want to spend the rest of my life with and then suddenly I had to contemplate losing her before we had a chance to begin."

Feeling the threat of tears behind his eyes, he took a breath to calm himself. Holding her away from him so that he could look into her lovely violet eyes, he said, "I love you, Lucy Penhallow. And I want to marry you."

A joyful smile broke across her face. "I love you too, Will. But I've already agreed to marry you."

He shook his head. "No, I mean I want to marry you now. Today. As soon as we can find a vicar who will perform the service."

"I'd love to," she said with a bemused expression, "but don't we need a sp—"

"Special license," he finished for her. Then reaching into his coat pocket, he pulled out a folded document. "I took the liberty of requesting one the morning after our encounter in the Leighton-Childe's library."

Her eyes widened in shock. "You did?" she asked, a pleased

smile curving her plump and oh-so-kissable lips. "But we barely knew each other."

"When a man knows, he knows," Will said, kissing the end of her nose. "Now, what will it be? A standing-room-only society wedding and St. George's Hanover Square with fifteen hundred of our closest friends in attendance? Or a small affair with just us, our mothers, a couple of witnesses, and a minister in your mother's drawing room?"

"The second one please," Lucy said with a heartfelt sigh of contentment.

"Had enough of being scrutinized by all and sundry, eh?" Gilford asked with a raised brow.

"I very much preferred my self-imposed wallflower status to being the center of attention from the ton gossips," Lucy said with a shudder.

"I can't promise you we won't draw the curiosity of society once we're wed," Will said with a sincerity that made Lucy's heart squeeze with affection for him. "But my darling wallflower, I can promise that I won't ever leave you to endure it alone."

"Promise?" Lucy asked, meeting his gaze with her own.

Will stroked a thumb over her cheek. "Absolutely. Now, let us leave this place and get you home. We have a very small wedding to plan."

Epilogue

One week later

I am just so disheartened by the fact that Vera—our Vera—turned out to be such a cold-blooded creature," Meg said from where she sat beside Lucy in the drawing room of the Gilford townhouse. "I know we've discussed it so many times at this point, but I shall never understand how thoroughly she managed to fool me. To fool all of us."

Elise, who was seated in a chair across from them, shook her head. "No more so than I am, my dear. When I think of how many confidences we exchanged with that, that utter villainess, I am positively livid."

Though Lucy and Will had assured Meg that she would always have a home in Gilford House, the younger lady had insisted upon giving the newlyweds some time to themselves in the house. Especially since the dowager had decided to make her move to her sister's home permanent. Not wishing to reside with her mother and aunt—who was not much better than the dowager when it came to disposition—Meg had accepted Elise's invitation to reside with her for the time being.

The friends had come to tea at Gilford House at Lucy's invitation, as much to discuss their lingering unhappiness over the fact that they'd all been betrayed by Vera Blackwood as to discuss the book that the Ems were meant to spotlight at their next meeting.

"She almost let that brute Hamilton kill you, Lucy," Meg said, gripping her by the arm. "I don't know how I should have managed if that had happened."

Though Lucy had not told either of her friends this, she'd been troubled with nightmares since the afternoon she had witnessed Hamilton's murder at Vera's hands. She was only too grateful that Will was there to offer comfort and reassurance to her when the terror visited her in her sleep.

"I have considered going to visit her in Newgate," Elise said with the air of one announcing a perfidy of some kind, "simply to let her know what I think of the way she betrayed us all."

"Did you think that we would shame you for it?" Lucy asked her with astonishment. "I certainly would not. Indeed, I think Vera is deserving of any and all shaming we can bring to bear upon her. Though I fear you have missed your opportunity."

Meg paused in the act of reaching for another ginger biscuit from the overloaded tea tray on the table around which they sat. "What do you mean?"

"I had a note from Cousin Andrew this morning," Lucy said, reaching for the teapot to pour herself another cup. "The government has reached an agreement with the Americans, and they have agreed to send her back to face trial in Philadelphia."

Elise's mouth dropped open in astonishment. "But her crimes were committed here. She deserves to face justice here."

"With the exception of her killing of Christopher Hamilton," Lucy said with a shrug, "none of the murders can be unequivocally linked to her. Hamilton murdered Sir Charles. And though Miss Fleetwood said there was a woman with Hamilton when he assaulted her, she could not identify Vera as that woman. Plus, there is the matter of the woman who posed as Hamilton's wife on his voyage to England."

"Yes!" Meg said at the reminder. "What became of that woman? If she wasn't Hamilton's wife, then who was she?"

"Vera told my cousin that she was the maid who had acted as courier between herself and Hamilton before she and her father came to London," Lucy said before taking a sip of tea. "Hamilton brought her with him on the journey here because he thought she might be useful to him once he arrived. He might not be able to show his face to her father, but he thought perhaps Mr. Blackwood would be more forgiving of the maid he'd sent off with a flea in her ear."

"From the way Mr. Blackwood spoke of her, I doubt he would have been so welcoming," Meg said with a snort.

"I fear Hamilton was outmatched by Vera when it came to cunning," Lucy said wryly. "Which is hardly a shock given how thoroughly she cozened us."

"But what became of the maid?" Elise asked, frowning. "Will she return to America with Vera and her father?"

"She has not been found," Lucy said grimly. "My cousin suspects from some hints that Vera gave that she believed the woman had seduced Mr. Hamilton."

"Oh dear," Meg said with a shudder. "I certainly hope Vera didn't do away with her, but given what we now know—"

"Precisely," Lucy agreed, in the silence following Meg's unfinished statement. "As much as we, none of us, wish to believe Vera capable of such things, I'm afraid I have firsthand knowledge of her ruthlessness."

The three friends sat for a moment with the unhappy awareness of just how easily they'd been hoodwinked by the American.

"In happier news," Lucy said with intentional brightness because the news was, indeed, good. "I also had word from my cousin that Silas King, the procurer who murdered Mary Crosby, has been found and is now sitting in Newgate awaiting his punishment. Thank heavens—"

The sound of footfalls on the stairs alerted them that their party was in danger of being interrupted. But instead of the butler, it was Will, followed by both Benjamin Woodward and Lord Cheswick, who entered the chamber.

"Ah, there you all are," Will said, though he had eyes for no one but Lucy. And feeling the flutter in her tummy that had by now become familiar, she rose to welcome him, as well as his guests, into the room.

"We didn't know you were entertaining Lady Gilford," said Mr. Woodward once he'd made his bows to the other two ladies. "As I was telling Gilford, I really can't stay. There's a pressing appointment that I cannot miss. Good afternoon, all."

And before Lucy could offer any protest the American had retraced his steps to the door and could be heard hurrying back down the stairs as if there was a vicious hound snarling at his heels.

"Goodness," Lucy said as she resumed her seat, and Will took Meg's vacated place beside her. "I hope it isn't serious."

Meg, who had dropped into an empty chair beside Elise's, made a snort of derision. "Somehow I doubt it."

Before Lucy could comment, Elise, who had not relaxed since Lord Cheswick entered the room, rose from her chair. "I fear that I too must go, Lucy. Thank you so much for the tea and conversation." To Meg she said, "You may stay and chat with your brother. I'll leave the carriage for you."

But Meg rose and said her goodbyes to both Lucy and her brother before following Elise from the room.

"I suppose that is my own signal to depart," Cheswick said with a bow to Lucy. "I have no wish to play gooseberry to a pair of newlyweds, thank you very much."

And just like that, Lord and Lady Gilford's once-crowded drawing room was empty of all save themselves.

"My goodness," Lucy said with a raised brow. "If I didn't know better, I'd guess that we are unpleasant company. But I know that is not the case because we are delightful company."

This last she said while looping her arms about her husband's neck.

To her surprise, he used the pose to lift her onto his lap. "We are delightful company, Lady Gilford. I suspect it is just that they fled because we are still newly wed. And if it is not too terribly bold of me, I suggest we behave as such."

"Lord Gilford," Lucy gasped in mock outrage, "you are a very bad man."

"My dear lady," he said as he rose with her in his arms and headed for their bedchamber, "is that not why you married me?"

About the Author

Manda Collins grew up on a combination of Nancy Drew books and Jane Austen novels, and her own brand of historical romantic suspense is the result. A former academic librarian, she holds master's degrees in English and library and information studies. She lives on the Gulf Coast with a squirrel-fighting cat and more books than are strictly necessary.

YOUR
BOOK
CLUB
RESOURCE

Visit **GCPClubCar.com** to sign up for the GCP Club Car newsletter, featuring exclusive promotions, info on other Club Car titles, and more.

Find us on social media: **@ReadForeverPub**

Reading Group Guide

Discussion Questions

1. Why do you think Lucy was so determined to find Vera after she was kidnapped? How do you think working in Eversham's office influenced her opinion about the police and their capabilities?

2. Being required to marry someone for the wealth they could bring to your family was a common practice before the nineteenth century, when marrying for love became more popular. But marriages of convenience are a favorite trope for readers of both historical and contemporary romance. Why do you think that is? Would you ever consider it an option for you or your family members? Why or why not?

3. Séances and attempts at communication with beloved family members who had passed became especially popular in the United States and Great Britain following the American Civil War, and then experienced a resurgence in the period between World War I and World War II. Do you believe in paranormal phenomena like ESP, clairvoyance, intuition, or any other concept that might be considered "woo woo"? Why or why not?

4. Because traveling across the Atlantic by ship or plane requires valid ID and passports, a major plot point of this

story would not have been possible today. What are some other ways in which the schemes employed by the perpetrators in this story would have been radically altered by modern technology?

5. The modern mystery story as we know it was born in the nineteenth century with Edgar Allan Poe's "The Murders in the Rue Morgue" and this is the sort of fiction Lucy and her Ems Book Club would be reading. What things about the present-day mystery and romance genres would come as a shock to Lucy and her book club friends? What wouldn't surprise them? Why or why not?